The Western Star

This Large Print Book carries the
Seal of Approval of N.A.V.H.

The Western Star

Craig Johnson

THORNDIKE PRESS
A part of Gale, a Cengage Company

Farmington Hills, Mich • San Francisco • New York • Waterville, Maine
Meriden, Conn • Mason, Ohio • Chicago

A Longmire Mystery.

Thorndike Press, a part of Gale, a Cengage Company.

Thorndike Press® Large Print Mystery.
The text of this Large Print edition is unabridged.
Other aspects of the book may vary from the original edition.
Set in 16 pt. Plantin.

**LIBRARY OF CONGRESS CIP DATA ON FILE.
CATALOGUING IN PUBLICATION FOR THIS BOOK
IS AVAILABLE FROM THE LIBRARY OF CONGRESS.**

ISBN-13: 978-1-4328-4102-7 (hardcover)
ISBN-10: 1-4328-4102-5 (hardcover)

Published in 2017 by arrangement with Viking, an imprint of Penguin Publishing, a division of Penguin Random House LLC

Printed in Mexico
3 4 5 6 7 21 20 19 18 17

For Lucy,
the sweetest pea of all the peas

ACKNOWLEDGMENTS

I know a lot of writers don't listen to music as they write, especially music with lyrics, because most find the words distracting. Not me, and I even put together a playlist that I listen to, a soundtrack, so to speak, for each book. *The Western Star* is no different, and in that there's usually a theme, the one for this novel is trains. Do you know how many train songs there are out there? From "Wabash Cannonball" all the way to the Doobie Brothers' "Long Train Runnin'," the one that had the greatest effect on me was the song I heard live at the WYO Theater in Sheridan.

I could tell you all about Chester, Montana, native Philip Aaberg, how he graduated from Harvard, bopped around Oakland cutting his teeth as a blues player, was a member of Elvin Bishop's Group, became a standard on Windham Hill, or how he started his own label, Sweetgrass Music, but I think what you should probably do is just listen to his music — that says it all.

Mr. Aaberg was introducing a song called "That Train" from his *Blue West* album and had explained how it had been influenced by "This Train," the old Sister Rosetta Tharpe rendition of the Florida Normal and Industrial Institute Quartette song. He went on to describe how he'd always loved the tune but had found it kind of exclusive and wondered if there wasn't a train out there for the rest of us.

Now, I'd be lying if I were to tell you that I haven't been influenced by Aaberg's music, and more important when I hear him play I can pretty much bring a Wyoming sheriff to mind, pounding the ivories in the same inimitable manner. The momentum that Aaberg builds in "That Train" is stunning, and when I listen to it, all I can think is that we're all going home.

I've always been intrigued by trains and never saw one I didn't wish I was on — I've even jumped a few. Every night there is a Burlington Northern Santa Fe that pulls coal a couple of miles from my ranch at about two in the morning, and if I didn't hear that rumble, I'm not sure I'd sleep well at night.

There are a couple of subjects that you

can count on getting grief about — history, guns, cars, and I'm guessing trains. Though I'm sure there are a few slip-ups in *The Western Star,* I can say honestly that the supporting cast I had in putting this excursion together was marvelous, and I'd like to toot a horn for them.

First and foremost is Cathy Norris of BNSF for all the hours of talk and, more important, the wonderful on-board experiences of riding the rails across Wyoming. Cathy introduced me to James L. Ehernberger for when I had questions and she didn't have answers, and to John and Lori Saunders, who filled out the research roundtable with details galore.

Scott Snowden, who appears as himself in the book, was instrumental in explaining the legal machinations surrounding compassionate release and continues to fork over some damn fine wine from the marvelous Snowden Vineyards in Napa. As Ned Pepper used to say, "I don't need a good lawyer, but I could use a good judge."

Thanks also to the Hotel LaBonte Bar, which needs to add to its law enforcement gallery, and to the Douglas Railroad Interpretive Center that allows you to crawl all over their exhibits.

Special thanks to Karma Osborn and Bar-

bara Bogart for the lowdown on the Wyoming State Hospital and its predecessor, the Wyoming State Insane Asylum.

I've been pulling the Walt Longmire Express for thirteen years now, but I never would've made the grade without Gail The Hiawatha Hochman or Marianne Marrakesh Express Merola. The roundhouse over at 375 Hudson Street lodges some of my favorites with Kathryn The Royal Scotsman Court, Lindsey California Zephyr Schwoeri, Victoria Super Chief Savanh, Brian Rock Island Rocket Tart, Jessica 20th Century Limited Fitzpatrick, Mary Streamliner Meteor Stone, and Ben Cannonball Express Petrone.

But the whistle that always thrills my heart and the train I'll never depart is Judy Orange Blossom Special Johnson, the express that runs through my heart every day.

1

I pressed in on the knurled end of my Colt 1911A1 with my thumb at the same time rotating the barrel bushing a quarter turn clockwise to free the plug and recoil assembly, my hands working from rote. "Business."

Joe Iron Cloud, the young Arapaho sheriff, held up my silhouette target, the fluorescent light beaming through the holes tightly grouped at the center with only one high and slightly off to the right. "I guess business was good."

I removed the mechanism, rotating the plug in a counterclockwise direction to free it from the spring. "I suppose."

Some of the other sheriffs came over to join Joe, who chewed his gum like a masticating machine. "When did you start carrying that thing?"

Concentrating on the work in an attempt to try to get out of the mood into which I was descending, I rotated the barrel bushing counterclockwise, disengaging it from the slide. "Vietnam."

Steve Wolf, the Wyoming Law Enforcement Academy's range manager, approached and handed me a clipboard. "Walt, I need you to sign off on these."

The younger sheriffs drifted away as I signed the forms, and the silver-haired man studied me.

"Mind if I ask why you do this?" Steve watched me continue to disassemble my weapon. "Come all the way down here every four years and requalify?"

I handed the paperwork back, shrugged, and leaned against the green felt bench. "A lot of these larger departments have facilities where they can do this stuff, but we're kind of small. The only range we've got is outdoors, and come November, my undersheriff really doesn't care for that."

The range manager smiled and glanced at Victoria Moretti, who was in the process of cleaning her own weapon. "I'd imagine." He was silent for a moment. "That, and the academy happens to be on the way to Cheyenne, where you go for a four-year parole hearing."

I glanced at him and then went back to working on my weapon. "Yep."

He waited a moment. "Lot of controversy surrounding that case."

"Yep."

"Lots of rumors."

"Yep."

Smiling, he pushed off the bench and started for his office, but then stopped to call back, "Hey, I heard a rumor that your daughter is working for Joe Meyer and that collection of outlaws down there in the attorney general's office."

Having reassembled the Colt, I finally turned to look at him. "Yep."

"She living in Cheyenne?"

"Yep."

"Well, maybe we'll see you more often?"

"Nope."

He shook his head and then turned away. "Really good talking with you, Walt."

As I took my time to carefully oil the exterior of my sidearm, I found myself staring at the forest-green felt, stained with the oil from thousands of weapons that had been taken apart and put back together on its surface. I wondered how many men had been taken apart and put back together in the process.

"You keep playing with that thing and you're going to wear it out." Iron Cloud barked a laugh. "At least, that's what my mother used to tell me." I turned and looked at him, his broad grin splitting his suntanned face like a shearing glacier. "How 'bout having a beer with us?"

I reloaded the one round in the pipe, filled the magazine, slipped it between the ancient, yellowed stag grips, and placed the Colt into the pancake holster at the small of my back. "Sorry, Joe, I have to get to Cheyenne. Besides, Lucian is waiting on us back at the hotel."

"How many times have we heard this fucking story?"

"I've heard it more times than you."

I had to admit the Rainier beer tasted pretty good, giving me time to think as my old boss, the previous sheriff of Absaroka County, regaled the younger men, who had waylaid us after all, with tales of derring-do from bygone days.

Vic leaned in, sipping her dirty martini. "Correct me if I'm wrong, but does it change every time we hear it?"

"Every time."

The perpetual frown was missing from his face, and his bushy eyebrows crouched over his nose as Lucian continued to hold forth. "I get this call that we had a cool one on the side of Route 16 out there on the edge of town. When I get there, this kid — Highway Patrol, he was — is standin' over the damn body, I mean practically standing *on* the damn thing. Well, he steps back when he sees me and says it's in my jurisdiction and what did I want to do?"

Vic nodded as she settled onto the piano stool beside me. "Yeah, it's changed from the last time already."

The first establishment near where we now sat was a tent town called Antelope that had popped up near Fort Fetterman and, appropriately enough, Antelope Creek in anticipation of the Wyoming Central Railroad back in 1886. Decamping and later moving their tents two miles west of the intersection of the Texas and Bozeman trails, the residents got serious and renamed themselves Douglas after Senator Stephen Douglas, the five-foot-four "Little Giant," most famous for losing the presidency to a then relatively unknown log splitter from Illinois, six-foot-four Abraham Lincoln.

I stared up at the old pressed-tin ceiling. The LaBonte Hotel had been built in 1913 as a replacement for the Valley House Hotel, which had been torn down when the Burlington Northern Railroad had cleaved Douglas in two. I often wondered why, with nothing but open land all around, they had decided to run the railroad right through the middle of town.

The LaBonte got its name from the first resident of Converse County, Pierre LaBonte. It had recently been updated but was still old school. Most of the younger officers, deputies, and Highway Patrolmen stayed at the more modern digs on the strip near the interstate, but Lucian had brought me here when he first hired me, and we were creatures of habit.

Near the piano, there was a pool table and a dartboard, where I had sometimes seen Lucian compete, the extra darts embedded in his fake leg — an intimidating gesture for the benefit of his opponents.

Noodling around on the battered upright, I watched as the old, one-legged sheriff sipped a Wyoming Whiskey, his preferred libation when away from home, where he kept a bottle of Pappy Van Winkle's Family Reserve twenty-three-year-old in the corner cabinet back at the Durant Home for Assisted Living.

"There was a big patch of blood at the back of his scalp, but I asked the HP if he was sure he was dead, and the troop said, 'As Kelsey's nuts.' So, I pull the kid's wallet and flip the body over, where I notice there are little blue threads all on the front of him.

Well, while we're waitin' for the medical examiner to come over, I sit in my car and have my dispatcher patch me in to the mother, who doesn't seem too upset about losing her baby boy. She says that her other son and another fellow went out with the kid rodeoing Saturday night and that they'd all hung one on."

He pushed the Open Road Stetson back on his head. "Well, I roll over to the mother's house where there's a beat-up old Chrysler in the driveway with shitty carpeting, a curious shade of blue. I drag the one kid out and show him the carpet and tell him I've got him red-handed and he better damn well start singing, and boy does he — a regular Frankie Laine. He says the decedent and this other fella got into it, and the other fella pulled out a Ruger Blackhawk single-action revolver and shot the young son in the back of the head."

Lucian took a swallow of the whiskey and licked his lips. "The one brother doesn't seem too upset about his dead brother, and I'm starting to think this family might be a little bubble off plumb, but I get the address of the shooter and throw Cain in back of the Nash. On the drive over, he's telling me that he didn't have anything to do with killing Abel and that he didn't even help the shooter dump the body — made him do it himself. Took some kind of strange moral stand on that one, I guess." The old sheriff rolled his eyes. "Well, Ludlow Coontz, the shooter, is this big, dumb-lookin' bulldogger, two hundred and seventy pounds if he was an ounce, and this is before I had yon man-mountain over there."

He gestured toward Vic and me, and I raised my glass at the enthralled dozen or so off-duty officers.

"So, I get Ludlow in the car, and all the way over to the jail I'm telling him how I've already got the story and if he wants me to go easy on him he might as well come clean and admit to the killing, but he doesn't say a word. I stick 'em in separate cells where I'm looking at this big bastard and figurin' I'm gonna have to beat on him all night to get a confession out of him. . . ." He paused. "Not that we did that type of thing a lot, but sometimes it was called for. . . . Anyway, I walk back into the office, tryin' to figure out what I was gonna do, when I spot the new photocopy machine we just got and unplug the thing and roll it back into the holding cells. I mean this was back in the day when those things were the size of a dishwasher. So, I plug it in and push it over and tell him to stick his hand on the glass, which he does, whereupon I cuff him to the bars and the machine and I close the lid. I ask him if he killed that boy, and he says no, and that's when I hit the button. Well, it lights up and goes back and forth with this hellacious racket and spits out a photocopy of his hand, and I pick the thing up and study it like it means some damn thing.

"Ludlow, I say to this dumb ass, this here is the newest state-of-the-art equipment in our ongoing battle with evildoers, the Xerox 914 Lie Detector. So, I hit a few more buttons, and I tell him that I've recalibrated the Xerox 914 so that if he lies to me again, it's gonna deliver about two hundred and twenty volts through his sorry ass.

"I hold my finger above the button and doesn't old Ludlow start sobbin' and tellin' the whole story of how he shot that kid and that the Ruger Blackhawk is under his mattress back home."

The other sheriffs broke out laughing, and Joe picked up his beer from the bar and sidled over, leaning on the piano as Lucian launched into another story. "You two might be stuck here all night."

"Well, if need be I'll stuff him in the backseat of the truck with Dog, and he'll sleep it off by the time we get to Cheyenne."

Vic and I touched glass to can, sealing the deal.

Iron Cloud glanced at some of the photos on the wall behind me. "There's a lot of history in here."

It was true. The bar's slogan is "Tell 'em I'll meet you at the LaBonte," and I'd spent many an hour combing the extensive collection of photos commemorating Wyoming peace officers that took in the history of the state from when it was an Indian territory to the present, a legacy that included small tintypes, 8×10s, and even a few movie posters. There were more than a few photos of Lucian, including the one of him in the hospital when they had just finished amputating the leg that bootlegger Beltran Extepare had attempted to remove with a shotgun in his own dynamic fashion. Lucian, with a nurse pulled onto his bed, is grinning widely and giving the camera a thumbs-up.

Iron Cloud fixed on a photo of Joe LeFors, the man who had famously gotten the murder confession from Tom Horn and been responsible for running Butch Cassidy and the Sundance Kid all the way to South America. "Was it tougher back then?"

"I wouldn't know — LeFors died in 1940; I'm old, but not that old."

He smiled. "No, I mean when you started working for Lucian." He looked back at the old sheriff and Doolittle Raider still holding forth. "Being a deputy couldn't have been easy with that old coot."

"He wasn't old then." I shook my head. "And he was a good teacher. I was going through a lot of stuff when I got back from the war, and he was patient with me."

"Jeez, Walt, you're one of the most patient people I know."

"Didn't used to be." Vic studied me as I sipped my beer. Joe's attention, however, was over my right shoulder.

"Is that the Star?"

I turned and looked up at an old 8×10 color photograph, overexposed in the sunlight. Twenty-five armed men in cowboy hats and gun belts were standing on the platform beside a locomotive. "No."

He sat up a bit in an attempt to get a better look. "Shit, that is it — that's Wyoming's The Western Star." He called to some of the other men, interrupting Lucian's story. "Hey guys, look at this."

They moved en masse toward the piano and peered at the photo behind me as I sipped my beer. Lucian had turned his stool and was watching me, but I ignored all of them and started playing Ravel's Piano

Concerto for the Left Hand in D Major, a relatively unknown piece.

Vic reached up, pulled the framed photo from the wall for a closer look before handing it to Joe, then let her tarnished gold eyes settle on me.

"Guys, this is The Western Star, the sheriffs' train that they ran from 1948 to 1972." He nodded his head in recognition.

"No, it's not."

They all turned to look at Lucian as he hefted himself off his stool and approached us, a little unsteady. "The Star was steam; that's a diesel, you pups. Some pecker head from the *Cheyenne Tribune-Eagle* had us all stand in front of that locomotive for the photograph because he was in a hurry and didn't want to wait till they could pull the real Star out of the Union Pacific roundhouse."

"Is that you, Lucian?" Joe asked.

He smiled a lopsided smile as he studied the photograph. "Front and center — that was '72, which turned out to be my first year as president of the Wyoming Sheriffs' Association." Lucian nodded and poked a finger like a truncheon onto the glass with a snapping sound. "Yep, and you might recognize that big son of a bitch on the end there."

Joe turned the frame toward me. "Is that you, Walt?"

The man on the far left was big with his hat pulled down low and his muscled arms folded over his chest. He was the only one looking to his right at something not in the frame. If the camera had been closer, you might've seen the grimace, but only I knew it was there because I remembered.

Joe held the photo out for a moment more, I guess in the hopes that I might say something, but I didn't. Then he turned it back toward himself. "Twenty-four armed sheriffs on a train."

Vic continued to study me. "And one deputy."

I glanced first at Lucian and then at Vic, as I shifted into playing the old spiritual "This Train" on the piano. "When we started."

"Trouble with that new wife of yours?"

I turned around and looked down at my boss and quickly dropped the ring I was holding into the pocket of my jeans. "Nothing I can't handle."

He studied me for a moment and then snorted, shook his head, and walked away.

I followed him as he codgered through the crowd of other sheriffs and their families on the loading platform outside the Union Pacific depot in Cheyenne. It was 1972, and I was going for a ride on a steam train. Not for the first time in the two weeks I'd been under Connelly's employ, I thought about shooting myself in the foot to get out of it.

I glanced back but couldn't see her, which was too bad, her backside being my second favorite view. I tried to remember what had set us off this time but couldn't come up with it — all I did know was the way it had ended: her wedding ring in my pocket.

Standing there as Sheriff Connelly talked with everyone on the platform, I studied on the fact that Martha had made the trip down here from Durant to see me off, even after I'd asked her not to. I'd explained that we were going to be gone for only a couple of days and that I wasn't even leaving the state, but she'd driven down in my friend Henry Standing Bear's Baltic blue '59 Thunderbird convertible to see me off — and now she was gone, in more ways than one.

Four months ago, she'd flown up to Anchorage, where I'd been working. I'd proposed to her in the Paris Club, and we were married three days later. We'd gone back to the hotel and celebrated in the grand style that had resulted in her pregnancy, a condition neither of us was ready for. By the time I'd gotten back to Wyoming a couple of months later, I had a wife, a child upcoming, and less than four hundred dollars in the bank, so I'd taken the job as a newly minted deputy of the Absaroka County Sheriff's Department. Two weeks later I had no wife, not much of a family, and even less in my bank account, and was having serious doubts about my choice of vocation.

"Did you get him at the sale barn?"

I glanced down at the man now standing with Sheriff Connelly. "Walt, this is Wally Finlay, the sheriff over in Niobrara County."

The older cowboy, who had massive silver eyebrows and a drooping mustache, stuck out his hand. I shook it, and he turned to my boss. "I hope you didn't have to pay by the pound for him."

I thought maybe I could find her. "Excuse me."

Sheriff Connelly called after me. "Where are you going — the damn train is leaving here in a few minutes."

I pushed open the double glass doors, and stepped into the depot, but she wasn't there. I walked past the ticket counter and a couple of long wooden benches where a few individuals loitered, one napping with a newspaper over his face. I exited on the street side of the building just in time to see Henry's Thunderbird disappear around the corner.

"Well, hell."

I stood there in the crisp autumn air and thought about just leaving, hopping a cab to the airport or setting out onto the open road to see if I could find her. I was antsy and indecisive, and I wasn't even sure if Wyoming was where I wanted to be anymore.

There was a bar across the street, but I decided I didn't want that, at least not yet. Walking back inside the depot, I veered in the direction of the newsstand and bought a roll of Reed's root beer candies and a paperback. Ever since I'd gotten back from Vietnam, I treated the company of books like life preservers.

I paid the old guy and stood there, trying to decide if I was getting on this train after all.

Stuffing the book under my arm, I sat on the bench near the man who was sleeping, peeled off a candy, unwrapped it, and popped it in my mouth. Pulling the ring from my pocket, I contemplated the diminutive diamond flanked by two chips, but ended up looking at the chemical burns on my left hand.

"You gonna eat all them yourself?"

I tucked the ring back in my pocket and glanced over, noticing that the drifter had pulled the paper from his face and was looking at me. He was incredibly thin, with a multitude of wrinkles around his eyes and about a three-day gray beard — he had only one arm, his left. "Probably."

He continued to stare at me. "It'd be gracious of you to give one up."

Not in the mood, I tried to brush him off. "Get a job."

"Got one."

It was odd, but he didn't seem intimidated by my gun belt or badge. "Sleeping at the train station?"

"Sometimes." He swung his legs around, placing his boots on the tile floor, and folded his newspaper with the one hand. "She sure had it figured out, didn't she?"

I glanced at the door and then back to him. "Excuse me?"

"Your book. Agatha Christie, is it?"

I looked at the cover. "Um, yep."

I'd barely looked at the title, let alone the author's name, when I bought it.

"There are only so many permutations — he did it, she did it, nobody did it, or they all did it." He set a pinch-front Stetson that had seen better days back on his thinning hair. "You read that book yet?"

"No."

He stood and dusted off his gray slacks with the newspaper and straightened a suit jacket with one elbow worn to a thin shine. "Well, look me up when you finish it and we'll talk."

I ignored him and glanced at the platform.

"Taking a train?"

I looked at the cover, trying to get past the fact that a bum had just used the word "permutation" — things sure had changed since I'd been away. "No."

He walked into my line of sight and stood there with his back to me, watching the locomotive as it pulled away. "Never seen a train I didn't want to be on."

I nodded and stood. "Well, if you're going to jump the next one you'd better do it outside of town, but I'd advise against it."

"Why's that?"

"The Western Star — it's the sheriffs' association junket — goes to Evanston and back once a year."

"A sheriffs' train, huh?"

"Yep."

He studied me. "You a sheriff?"

"Deputy."

"How come you're not getting on it?"

"You ask a lot of questions for a guy who

sleeps in train stations."

"Asking questions is how you get answers, Deputy," he said with a slight smile. Figuring I wasn't going to give up a candy, he strolled off toward the public restrooms.

I watched him go, then started off to the platform, pushing my way through the heavy glass doors and back out into the crowd of Wyoming law enforcement.

The bum had a point about trains. I was in a mood to travel, and why not have the sheriffs' association pay my way across Wyoming? What the hell, I could always take the train to Evanston, get off there, and just keep heading west, jump a tramp steamer, reenlist in the Corps. . . . The options were endless.

"Walt, get over here. I want to introduce you to some fellas."

I went over to where Sheriff Connelly was standing, along with two other men in gun belts and hats. The men were both large, so at least I didn't have to worry about being looked over like I was a prize steer. "Howdy."

Lucian did the introductions. "This is Bo Brown out of Natrona County."

He was the older of the two, with a big, open, farmer face and sad eyes, and was wearing a broad-brimmed hat and an Indian blanket coat. "Hey, so you're Lucian's new whipping boy, huh?"

"And this is George McKay from down here in Laramie County."

The other man stepped forward with a slight smirk on his face and a great deal of assurance in his eyes. I'd seen the type numerous times, good ol' boys who were never satisfied unless they were bending rules or breaking heads. He was almost my size with maybe a little more weight on him, and he gripped my hand like a hydraulic press.

I studied his fringed jacket and pencil-roll hat, stylish for a thug.

"Lucian says you were some kind of big Marine detective over there; you find out who shot the Archduke Franz Ferdinand?"

"We think it might be a member of Young Bosnia or an affiliate of the Black Hand."

McKay nodded, smiling at Sheriffs Connelly and Brown. "Well, he's not just big, but well read, too."

An odd-looking woman with an extravagant ash-blond hairdo and dressed in a striped pantsuit squeezed in and took his arm. "George, those hateful men over there say I can bring only two bags on the train, and there's no way I can be gone for that long without all my things." Then she glanced up at me. "Well, hello."

I slipped my hat off, the paperback, which I still had under my arm, dropping onto the concrete as I did.

Brown scooped it up as the woman studied me and in a husky voice asked, "And who are you?"

"Longmire, Walt Longmire, ma'am."

She glanced back at McKay. "Did you see that, George, the way he took off his hat? Now, that's how a gentleman treats a lady." She started off but not before giving me a wink. "See you later, handsome."

"Don't worry, youngster, you won't have to take off your hat again — not too many ladies on this train." He looked at my boss. "Right, Lucian?"

He went after her, and we watched as the couple made their way through the crowd, McKay looking like a pulling guard, the woman wobbling on high heels as they went off to give the porters hell.

Brown handed me my copy of *Murder on the Orient Express*. "Studyin' up?"

"No, I just needed something to read."

He glanced around. "You'll have to meet Leeland. I think he's read every damn book that's ever been printed."

Lucian looked up at me. "Sheriff of Uinta County and the current president of the

Wyoming Sheriffs' Association." He gestured around us. "This is kind of his going-away party."

I nodded. "What did that fellow McKay mean about not meeting any ladies on the train?"

"I'll see you fellas on board." Sheriff Brown seemed embarrassed and quickly departed.

"I say something wrong?"

"Nope." Pulling a pipe and a beaded leather tobacco pouch from his jacket, he walked toward the rails. "When we first started running the Star back in '48, it was just a sheriff from each county, but then some of 'em started complainin' about how they wanted to bring either their wives or undersheriffs — so we loosened up the rules and started letting each sheriff bring a guest." He stuffed his pipe, clamped the stem between his teeth, and returned the pouch to his pocket. "Well, one thing led to another, and pretty soon some of the fellows started showing up with women that they weren't particularly married to."

"Oh." I glanced back down the platform. "Am I to take it then that the woman with Sheriff McKay is not Mrs. McKay?"

He struck a match and puffed on his pipe, getting it started. "You are to take that, yes."

"What about you?"

He froze for a second and then glanced at me with one of those mahogany irises of his. "What about me?"

"You ever bring any female guests?"

He puffed on his pipe some more and then blew out the flame, flicking the dead match onto the cinder bed of the gleaming rails. "If I did, it wouldn't be any of your business, now, would it, Troop?"

I smiled at my boots. "I suppose not."

He smoked his pipe. "I gotta go say hello to more of these fearless lawmen. . . . You wanna join me or have you had enough?"

I took out another Reed's candy. "I think I'll pass. I figure I can meet the rest of them on the train. When does it get here, anyway?"

"They're pulling it up from the side rail, and it'll be any minute."

I looked at my wristwatch. "Should I go get our bags?"

"Already had the porter deposit 'em on the train, and then it'll be your job to get 'em to our cabin. Now, normally I always take the bottom bunk, but I don't want to chance that you might collapse yours and land on top of me, so just this once I'll take the upper and you can have the lower." He turned to walk away but then hesitated.

"You don't snore, do you?"

"No."

"Good, 'cause I do, and I don't need competition."

"I don't suppose you'd like to tell me which car we're in?"

He smiled. "You can't miss it; the coaches are divided into Wyoming mountain ranges — the Laramie, the Medicine Bow, the Absaroka, the Wind River . . ."

I called after him. "Which one are we?"

"The Bighorn, of course!" He disappeared into the crowd, and I looked for somewhere to sit. A little ways down the platform, I spotted another wooden bench, only to see the same one-armed vagrant who had been sleeping inside now sitting there, reading his paper.

Thinking I'd do a little fence mending, I walked over and sat beside him. "Hey, um . . . I just wanted to say I was sorry for the way I acted a few moments ago."

He looked up from his article on the president's reelection. "Oh, that's all right. I figured it had something to do with that girl you were chasing after." I remained silent, and he gestured with the paper. "Can you believe we're stuck with this sad sack for another four years?"

I held the roll of candies out to him, and

he looked at me for a moment before taking one. “Mmm . . . root beer. You know, I met Eisenhower one time.”

I decided to play along. “Really?”

“Yes, and he told me he wasn’t the one that chose Nixon as his running mate back in ’52, that it was one of those smoke-filled backroom deals in Chicago. I guess he softened to him after their kids got married, but when I met Ike, he said he wouldn’t hire that man to serve drinks at a party, let alone be vice president of the United States.”

There was a thunderous noise, and the ground shook.

The vagabond stood and looked down the rails. “Well, son, here’s your train.”

I followed him toward the tracks to take in the spectacle.

As you begin your life there is something that attends you, something that will be an image of yourself and will meet you somewhere in that journey. It can take many forms, but for me, I will always remember mine as an FEF-3 class, 844 “Northern,” the Union Pacific’s oldest serving engine and the only steam-powered locomotive that held the distinction of never having been retired from a North American Class 1 railroad.

We watched the twin billowing clouds erupting from the jungle of black iron, small puffs pushing past the massive steel wheels as they slowly turned, and the majestic beast rolled into the station.

Designated UP 8444 so as to not be confused with the 844 diesel engine already in service, Wyoming's Western Star was a legend of a bygone era. But at the moment it was a living, breathing reality, a 907,890-pound behemoth that rolled into my life like a mechanized buffalo, snorting and lumbering destiny in every rotation of its steel wheels.

"I've lost count of how many times I've seen this beauty, but it never ceases to amaze me." The admiration in the old man's voice was evident. "Lord almighty."

The vagrant turned and offered me his only hand. "Nice to meet you, Deputy Longmire. Marv Leeland, president of the Wyoming Sheriffs' Association."

2

“You gonna stand there looking at that damn locomotive for what’s left of the night?”

Breathing a deep sigh, I watched the fog collect at my face and then blow away. “You finally woke up.”

“Hell yes, and I’m freezing my aged ass off. If it wasn’t for your dog here, I’d be a goner.”

It was late, and I turned back to the refurbished engine sitting outside the Union Pacific roundhouse in Cheyenne. “Let him out so he can pee.”

“What about me?”

“You can pee, too.” A few seconds later I heard the door of my truck open and the creature known as Dog, an animal that would probably have been better suited for the Pleistocene period, hiked a leg up on the chain-link fence and saluted the 844 Northern in his own particular fashion.

He came over and sat on my foot, and I gestured toward the massive engine. "Look, something bigger than you."

Built toward the end of the Second World War, the 844 was one of ten locomotives ordered by the Union Pacific. The quintessential result of dual-service steam engine development, the Northern turned out to be its swan song, designed to burn coal but converted to fuel oil even as research and development concentrated on the diesel-electric engines that dominate the tracks even today. Capable of speeds as high as 120 miles an hour, the passenger puller was a workhorse that had towed such legendary trains as the Los Angeles Limited, Portland Rose, and Wyoming's The Western Star.

The old sheriff nodded, walked over to the chain-link fence, and began urinating, marking his own territory at the exact same spot as Dog's. "What time is it?"

"Almost two." I turned to look at him. "Vic still asleep?"

"Yep." He turned back to the engine. "There any particular reason why we're standin' here in the middle of the rail yard lookin' at a piece of scrap metal?"

"They refurbished it and put it all back together like new." I gestured with my chin. "They're using it to pull excursion trains."

The old sheriff barked a laugh. "Excursions, huh?"

I ignored the response. "I wonder where we could go to get refurbished?" I stood there looking at the lines of the thing; like a woman with a broken nose — you can love her, but she ain't lovely. "Do you ever wonder if, like this piece of scrap metal, we were better then than we are now?"

Wavering a little, he zipped up and came back over to stand with Dog and me. "You havin' some sort of crisis of conscience or something?"

I stood there awhile longer, breathing out clouds. "Maybe."

"Well, don't."

I had to smile at the magnificent simplicity of Lucian Connelly's worldview. "Why did you hire me all those years ago, Lucian?"

" 'Cause that girl you had just married was some kind of cute." He blew a deep breath from his nostrils and stood there, deliberating a real answer. "Because you needed it."

I studied him for a moment more and then went back to looking at the big machine with its elephant ears — side panels that channel air closer to the steam engine at lower speeds in order to divert smoke away from the operators. "In case I've never said it . . ." I pulled my eyes away from the antique and glanced over at another piece of history. "Thank you."

He stared at me for a moment and then began hobbling back toward my truck in a serpentine fashion, grumbling and gesturing in the direction of the state capitol. "Have we got someplace to stay in this den of thieves and hucksters?"

"With Cady."

He called back, "Am I gonna have to climb steps?"

"That, or I can throw you over my shoulder and carry you."

"I'll climb, thank you very much."

We got back in the truck, and I navigated my way through the empty streets to my daughter's place, a carriage house with an alley alongside.

Lucian studied the large Victorian adjacent, a Queen Anne structure complete with a rounded corner tower and witch's hat turret. "That Joe Meyer's place?"

"Yep."

He continued studying it. "Damn, we should'a been attorney generals."

A voice rose from the backseat. "Jesus, are we there yet?"

Lucian turned. "Good morning, sweet pea."

"Fuck you."

I got out. Dog followed at a gallop and shot straight up the outside metal steps leading to the second floor, where a familiar shape stood backlit in the open doorway.

He stooped and caught the beast as Lucian and Vic began the ascent with me bringing up the rear, carrying our three duffel bags. "Lola is asleep, as is your daughter." We made the first landing, and he reached over the side to heft two of the bags. "I told her I would stay up and wait for you."

"How are you, Ladies Wear?"

"Tired, old man." Henry Standing Bear smiled and ushered us in, setting the duffels on a nearby chair and closing the door behind us. "You are late."

Lucian ambled over to the worn-out sofa that my daughter had hauled from Wyoming to Berkeley, to Seattle, to Philadelphia, and back again to her native state. "Well, big boy here wanted to stop by the Union Pacific roundhouse and have a gander at his ill-spent past."

Henry glanced at me, dark hair threaded with silver strands covering one side of his face. "There are two single beds in one guest bedroom and a single in the other to the right, but one of us will have to sleep on the sofa."

Upon hearing that information, the old sheriff redirected toward the left bedroom, veering around the piano that occupied most of the space. "Boy, have my bags brought to my room; there'll be something in it for you later."

The Bear waited till Lucian was gone before folding his powerful arms. "He has been drinking?"

"That's the real reason we're late."

Vic, sensing the party was over, took her bag and made for the single-bed guest room to the right. "I'm turning in; anybody want to join me?"

Not waiting for a response, she shut the door behind her as I rubbed my eyes one more time and then, stretching out another yawn, collected my bag and Lucian's from the chair beside the door. I looked around the room at the newly painted walls. "Sofa or bed?"

"As I recall, Lucian snores?"

I stood there waiting for him to make up his mind. "Like a Husqvarna chain saw."

"I will take the sofa."

Standing in the train's narrow passageway with a bag in each hand, I studied the small brass numbers on the eight berths per car

— Lucian having neglected to tell me which number was ours.

"Can I help you, sir?"

A small man with a lean face was standing beside me in a very white jacket that contrasted greatly with his black complexion. "Are you the porter?"

"No, sir. The porter is busy. I'm Mr. Meade Lux Gibbs, the head chef. Can I be of assistance?"

"That is a significant name, Mr. Meade Lux Gibbs." I glanced up and down the wood-paneled Pullman. "I'm trying to find the berth for Lucian Connelly?"

He retreated and gestured for me to follow. "And what county is he the sheriff of, sir?" Stopping at the end of the car, he stooped down and peered at an electric panel with a brass facing where pieces of paper had been slipped behind glass, each one corresponding with, evidently, a county.

"Absaroka."

"Hmm . . ."

"Is there a problem?"

He glanced up at me. "Are you travelin' with Sheriff Connelly, sir?"

"I am."

"Well, there seems to be some sort of confusion in that he has been given a single berth."

"That's not right. I gave him mine."

We both turned to see the man I'd mistaken for a bum, who had turned out to be the president of the Wyoming Sheriffs' Association.

The chef immediately brightened. "Mr. Leeland, how are you, sir?"

"I'm traveling alone and traded with Lucian when I found out he had a companion this trip." The affable individual leaned his armless shoulder against the doorway nearest us and turned the knob with his only hand. "I see you've met the real center of this train, Deputy Longmire. Mr. Meade Lux Gibbs here has told me he's originally from Belzoni, Mississippi, which was also the birthplace of Pinetop Perkins, one of the finest blues pianists of all time." He smiled. "Am I to understand from Lucian that you are known to tickle the ivories?"

I smiled back. "Pound is more like it, I'm afraid."

The chef gestured for me to take the nearest cabin. "Then numbers one and two are yours, Mr. Longmire."

"You don't sound particularly Southern, Mr. Gibbs."

"My family moved to Chicago when I was young, sir."

I looked through the doorway. "But this is

two rooms."

"It's a suite." He gestured toward Leeland. "You have this gentleman to thank for that."

I ducked inside, dropping Lucian's suitcase and my duffel on the sofa, but then leaned back out in time to catch Leeland, who was still talking to the head chef at the back of the car. "Sheriff?"

He broke off with the man and met me halfway. "You're going to have to come up with some other designation to get people's attention on this train."

I stuck out my left hand, seeing as how he was missing his right. "Longmire, deputy, Absaroka County. I didn't have a chance to introduce myself properly before."

We shook. "As I said, I've heard about you." He grinned the shy smile. "Lucian says that, besides playing piano, you were involved in the current conflict?"

"Yes, sir."

"I would imagine you didn't have much opportunity to play over there."

"You'd be surprised."

"Well, Lucian's a good man." He glanced around at the empty car. "Just between you and me, I'd like to see him as the new president of the sheriffs' association, but there appear to be a lot of individuals around here with other ideas."

I smiled. "You don't get to name your own heir?"

"No, no, no. . . . The Wyoming Sheriffs' Association is a democracy, which usually results in us settling on the worst possible candidate." He thumbed his lapel with a satisfied smile and you couldn't help but like the old guy. "Including yours truly."

"How long have you had the job?"

"Since a couple of years after my, um . . . conflict." Unconsciously, I let my eyes slip to his missing arm, and he noticed. "Peleliu."

I started to salute before catching myself and stuck my hand out again. "Lieutenant Walter Longmire, First Division."

"Corporal Marvin Leeland, First Division." He saluted in a jaunty fashion and then shook. "If I am to understand it correctly, you were one of the first Marine investigators over there?"

"Yes, sir. I was."

"Interesting." He nodded as he studied me. "I've got a few things to take care of, but wait for me in the dining car — it's the last one just before the caboose; the bar is small, so it's not as popular as the parlor car, where all the professional drinking will be going on. By Elk Mountain, we'll likely be the only two sober men on this train and maybe that'll give us a chance to talk alone."

"About?"

He smiled again. "Well, if I told you, then there wouldn't be anything to talk about, would there?" I watched as he turned and went in the same direction as the head chef, amazed at his physical ease despite the impairment.

Careful to leave Lucian's bag on the upper berth, I unbuckled my gun belt and placed it on my duffel. The newspaper had wanted us in our semiuniforms for the photograph, but I didn't see any reason to be walking around the cramped quarters like Bat Masterson.

Someone had passed by my door humming the old gospel tune "This Train," and now the tune was stuck in my head.

I couldn't help but be intrigued by the older sheriff's invitation, and I also couldn't help but wonder why he wanted to speak with me alone. Maybe it was just the camaraderie of the Corps.

I opened the small door to my left.

"I don't think you'll fit in that shower."

I turned around to see the woman I'd met on the platform, the one with the gravity-defying hairdo who was accompanying Sheriff McKay from Laramie County, standing in the doorway. "I think you're right."

"Kim LeClerc." She adjusted the scarf at her throat and extended a hand and we shook. "I'm a singer, mostly Peggy Lee stuff — you know, ballads and torch songs. I get a lot of work up at the Sandbar in Casper."

I didn't say anything.

She cocked her head, and her eyes shifted back to the shower. "We could soap up and see if we could both get in there."

"Are you in 3?"

She nodded and grinned. "With Georgie." She studied me, adjusting the belt on her pantsuit. "What's your name again?"

"Walt Longmire."

"Glad to meet you. . . . And where are you the sheriff again?"

"I'm not. I'm a deputy up in Absaroka County."

"Guess that makes you the low man on the totem pole around here, huh?" She entered the compartment unbidden and sat on the sofa with her legs crossed. "So, you kill many babies over there?"

"Over where?"

She flapped a hand. "I don't know, Swaziland, or wherever we're fighting."

"Vietnam." I sighed and leaned against the folded upper bunk. "Hardly any, they're small. . . . Hard to hit."

She shook a cigarette from the pack. "Got a light?"

"No."

She pulled out a lighter and lit it herself. "Want a smoke?"

"No, thanks."

She leaned back and exhaled toward the upper bunk. "Not a Mormon, are you?"

"No, ma'am."

"Neither are you." We both turned to see George McKay occupying the open doorway. He reached down, took her by the arm, and none too gently pulled her into the passageway. "C'mon."

I was preparing to close the door when he reappeared and, staring at the carpeted floor, leaned into the compartment. "Let's get something straight."

I folded my arms over my chest so that he wouldn't be tempted to replicate the Gottlieb Grip Tester from our previous meeting. "Okay."

He continued to look at the floor but craned his neck, exposing the muscles there for my benefit. "We're all going to be on this train for the next couple of days and nights — close quarters."

"Yep."

"Well, we'd probably all do a lot better if

we were careful of each other's property: I may have only known Miss LeClerc for a short time, but she's mine." He raised his eyes and squinted. "You read me, Sergeant Rock?"

"Like a comic book."

He stared at me a moment longer and then tattooed a quick beat on the door with a few knuckles. "Okay." He smiled a broad grin, revealing a little gold dental work. "Baby killer." And was gone in her direction.

I sighed and was about to sit down when Lucian appeared in the hallway. "What the hell was that all about?"

"Your buddy, appropriating his property."

He shrugged, unbuckled his gun belt, and handed it to me. "His what?"

"Nothing."

"Well, c'mon then, we need to get to the parlor car and meet the populace."

I stood there examining the utilitarian holster and the vintage Victory Model .38, replete with a lanyard attached to the butt of the revolver. "What do you want me to do with this?"

"Stuff it in one of those cupboards along with yours."

"They don't lock."

He stepped into the hallway, pulling back

a curtain to confirm that we hadn't yet left the bustling platform. "They never have."

I glanced around. "Well, I'm not leaving my sidearm in here unsecured."

He shook his head. "There are porters, conductors, and every other damn thing running up and down these corridors, not to mention every sheriff in the state of Wyoming, so I wouldn't worry about it if I were you."

I bit the skin on the inside of my cheek, shook my head, and put our gun belts in the highest cabinet above the shower.

"Criminy, if there's a problem do you promise to get my gun down for me?"

I paused for a moment, thinking about how weathered the leather of his holster was compared to mine. I wondered how many years he'd carried the thing, and whether I wanted to commit to carrying that long.

I closed the cabinet door. The next thing I was aware of was Lucian's voice, which seemed to come from a long ways away. "Hey, you all right?"

"I'm not so sure I can take this job."

His dark eyes narrowed, but a smile stayed on his lips. "Well, it's a hell of a time to tell me that." He cocked his head. "How long you been working for me now?"

"Coming up on two weeks."

He crossed his arms and glanced over his shoulder to assure we had at least a semblance of privacy. "I believe that would be the shortest on record, aside from that one kid ten years ago that ended up shooting himself." He laid his eyes on me like a blanket. "You aren't planning on shooting yourself, are you?"

"I'm just not sure if this is what I need to be doing with my life."

"I can see that, God help me." He reached out and pulled on my arm. "C'mon, I've got a bunch of fellas in the parlor car who aren't sure if they're doing what they're supposed to be doing with their lives, either — but they're all gonna be drunk as hootie owls by the time we get to Laramie, so who cares."

"I've got an appointment."

He glanced down the hall and then back at me again. "With McKay's property?"

"Hardly. I owe Sheriff Leeland a drink and promised him I'd meet him in the dining car."

He studied me for a moment. "Well, you can stop and have a beer with the boys as you pass through."

"All right, but not for too long, if that's okay with you." I closed the door and pulled up short. "Hey, how do you lock this door anyway?"

"With the key Mr. Gibbs gave me, but I've never locked a cabin in my life."

I stared at the door.

"Here, you take the damn thing, then."

I locked the door, pocketed the key, and started off after him.

"Look, I'm not one to tell a grown man what to do, but be careful with Leeland."

It seemed like a strange statement. "In what way?"

Summoning up a response, he stared at the lush carpeting. "He's something of a politician."

"And you're not?"

He studied me, and I marveled as I had a number of times in the last two weeks at the absolute darkness of his black pupils. "There are probably a lot of things you can learn from the men on this train, Troop, different things they can all teach you — or you can not learn a damn thing. Suit yourself." He sniffed a laugh and started off, seemingly unconcerned if I was following.

"Whiskey or bourbon?"

I stared at the tall, empty glass in front of me, looking the entire world like a water tower. "You're kidding, right?"

The parlor, or bar car, of The Western Star

looked to be circa 1880 but had actually seen its share of updates. The thick leaded-glass skylights allowed the afternoon sun to cast a golden light through the car as it sat there at the station. There were oak-paneled walls and green velvet curtains with gold sashes that matched the oriental carpeting. There were a few miniature oil paintings and an honest-to-goodness baby grand piano crouched in the forward corner.

The young woman waited for an answer without a hint of exasperation at my dithering. "Whiskey or bourbon?"

"Um . . ." I placed a hand over my glass. "Neither."

She shook her head as she moved on. "You're not a Mormon, are you?"

I glanced around at the collective senior law enforcement of the state of Wyoming as Lucian pointed out a few of the men I hadn't met, including one particularly wizened individual. "That's Anson Tillman, our neighbor from Sheridan County." We walked over, and he gestured to the two men at the table with him. "Meet Bill Wiltse, newly elected from Fremont County, and Wayne Hanna of Sublette."

"Nice to meet you, gentlemen." I tilted my head in the direction of a tall, thin individual by the door, who was talking to a heavyset man. "Those two?"

"Sundown Nolan of Campbell and Otis Phelps from Platte County."

"You're kidding. Sundown?"

He sipped his bourbon. "Meaning if you aren't white, you need to be out of his jurisdiction by sundown." He noticed the look on my face. "What?"

"In case you haven't noticed, there's been something of a cultural revolution going on in this country lately."

"And in case you haven't noticed, John's dead, Bobby's dead, and Martin's dead, and not a damn thing has changed — people still hang by their tribe. That's all we are, just a loose coalition of tribes." Lucian sighed and stared at me. "Speaking of, how's that outlaw buddy of yours, that Cheyenne? Ladies Wear, was it?"

I thought about my best friend in the world, a man I hadn't spoken to in over a year. "France."

"Come again?"

"Standing Bear, Henry Standing Bear, he's in France last I heard."

"What the hell's he doin' over there?"

I smiled. "A woman."

"Well, that's a better reason than most." He waited a beat before pointing at my left hand. "I'm guessing those scars wasn't from

France."

"No." I sighed, figuring he'd want the story sooner or later. "Johnston Atoll — I was given a rehabilitation duty, punishment by the provost marshal."

"Johnston what?"

"Johnston Atoll." I was surprised the old Doolittle Raider hadn't heard of the place. I figured with his extensive travel in the Pacific he'd heard of every speck of land that was there. "It's an atoll in the north Pacific Ocean."

He half shut one eye and considered. "Little airstrip located on a coral reef about eight hundred and sixty miles southwest of Hawaii?"

So he had heard of it. "Yep."

"Never been there, but it sounds like a paradise."

"Probably was before we started dropping atomic bombs on it and using it for storage of chemical and biological weapons."

He nodded and leaned in. "Had a civics teacher in high school who fought in the Great War." He tugged at his collar with a hooked index finger. "Had scars not so different from the ones you've got on your left hand."

I nodded. "Mustard gas."

"So, I take it your time there was not

entirely recuperative?"

"Lucian Connelly."

The sheriff extended a hand to the sad-looking man in the suit who now stood by our table. "Joe Holland, how did you get on this train?"

"The UP figured you fellas needed somebody to protect you from yourselves."

Lucian glanced around the car. "They might be spot-on in their concerns." He patted the seat next to him as I studied the man's face, bulbous and heavy. "Wanna sit down?"

"No, I've got to make my first pass of the train before we head out."

"Well, we'll catch you on down the tracks."

"Deal."

The man moved off. "What county is he?"

"Special officer. Whenever the stationmaster sends out a special like this, the UP always provides its own on-train security."

"What's the matter, young'un, too good to drink with a bunch of sod-busting sheriffs?" A man in black-framed glasses pushed my boss aside and sat down across from me. "Jeez, Lucian, you're not training him right." He glanced at me again. "You're not a Mormon, are you?"

"That's not the first time I've been asked that today."

He glanced around, seemingly embarrassed. “Jeez, you’re not, are you?”

“No, just cutting back as of late.”

He raised his eyebrows at Lucian. “Boy, did you bring the wrong deputy on this train.”

I glanced out the window. “Speaking of, does this thing ever move or do we just stay here at the station the whole time?”

“Oh, it’ll get moving here in a minute.” Sheriff Connelly did the necessaries. “Walt Longmire, meet Bruce Eldredge, sheriff up in Park County.”

We shook, and he glanced around, finally settling on Lucian. “Hey, did you hear about that house breaker in Albany County eleven months ago?”

Lucian sipped his king-size bourbon. “No.”

“Black fella strung up in a barn south of Bosler, dead as a stone.”

My boss nodded but said nothing.

“Somebody hung somebody for breaking into a house?”

Eldredge glanced at me, nodded, and sipped from his vat of whiskey. “After breaking in, robbing, and killing a sixty-three-year-old woman.”

Lucian leaned back in his chair and reached up to lower the window shade at his side. "How did they know it was this fellow?"

Bruce hunched his shoulders over his drink. "Found all the stolen jewelry in his pockets."

"After he was dead?" Connelly sighed. "Convenient."

The bespectacled man nodded. "Maybe." He studied Lucian and then looked around and leaned in. "You hear about Pixly?"

Connelly sipped his bourbon. "I heard he was dead."

"That he is, but did you hear how?"

I looked at my boss. "Who's Pixly?"

He made a face. "Fella that climbed in the window of a hotel in Jackson and abused and killed two young girls." He turned back to the Park County sheriff. "How?"

"Somebody cut his dingle off; tied him up in a motel room in Alpine, taped up his mouth, and left him there to bleed to death on the carpet."

My boss looked out the window. "Well, a tragedy in some very small and deeply disturbed circles, I suppose."

"There are more, Lucian."

The sheriff of Absaroka County turned and looked at the other man with his full attention. "How many?"

"In damn near all the counties." He shook

his head. "Have you had anything happen up in yours?"

"No."

"Nothing at all?"

Lucian's response was stronger this time. "No."

"Well, you're one of the only ones." Eldredge took another sip. "That's likely to raise some questions in itself." Lucian kept looking at him, and the ill ease became palpable to the point that the other sheriff stood and excused himself. "I just thought you ought to know."

I watched the man depart. "What's going on?"

"Hmm? Nothing. Nothing you need to be concerned with, at least." His eyes didn't move from the surface of the table, but his hand lifted the glass, holding it away from his mouth like a promise. "Lots of time to think on a train. . . . Maybe that's why people don't take 'em anymore."

It was at that moment that a whistle sounded long and loud enough to rattle teeth — and the world began moving.

3

"Glad you could make it." Marv Leeland sat in the next to last seat of the next to the last car of The Western Star, his pale blue eyes focused on the gently rolling hills glowing a faded amber in the afternoon sun west of Cheyenne. "Hard to get lost on a train."

"Oh, I think I could manage, if I set my mind to it."

"Well, this is the end — the only thing farther back is the caboose." He smiled. "Normally there wouldn't be a caboose, but Gibbs won't travel without one." He took off his hat and rested it in his lap alongside the cuff of his pinned sleeve. "Have a seat."

I sat at the table opposite him. "I don't see a bar in this car."

"I lied about that part."

"Oh?"

"Liquor is easy to find, but a quiet place . . ." He let the thought trail off. "I've got a question for you."

"Yes, sir?"

"I seem to remember a Walt Longmire who was the offensive tackle for the University of Southern California team that played in the Rose Bowl and handed Wisconsin their ass a few years ago."

"Yes, sir."

"I was a wideout for the University of Wyoming, myself, back when I had two good hands." He chuckled, and his eyes came up to mine. "You're a hell of a ballplayer, son."

"Thank you."

"How come you didn't go pro?"

I sighed. "I had an obligation with the United States government."

He widened his eyes for comic effect and nodded. "Well . . . and now you're toiling in the fields for Lucian?"

"A couple of weeks, so far."

He made a point of staring at the scenery again. "Not looking to make a career in sheriffing?"

I thought about it. "I don't think so, sir."

"Well, I'm sorry to hear that, but it might be better for my purposes in the long run."

I studied him as he continued to look out the window. "In what way?"

"I'm looking for a short-term partner, and I thought you might suit the bill."

"A partner in what?"

"An investigation."

I glanced back at the empty car. "Why me?"

"You're young, and you seem damn capable." He looked at me. "And because, son, I've got a relationship with every man on this train, and I'm looking for a fresh set of eyes — eyes I can trust."

I waited a moment, trying to figure him out but not having any luck. "On a train full of sheriffs you know."

"Yes."

I shook my head. "Am I to gather from that that your suspect in this investigation is a sheriff?"

"Quite possibly."

I slumped back against my cushioned seat. "Why would you trust me? You don't even know me."

"Call it a hunch." He smiled. "Lucian trusts you."

"Well, following that line of thought would suggest you trust Lucian."

"But I don't."

I studied him for a while, the sway of the rails the only soothing thing in the conversation. "I'm not so sure I should be having this talk with you."

"Maybe not."

"Do you mind if I ask what crime you're —"

"Murder."

The two of us sat there listening to the rail joints as they composed their own rhythm. "And this murder took place in Uinta County?"

He was slower to respond this time. "Not exactly."

"I'll need you to be exact if I'm going to assist you." A thought dawned. "I'm not so sure I like where this conversation is heading."

"And why is that?"

"Well, I've been working for Lucian only a couple of weeks, but I've known him most of my life."

"Do you trust him?"

"Trust him to what?"

"To not kill someone. Just about every man on this train has killed, some more than others, and if you're looking for a killer, I figure one who has already killed is a pretty good place to start."

"Well, why don't you tell me about this murder?"

"Actually . . ." His eyes went back to the darkening sky as the train rumbled on. "There's more than one."

■ ■ ■ ■

Cady lifted her head and looked at me as she attempted to clean my granddaughter's hands. I'd made pancakes; it was something I did for my daughter in the mornings when we were together, especially rewarding because now there were three of us again.

"What is she doing?"

"She's humming."

I rested the spatula on the edge of the frying pan and turned off the burner. "Does that mean she likes my pancakes?"

"She likes the syrup."

"More!" Lola laughed, giggled, and clutched another flapjack, stuffing part of it in her mouth and dropping the rest for Dog, who knew a good deal when he ate one.

Cady watched her and then held up her own blob of fried batter by the edge. "By the way, what is this supposed to be?"

"I think . . ." I studied my creation. "It's a bear."

She turned it and looked at it, pulling off what for me passed as a leg.

I sat at the table with my tiny family. "Okay, I'm a little out of practice."

"Maybe you and Dog should come to Cheyenne more often, then."

Lola pointed at the beast and said, "Dog."

"Maybe the two of you should come to Durant more often."

We sat there in a three-hundred-and-seven-and-three-quarter-mile stalemate.

She sipped her coffee and deflected. "Where's the gang?"

"Henry and Vic drove down to Denver, but I'm supposed to meet them in Fort Collins at around four o'clock to pick up your sofa. Personally, I think they just wanted to give us some time alone."

The cool gray eyes studied me over the rim of her cup. "Where's Uncle Lucian?"

"Still asleep." She glanced at her wristwatch and then at me in turn. "He had a long night."

"Mama. Down!"

Cady picked my granddaughter up from the high chair. "Say please, Lola." She sat her on her lap. "Showboating for the young sheriffs, was he?"

"He had a good time."

She kept looking at me, which always made me a little nervous, feeling that she might be thinking of trading me in on another dad. "You seem a little out of sorts."

I shrugged.

"Is it the hearing?"

I stood and went over to the sink to rinse

out my mug. "I suppose." Lola began reaching for her mother's coffee cup, so I went over and took her, lodging her on my hip, and then twisted back and forth until she began giggling again.

Cady straightened her bathrobe and watched us. "As I recall, last time it took less than an hour."

Taking Lola's hand, I made like I was going to bite it but then kissed it instead. "Forty minutes."

"I don't understand why you even have to be there."

I turned and looked out the kitchen window at the treetops in Lakeview Cemetery. "It's a promise I made." Spinning my granddaughter around, I bounced her a few more times as the other sheriff of Absaroka County, looking a little worse for wear, appeared in the doorway. "Good morning, Sunshine."

He struggled toward my empty chair and sat, his silver hair, still in a crew cut, doing its best to look sideswiped. "Coffee."

Cady trailed a hand across his shoulders and poured him one, placing it carefully in front of the old man like a life preserver. "Here you go."

"Hangover?"

He slurped the coffee. "More like a cliffhanger; I'm still not sure if I'm going to make it." He looked up and mustered a smile for Lola. "I figure me and the baby both can spend the day sleeping, puking, and shitting our pants."

Cady smiled. "The babysitter will be here in about twenty minutes, and I'll tell her she's got two today." My daughter stood. "I've got to go take a shower and get to work."

"If you're still working for those shysters over at the attorney general's office, I wanna file charges against an individual who was supposed to take care of a delicate senior citizen such as myself."

She kissed the top of his head as she passed, disappearing around the corner. "Delicate like a bristly old badger."

He called after her, "Well, thank God I got some coffee, 'cause it looks like I'm not getting much sympathy around here!" He turned and looked at Lola and me. "Gimme that baby."

"Are you sober enough to hold her?"

He stuck out his hands. "Gimme that damn baby; I know where I can get me some lovin'." I handed her over and watched as he folded her up in his arms, then left them there to discuss the state of the world.

As I passed through the living room, there

was a knock on the door, so I changed course and opened it to find a very large woman practically looking me in the eye, with two young men standing behind her. "Howdy."

"Sheriff Longmire?"

"Yes, and you must be Alexia Mendez." I swung the door open and invited her in, but by that time Dog was standing beside me, which apparently gave the group pause. "Don't pay any attention to him, he's friendly."

No sooner had I said these words than Dog began a low, vibrating growl.

I swatted him and turned back to them.

She entered, but the two young men stood outside, looking at each other and then at Dog. "This is my nephew Ricardo and his friend David; they are living with me in my house and I asked them if they could be here to help with the sofa that your daughter is getting?"

"Oh, we haven't picked it up yet." I stuck a hand out to Ricardo, a rather thin young man with deep-set, dark eyes not unlike his aunt's. The other young man was more muscular, with shoulder-length blond hair. "David . . . ?"

He spoke with a Southern accent. "Um, Coulter, sir."

Something about his manner tipped me off. "Military?"

"Army — used to be."

"You?"

"I play guitar."

We stood there for a moment. "Well, that means you'll get all the girls."

He nodded, relieved at not having to prove his manhood. "You want us to hang around and wait?"

"You're welcome to come in, but I have to run down to Fort Collins to meet them and don't know when we'll get back."

He glanced at Dog and then his aunt, and there was a brief exchange in Spanish. She turned back to me. "I have his number, so we can call them when the sofa arrives?"

"Sure, that'd be great, but I think we can probably handle it, if they have other things to do."

They departed, and I gestured toward the kitchen. "Lola and her Uncle Lucian are in there, and Cady is getting ready for work."

Dog approached, and she ran a hand over his head, winning him over with a scratch behind the ear. "Miss Cady has an uncle?"

"Well, not officially. Anyway, you'll see. I'm going to go speak with her, and then I'll join you."

She smiled again and disappeared with

Dog following behind.

I tapped on the partially open door of my daughter's bedroom. "Alexia's here, but if you need any extra help today . . . with Lola, I mean?"

The door opened, and she hung on it, looking up at me. I had a momentary flashback to the many conversations we'd had in the doorway of her bedroom in the little rented house she'd grown up in back home. "Not really. Why, are you looking for something else to do?"

"Maybe."

She studied me, pulling a reddish butterscotch lock from her eyes and depositing it behind her ear. "You really hate this, don't you?"

"I guess I do."

"Then don't do it."

"It's not that easy, Cady."

She straightened my collar. "With you, it never is."

I decided I needed a drink after all.

Leaving Sheriff Leeland in the rear, I found my way back to the lounge car where the party, along with the train, was well under way. Sidling up to the bar, I got the attention of the bartender, the same diminutive brunette as before. "What's a man got to do to get a beer around here?"

She smiled. "Boy, are you on the wrong train."

"So I've been told." I pulled the Agatha Christie from my jacket pocket and thumbed to the beginning in hopes of insulating myself from any company.

She leaned forward with an air of confidentiality. "The crew has a case of Rainier they smuggled on board back in the dining car. When I get a second I'll go liberate a six for you, just 'cause you're cute."

"Or because I'm less than thirty years old?" She smiled, ran her hand through her hair, and turned to another sheriff whom I hadn't met, as I feigned reading.

"Just a branch water on the rocks, if you would, please." He leaned toward me and shifted his buckaroo hat farther back on his head. He was younger than the rest of the sheriffs with one of his eyes larger than the other, giving the impression that he was studying you with only half his faculties. "John Schafer."

"How do you do."

"I'd do better if I wasn't on a train full of drunks." He gestured toward my empty hands. "Good to see another man with some restraint. You a Mormon?"

"Um, no." As we watched the young

bartender set his water on the bar and then disappear, I came clean. "Actually, I just ordered a beer, but evidently she has to go find some."

"Oh." He studied me for a moment with his larger eye. "You're new."

"Yep. Deputy sheriff up in Absaroka County under Lucian Connelly."

He glanced over his shoulder to where Lucian had moved to a row of chairs facing the windows. He had been joined by some of the other men, who were laughing uproariously at something my boss had just said. "He appears to be having a good time." He shook his head. "Hey, hey, hey, you see that piece of work that McKay brought on board — a real cruiser-crawler. She made a play for me about a week ago, but I told her to take a hike." He studied me some more. "You're a big one, aren't you?"

"Yep."

"Six-four?"

"Five."

He nodded and sipped his water. "When we get to Evanston, I might need a favor."

"A favor?"

"Yes." He looked out the window. "If I need you, I'll tell you about it when we get there." He looked a little embarrassed at asking, and then, changing the subject, gestured outside. "What do you make of this country?"

I dipped my head to look out the window at the unfamiliar terrain. "I'm not sure where we are."

"Hermosa — it used to be a cattle loading depot, but it's just a ghost town now."

"Looks like godforsaken territory."

I got the eye again. "Albany, my county as of eight years ago."

I glanced back out the window. "It has a subtle beauty."

He nodded, and a slight smile snuck onto his lips. "We'll start climbing here in a minute and finish off at Sherman Hill, the highest point on the transcontinental railroad."

The young woman returned and handed me a bottle of beer with a smile and a tilt of her head.

"Thank you." She eyed me a moment more and then I turned back to Schafer. "Well, that should be a sight."

"Not really, we'll be going through the tunnel, so it'll be mostly dark as ten feet up a bull's ass."

I nodded, thinking it best if I said nothing, still wondering what kind of favor he might have in mind. I was relieved when

Holland, the special agent from the railroad, joined us. "Gentlemen, what are we up to?"

Schafer sipped his water. "I'm attempting to educate the new guy."

"Concerning?"

"Just about every damn thing." With that, he pushed off the bar and moved away.

"I don't think you impressed him with your breadth of knowledge, Deputy," said the sad-looking train dick.

"No, I suppose not." I gestured out the window. "Have you ever wondered why all of the major cities, or what passes for major cities in southern Wyoming, are almost exactly two hours apart by train?"

"Can't say that I have."

"They started out as water stops for when all the trains were steam."

He cocked his head. "I'd say Sheriff Schafer has underestimated you, Deputy Longmire."

"I'm careful who I share my intellect with, Mr. Holland." My eyes went back to the window — we were, indeed, climbing. "You know about the raffle?"

"Excuse me?"

"The raffle. When Wyoming moved from being an Indian Territory to becoming a state, they knew they needed towns every two hours for those water stops, so they put up a raffle to divide the state government. The towns would get their choice of the capitol, the university, the prison, or the psychiatric hospital."

"Who won?"

"Rawlins."

He looked at me, doubtful. "The prison?"

I nodded. "First choice, the theory being that they weren't so sure how the state government or higher education thing would work out, but we'll always have prisoners here in Wyoming."

He pulled at an elongated earlobe. "Well, they had a point." He glanced over his shoulder. "That might be one of the reasons Schafer's not too sociable."

"He lives in Rawlins?"

"No, but he's got a brother that had a short stop there before they shipped him off to Evanston."

I raised an eyebrow — maybe this had something to do with the favor Schafer had mentioned.

Holland looked around to make sure the sheriff of Albany County was well out of earshot. "This brother of his, Ed, got into some trouble back when he was a kid and did a juvenile stint. When he got out, they figured he was okay, but pretty soon some coeds started disappearing around the university in Laramie. I guess he killed a half dozen before they figured out it was him. He was an adult by that time, and they sent him to Rawlins on a life sentence, but when he killed a guard there, they stuffed him in a hole underneath the Wyoming State Insane Asylum."

"Black sheep, huh?"

He nodded. "They tested him and they say he's got an IQ of over a hundred and forty." He glanced around and remained silent as another sheriff passed us holding two drinks. "Arrested by his own brother. Strange, too — even with more than a couple of years between 'em, they look remarkably alike with the same proptosis."

"The bulging eye?"

He nodded. "But in opposite eyes; John's is the left and Ed's is the right. Even though they aren't twins, there are some folks who said that was the only way you could tell the two apart."

"Before they lodged Ed under the insane asylum?"

"Yeah." He nodded toward the man who now stood near Lucian and was listening to the stories. "John's one tough hombre. He still goes and visits his brother every month over there, and I was on this train with him a year ago and he invited me to go along."

The man shuddered. "My God, I've never been in a place like that. They slid that grate aside, and the two of 'em talked through a hole in the door." His face turned back to mine. "I've never seen anything like that. There just aren't words for it. Ed just kept telling his brother that he was innocent, and he had to get him out of there."

"Unfortunate."

"Is that what you call it?" He shook his head. "They should've taken Ed out and shot him in a ditch and left the body for the turkey buzzards."

"Unless he really is innocent."

He chuckled. "Don't you know? Everybody's innocent in there." He stared at me. "You're a true believer, huh?"

"Define true believer."

"Someone who thinks there is an equal and all-encompassing justice."

I took a sip of my beer before answering. "No, I don't think there is, certainly not after Vietnam."

He studied me a few moments more. "Yeah, you're a true believer all right."

"You ought to get one of those phones that tell you where to go." Lucian stuffed the bowl of his pipe from the beaded tobacco pouch as I drove.

"I know where I'm going."

He glanced around as I parked in the municipal lot. "This ain't the way to the Office of Probation and Parole."

"I know that, too."

I cut the ignition.

"Then where the hell are we going?"

"Wyoming Court of Appeals."

"Hell, what's being appealed?"

I pulled the handle and opened the door of my truck, glad to get him out before he started smoking. "We're going to find out."

Declining my assistance, he exited from the other side and eased the prosthetic leg to the pavement. "You need to get a lower truck."

I helped him around the door and closed it behind him, handing him his four-prong cane. "You seem to have a lot of ideas about what I need."

He glanced around. "Well, you needed to park closer, too."

"Uh huh." I shook my head and guided him in the direction of the office. "How about you get one of those handicapped mirror danglers? That way I can park right by the door." He didn't say anything. "Or I could go get one of those complimentary wheelchairs they've got inside. . . ."

"How would you like to kiss my ass for a

big red apple and then not get it?"

I assisted him in stepping up on the curb. "Well, I don't think I'd like that very much at all." I spotted one of the court-appointed attorneys on his way out of the building. "Dick Davis?"

He joined us. "Hey, Walt . . . Lucian."

"Where are you headed?"

"The convict had what they're calling a heart episode, so they hauled him over to Cheyenne Regional Medical; we're in a holding pattern."

Lucian poked at one of the silver-haired lawyer's boots with his cane. "There are a lot of folks who would contest the fact that the convict has a heart at all."

Dick nodded and started past us. "I've got more cases that need attention this morning, certainly ones that pay better, so . . ."

I called after him. "What are we supposed to do?"

"I guess you've got to wait until the court decides when the hearing will convene."

"Well." I turned back to Lucian. "Do you want to get Lola and go to the zoo?"

He ignored me. "No, by God, I'm goin' to find out what the hell is goin' on."

I followed, figuring the least I could do would be to keep Lucian from being incarcerated himself.

Ushering him through the glass doors, I got that feeling I always did when walking on the marble floors past the wood-paneled walls of the grand government building — that I was some country cousin from the hinterlands, unworthy of sullying the halls of justice. We were making our way down one of those halls when we ran into the one person in Cheyenne I was hoping to avoid.

"Walt Longmire, you haven't been returning my e-mails."

I looked down at the frizzy mop of chemically dyed fuchsia hair, a color approximating nothing in the natural world. "Libby, I don't have a computer."

She propped a fist on a hip obscured by an extremely loud, printed caftan and swung a scarf as large as a Hudson's Bay blanket over a shoulder, her jewelry rattling like a sheep wagon. "Do you have a phone?"

"Sometimes."

Libby Troon was the owner and operator of Liberty Bail Bonds and living proof that the spirit and style of the sixties were far from dead. "Well, I've got some opportunities for you and that delicious Henry Standing Bear."

I watched as Lucian, who hadn't paused, kept walking. "We've got enough official work to keep us busy, Libby."

I tried to move past her, but she stepped in my way. "Um, there's something I'd like to talk with you about."

I stifled my sigh. "Go ahead."

"Abarrane Extepare."

One of the patrician Basque ranchers from my county. "He's, what, a hundred years old?"

"Well, almost, I guess, but there's a situation developing with his great-grandson."

"What kind of situation?"

"He keeps taking him off on unscheduled trips."

"Unscheduled trips. Like what, fishing?"

"Now that you mention it, yes. The parents filed charges. Abarrane had taken the kid to Elko, Nevada. The charges were dropped, but I've got a funny feeling on this one."

I glanced down the hallway where Lucian had disappeared. "Libby, if you've got something to tell me, I'd appreciate it if you just got to the point."

"I've seen this pattern before where they test the limits, seeing how far they can get before they finally take the child and vanish."

I stuffed my hands in my pockets and looked at her. "Abarrane is one of the largest landowners in the county and he's older than dirt. Where would he run off to, the Sunnydale Home for Assisted Living? And why would he kidnap a kid in his own family?"

With her hands waving in a flurry of jewelry jangling, she dismissed me and continued past. "I'm just warning you, Walt."

I caught up with Lucian at the office of the court of appeals, turned the knob of the glass-paned door, and swung it open, stepping inside and pulling it closed behind me.

The old sheriff was standing in front of a young woman at a reception desk who looked as if she wished she were anywhere else but under Lucian's scathing gaze as he stared at her from over the piece of paper he was holding. "What the hell does that mean?"

The young woman reached up and tapped the paper he held. "It's all right there."

Lucian turned and looked at me. "Will you please tell this young woman that I know how to read, I just need to know what it means?"

I took the sheet and paraphrased. "The prisoner's lawyers have filed for a compassionate release, petitioning the warden in Rawlins and the court to the effect that the subject is terminally ill and would benefit from obtaining aid outside of the prison system, or is otherwise eligible under the relevant law."

I handed the woman back the paper and turned and walked out, not trusting myself with human company at that moment.

I don't remember slamming the door, but the glass exploded into the carpeted office like it had been hit with a fragmentation grenade.

Waves of emotion roiling my mind, I didn't stop to look at the damage I'd done. Instead, I stalked down the hallway through a cluster of suited men, blew open the brass double doors, and stepped out into the free air.

I stood there looking at the state capitol, taking deep breaths in an attempt to control the tide of emotion that was overwhelming me.

Feeling someone approaching from behind, I whirled with a snarling anger that caused Lucian to step back, whereupon he stumbled and almost fell, catching himself on the railing. Luckily, there was a bench nearby and he redirected the fall into a seat.

I stood there with my fists clenched.

"You ain't gonna hit me, are you?"

"No."

"Wouldn't be the first time."

After another breath, I turned and sat beside him, finally feeling a little cooler, the angry, red tide subsiding.

He studied my face. "You all right?"

"No."

He nodded and re-produced the piece of paper. " 'Compassionate release is most often granted to inmates with terminal illnesses that cause life expectancies of less than six to eighteen months, depending on the jurisdiction. Other allowable causes for compassionate release may be medical but nonterminal, such as incurable, debilitating mental or physical conditions that prevent inmate self-care, or a combination of advanced age and irreversible age-related conditions that prevent functioning in a prison setting.' " He stopped, cleared his throat, and turned to look at me again. "What in the hell is that supposed to mean, anyway?"

"They're going to try and set him free."

4

Henry and I negotiated the second corner of the staircase and were trying to figure out how to navigate the next. I was starting to regret not taking Alexia's nephew and his friend Coulter up on their offer. "It's not going to fit."

The Bear smiled and shook his head. "You said that the last time."

I shifted the weight of the thing in an attempt to relieve the pressure on my shoulder. "Maybe I'm not meant to be a furniture mover."

"Then you should not have had a daughter."

"Hold on a second." I moved to the landing and extended the sofa out over the backyard, wedging my legs against the railing. "I have to get arranged here."

He patiently waited as I prepared to bear the brunt from below. "So, 'particularly extraordinary or compelling circumstances which could not reasonably have been foreseen by the court at the time of sentencing'?"

"That's what the letter says."

"He had a heart attack?"

"Episode. Supposedly." I shifted to one side. "Are you pulling on this thing at all?" He made headway, and we turned the corner like two men in a horse suit. "All right, put it down — I need a breather."

He did as requested and then sat on the arm nearest him.

I pushed my hat back, giving the sweat in my hair a chance to dry. "For years I've been coming down here to make sure this didn't happen."

"Perhaps it is time to let it go."

"No."

"You will not entertain the thought?"

"No." He said nothing. "What, you're not going to argue with me?"

"No."

"It's a moral issue — you always argue with me about moral issues."

He looked down at me from an eight-step advantage. "I am tired of arguing with you about moral issues."

"Well, what are we going to talk about for the rest of our lives?"

He glanced around. "The weather."

"Hey, when are you lollygaggers gonna get the job done, huh?"

I looked up. Vic was sipping a glass of red wine; Lucian was hanging over the deck railing with a bourbon in one hand and Lola in the other. "Old man, if you drop my granddaughter, could you make sure she lands on the sofa?"

"There ain't anywhere for the lady, me, and the baby to sit up here, so speed it up, will you?" With that pronouncement he and a couple of the loves of my life disappeared.

I went back to looking at Henry. "You know what happened."

"Intimately."

"Then you should understand that there are some sentences that can't be broken."

He stooped to pick up the sofa again.

"Hey, what's the holdup down there?"

I looked up to see my daughter with her own glass of red wine.

"Your father is wanting to have a conversation."

"No, I'm not."

"Well, your granddaughter wants you to play the piano for her, so maybe you should get moving."

With nothing else to do to entertain myself, I sat at the baby grand — a 1938 Wurlitzer

Butterfly, so named for the twin top boards — in the corner of the parlor car and lifted the lid. The last time I'd played was in Vietnam; hell, I wasn't even sure I still could with my hand scarred as it was.

A drunken sheriff who was leaning against the wall nearby yelled, "Play 'Melancholy Baby.' "

Another laughed. "How 'bout 'Wreck of the Ol' 97'!"

I ignored them and laced my fingers together, cracking my knuckles in a fashion that the great pianist Arthur Rubinstein would have abhorred — or maybe not. I tested a few fingers on the keys; the piano was a slight bit out of tune and the action on the soundboard a little dead, but I doubted the drunken sheriffs would be able to tell the difference.

"Let me get back there with you. I can play 'Chopsticks' with the best of 'em."

Just for fun, I saluted Mr. Rubinstein with a little of Chopin's Waltz in C-sharp Minor, but that made my audience go silent, which wouldn't do.

I adjusted myself on the bench and slowly began playing a trainlike rhythm that changed into a boogie-woogie beat. I vamped on this and then began bringing in my left hand to follow the chord changes at eight to the bar.

"Holy shit!"

The second drunk gestured toward my boss, who was standing nearby. "Hey, Lucian, this boy's actually got talent."

I had just finished up with an improvised "Western Star Boogie" when I noticed Sheriff McKay's property standing by the doorway with that look that singers get when they want to join in but can't figure out how.

I raised my hands and began snapping my fingers, and even in its inebriated state, the audience joined in. By the time I lowered my hands to the keyboard, about half the train was snapping. I overemphasized my left hand in an attempt to make up for the lack of bass and drums.

I watched the smile slink onto Kim LeClerc's face as I circled around and gave her the intro again, nodding my head for her to take the impromptu stage. She moved forward and out from under George McKay's arm.

Davenport and Cooley wrote the song in 1956, the first version being recorded by Little Willie John, but I first became aware of it when this chick from North Dakota picked it up, added some lyrics of her own, and emphasized the beat, making it into a monster hit back in '58.

LeClerc was surprisingly good, with her husky voice, and I redoubled my efforts to match her phrasing, which was slightly different from Peggy Lee's.

I looked up the length of the car and noticed that even Marv Leeland, peeking over the heads of the other sheriffs, was standing in the near doorway of the packed Pullman.

LeClerc was feeling her oats by this time and had begun swiveling her hips, providing a percussion all her own, as George McKay advanced and reached a hand out for her. "C'mon, that's enough."

She slipped away from him and, having moved toward the chairs that faced the windows, continued to sing like a cornered cat. *"Fever! In the morning, fever all through the night . . ."*

McKay moved toward her again. Even after a number of the sheriffs yelled for him to clam up and sit down, he kept reaching for her, obviously upset that she was sharing her charms with the other men. When he got close enough he made a grab for her but instead knocked the hat off an individual I hadn't met yet, who took exception and stood. There were words, and McKay shoved the man out of the way. I started to get up.

Suddenly a hand was on my shoulder, and I turned to find Sheriff Leeland sitting next to me. "Not your fight. At least until somebody gets out a set of bongos or an accordion. God, I hate accordions."

Bo Brown, the big farmer type from Natrona County, grabbed McKay by his collar and pulled him away from the other man, pushing him into the crowded aisle where a number of other sheriffs, including Sundown Nolan and Wayne Hanna and Holland, the security man, held him still until LeClerc and I finished the song.

I struck the final note, and the car erupted in a roar of applause as Kim took a bow and blew a kiss toward me; I nodded my head and gestured back to her, and she curtsied.

The group of men had released McKay, and he started toward his property just as Lucian stepped forward, intercepting him.

McKay loomed large over my boss, but the smaller man had lived entire lives that most men only hear about, and he stood there like a rock outcropping in a high tide.

I moved to get up, but Leeland stopped me again.

"In case you haven't noticed, he's about

twice Sheriff Connelly's size."

Leeland chuckled as he glanced over his shoulder at the two would-be combatants. "Maybe, but my money would still be on Lucian — he fights dirty. Besides, this'll be a nice audition for the presidency."

I thought for a moment McKay was going to punch Sheriff Connelly, but then more words were exchanged and McKay seemed to deflate a little. Finally he turned, pushed some of the others out of the way, and exited through the front of the car, giving me a particularly hard look as he passed.

"Well, scoot over." Marv glanced at me, and I did as he asked. "I think the biggest crime right now would be for you to rob this train of your talent." He placed his hand on the keyboard, softly trilling a few notes. "Have you ever heard of Paul Wittgenstein?"

"I've heard of Ludwig Wittgenstein, the philosopher."

"His brother. Paul was the seventh child of nine. Now, the Wittgensteins were one of Vienna's most remarkable families and were so obsessed with music that they had seven grand pianos. Paul made his debut in 1913 and was already deemed a successful pianist and promising virtuoso when he enlisted in the Austrian army."

I had a funny feeling I knew where this

was going.

His hand trailed up the keys, ending on a grim chord. "A few months later he was wounded on the Russian front and taken prisoner, where they amputated his right arm. In a Siberian prison camp, he practiced Chopin on a wooden box, improvising ways for one hand to play both melody and harmony."

Sheriff Leeland began playing in a waterfall of five fingers, and I'd never witnessed anything like it.

"After the war, Wittgenstein returned home and commissioned more than a dozen pieces from some of the greatest composers of his time." He chuckled. "He wasn't particularly fond of any of them but decided that Ravel's Piano Concerto for the Left Hand in D Major wasn't bad."

He swelled into the piece, his hand flat-hatting across the keyboard and thundering the lower notes like a trip-hammer. Finishing what I assumed was the first portion of the piece, he turned to look at me with his sad eyes. "Personally, I think it's a masterpiece."

We sat there smiling at each other until we became aware of the silence and looked up once again to find the onlookers dumbstruck.

I leaned his way and spoke in a low voice. "Maybe not a highbrow crowd."

Leeland immediately launched into a jazzy blues version of "This Train." "Boy howdy."

"How was your day?"

I sat on Cady's newly arrived sofa with Dog snoring at my feet and Lola snoring on my daughter's lap as the radio played in the background. "Great."

She stared at me over the lip of her glass.

"Okay, not so great."

She put her wine down and cradled Lola's head in the crook of her arm so that she would stop snoring. "So, is this a medical release, medical parole, medical furlough, humanitarian parole . . . ?"

I nudged Dog with my boot. "I'll find out tomorrow morning in the judge's chambers."

"In these cases, the eligibility usually is a result of terminal or chronic illness."

"Yep."

"So, he's dying."

"Maybe." I stood and walked toward the door.

"Where are you going?"

"I just need some air."

I pushed it open and stepped out onto the deck that overlooked the alley and the backyard. Carrying my tea to the balustrade, I stood there for a while looking at the nearby park and cemetery. Vic, Henry, and Lucian had gone to bed, and since Cady and I had occupied the new sofa, the Bear had made the supreme sacrifice of attempting to sleep in the same bedroom with Lucian, who had been snoring louder than Dog and Lola combined. In the distance I could hear a train whistle and, with the music in my head, I tapped a rhythm on the railing with the fingers on my left hand as I sipped my tea.

"What's the song?"

I turned to find her wrapped in an old hippie blanket her mother had given her. "I put Lola to bed."

"Where's Dog?"

"Asleep beside her crib." I smiled, and she asked again, "What's the song?" She placed a hand over mine.

I sighed. "It's called 'This Train' — so old nobody knows who wrote it."

"Oh, that old."

"The first recording was done in 1922 by the Florida Normal and Industrial Institute Quartette. Their version was called 'Dis Train,' with a 'D,' but it was Sister Rosetta Tharpe's version, called 'This Train,' for Decca in the early fifties with accompaniment from a newfangled contraption called the electric guitar that really kicked the song off."

"And it's about a train."

"Bound for glory, but the thing that always bothered me about it was the exclusivity — it's basically a list of all the people who aren't going to get to ride the train to heaven, and if you're a certain type of person, you don't get to go."

"Like who?"

"Lawyers are the first ones mentioned."

"Oh, I don't like this song already." The Greatest Legal Mind of Our Time looked up at me. "Who else doesn't get to go? Anything about sheriffs?"

"Not specifically. . . . It's mostly concerned with false pretenders, backbiters, whiskey drinkers, and crapshooters. As I recall, no jokers, no tobacco chewers or cigar smokers, either."

I sighed and looked back at the scattered lights of the state capitol. There were no lights when you looked out my windows at home, unless you count the ones on the Hanging Road in the Milky Way.

She nestled in close and took my arm in hers, pulling me in tight, her voice muffled against my shoulder. "You seem to be thinking about redemption a lot lately."

"I suppose."

She tilted her head back. "Maybe you should go see the object of this compassionate release?"

"Now?"

She traced a fingernail at the side of my jaw. "You see this muscle right here? I used to see it a lot when I was a teenager. I used to look for that muscle, because it told me that I was probably not going to get what I wanted. Well, that muscle is there now, and it tells me that you're not going to go to sleep, so why don't you go over to the hospital and take a look at him and decide for yourself if he's worthy of the compassion of the state." She nudged me. "I'm sure they'll be more than happy to let the celebrated sheriff of Absaroka County have a look at the prisoner."

I thought about it. "You want to go with me?"

She shook her head. "I've got a baby in bed and a job to go off to in the morning. Anyway, I'm thinking this is a train you should maybe ride alone."

I lay there trying to read Agatha Christie and listening to Lucian snoring from the upper bunk as the train pulled into Medicine Bow to take on water and maybe to top off the fuel oil as well; we would stop every two hours, just like they used to, as we rolled across the state to Evanston.

Someone was whistling "This Train," the tune drifting along the passageway as I slid my boots on. There was a tradition that if you left the boots in the cubby by the compartment door, the porters would have them polished by morning; I figured the porters had enough to do, and besides, I liked polishing them myself. I slipped my horsehide jacket on, straightened my hat, and stepped into the hallway.

There was a surreal glow coming from the work lights that the crew used so that they could see to load the water, check the fuel, and who knew what else. The old train depot was to my right, its tile roof looking like it had escaped the Southwest, and beyond the tracks I could see the Virginian Hotel, a three-and-a-half-story Renaissance Revival building that was a little incongruous in a town of less than five hundred.

Owen Wister had used the hotel for the title of his book and Medicine Bow for the setting of his quintessential western, *The Virginian: A Horseman of the Plains,* and even though he actually had written the novel in Philadelphia and had never written another about the West, the book was credited with raising the genre from pulp to true literature.

Making my way to the nearest end of our car, I tried to keep quiet so that I wouldn't disturb anyone, but I needn't have bothered since about half the train was out smoking and talking near the adjacent track.

I wasn't looking for conversation, so I climbed back up and got out on the other side, away from the town proper.

"Takes a while, getting used to sleeping on a train."

A glowing ember illuminated the covered face of the sheriff of Laramie County.

"I guess so."

There was a pause. "You guess so, huh?"

I stood there for a moment more, looking at McKay, the tip of his cigar glowing orange, and then started toward the front of the train. "I'll see you later, Sheriff."

He spoke quietly, but I still heard him. "Yes, you will, Deputy."

Figuring if I couldn't be alone, at least I could learn something, I walked up to where the crew was pulling the spout from the water tank on the back of a tanker truck.

The closest workman turned and looked at me. "You're not allowed up here." He gestured toward the operation. "It's the union and insurance stuff — they don't want anybody around in case something happens."

"What, you're afraid I might drown?"

"Son, that's 23,500 gallons of water and a lot of very hot steam under a lot of pressure, and seein' as how we're operating an antiquated piece of equipment, you never know what might happen."

I didn't move.

He pushed his engineer cap back. "Foamer, are you?"

"Excuse me?"

"Foamers, that's what we call train buffs — the guys that get all excited about trains and start foamin' at the mouth."

I stared up at the big beast humming and blowing like some living thing. "Well, I can see the attraction, but for me it's just a part of where I'm from; my family has a ranch up on Buffalo Creek in the northern part of the state and I used to hear these trains going by the place when I was a kid." Laughing at myself, I told him something I hadn't told anyone in a long time. "I jumped one when I was six years old, rode it all the way to Livingston, Montana. A switchman in the rail yard saw me and stopped the train and called my family to come and get me."

He adjusted his glasses and looked me

down and up. "You been somewhere since then?"

"Overseas." I studied the locomotive; it was easier that way. "And a couple of places nobody's ever heard of."

He extended a hand. "John Saunders. I'm the engineer of this train."

"Walt Longmire, freight."

He nodded at me and then at his battered, steel-toed work shoes and started off toward all the commotion. "Well, c'mon." He smiled as he turned back when I didn't follow. "This ain't the interesting part." He headed off again, and I followed after him as we ducked under the surface hose, passed the tender, and approached the steps that led to the cab of the Union Pacific 8444. "You ever been in the cab of one of these things?"

"Nope."

He started up the ladder. "Well, I'm breaking about every rule in the book by bringing you up, but it ain't like anybody from the line is gonna be out here in the middle of nowhere this time of night."

I followed him up the ladder and stepped inside, where another man sat on the seat to the left. He extended a hand. "Rich Roback. I'm the fireman."

We shook.

"You one of them sheriffs?"

"Deputy."

"How come you aren't drunk like the rest of them? You ain't a Mormon, are you?"

I smiled. "Nope." I looked at the backhead of gauges, levers, handles, and other instruments that I didn't even have a name for. "Jesus . . ."

Saunders chuckled. "Looks complicated, doesn't it?"

"Yep."

"Any questions?"

I thought I should ask something just as a courtesy, so I pointed at a brass handle. "What does that do?"

"That's the train brake."

I pointed to one above it. "And that red one?"

"Engine brake for the drivers and tender."

I pointed at the only gauge that looked familiar. "Speedometer?"

"Yeah, added in the fifties. She went a hundred and twenty in her prime."

"That's pretty fast."

"This ol' girl isn't in a walker just yet." Roback laughed. "She's faster than you want to go, I can tell you that."

"What did they do before the fifties, to tell how fast you were going?"

Saunders laughed this time. "Nobody

cared — it wasn't like there were any speed limits. You kept a schedule and ran as fast as you needed to keep it."

I pointed to a lever. "This?"

"Throttle — forward is off, backward is full."

I noticed a large handle in front of Roback. "What's that?"

"Firing valve; it's what introduces oil into the burner down there. Nobody shovels coal anymore." The fireman patted the lever. "She's been converted to a heavy heating oil so as not to set the countryside on fire every time she heads down the tracks." He gestured toward the tender behind us. "That's about six thousand gallons of oil back there, and when you're whistling along in front of it with close to five hundred tons and that's just the weight of the loco and tender — it's kind of hard to forget."

There was a red wooden handle hanging by a chain. "What's that?"

"The whistle." He leaned out the cab, looking back to where the crews were finishing up their work. "You wanna pull it two times?"

"Sure." I pulled the chain twice. "Loud."

"Yeah, well, it's going to get a lot noisier." Roback started feeding the oil into the burner, and the great engine began churning louder than a 707. "You might want to get back there where it's a little more comfortable."

"Thanks for the tour."

Saunders came over as I climbed down. "You can come up and visit us again, if you don't mind climbing over the tender."

I waved good-bye and, noticing that the crews had already pulled away and that there was no one else trackside, I started back at a clip. I jogged down the line and was about to turn and climb up the ladder to my car when something struck me hard on the side of my head, and that's the last thing I remember.

Parking at Cheyenne Regional Medical Center was usually a headache, but it wasn't much of a problem at this time of night, the only signs of life being near the emergency room entrance. I turned and looked at Dog, the only occupant of my daughter's house who had elected to join me. "They don't allow dogs."

He stared at me with soulful eyes.

"It's not my fault."

He continued to stare.

"They aren't going to buy the service dog thing."

I felt guilty abandoning my backup. "We'll

have a ham sandwich tomorrow, I promise."

It was a bit of a relief walking in the front entrance as opposed to the ER and asking the receptionist at the front desk where, exactly, I needed to go.

Arriving on the fourth floor, I approached the nurses' station to find a Cheyenne city police officer leaning on the counter, chatting up a pretty nurse with too much makeup. "Howdy."

"Can I help you?"

"I'm looking for room 426."

The youngish patrolman turned around, giving me a hard look. "Then you need to talk to me."

I sighed, pulled my badge wallet from my jacket pocket, and flipped it open. "Walt Longmire, sheriff, Absaroka County."

He studied it, then looked up at me. He was so young, I wondered if he shaved. "Mind if I ask why you are interested in room 426, Sheriff?"

"Ask all you want, but I'm not sure myself."

"It's awfully late."

"I'm a night owl. . . ." I read his nameplate. "Officer Keith."

He gestured down the hall to my left. "Help yourself."

"You mind if I ask why you're not doing

your duty and guarding the prisoner?"

His face turned a little red. "Um, because he's had a heart attack and looks like he might croak in the next five minutes?" He shook his head. "And he's handcuffed to the bed rail and has a catheter."

The room was at the far end of the hallway on the right. It was easy to spot since it was the only one with a chair by the door.

I gently pushed it open and, letting my eyes adjust to the dimly lit room, stepped inside. I guess there were privileges when you had spent half a century behind bars, a corner view in the last room you would ever occupy being one of them. My attention settled on the bed, where he lay surrounded by a ton of machinery, all of it focusing on keeping a man alive that I'd just as soon be dead.

I stood at the foot of the bed and watched the shallow rise and fall of his labored breathing.

He looked a lot more fragile than I remembered from our last meeting in Cheyenne four years earlier, and I wondered what it was that had kept him alive, a man who should've died a long time ago.

Of course, when you finally sit down at the table, the game is already crook.

House rules, and it never loses in the end. Ever.

5

I woke up on the side of the tracks just as the engine of an eastbound freight rumbled by a couple of yards away.

I stayed still with my arms outstretched and watched the train pass, my hat skipping down the ballast roadbed in the wind it kicked up, finally sliding to a stop in a cluster of sage. I took a deep breath as the fifty or so cars raced by, causing the swirling snow to blow in a tunnel-like vortex that chased after the train like a borehole. It disappeared with a long, low whistle, and I stood stiffly in the dark and cold.

"Well, hell."

Wavering a little, I saw that the buildings on the side of the track were dark, and all the vehicles that had been around when the crew had been refueling were gone. I looked toward the town of Medicine Bow but could see only one set of lights, just to the right of the grand hotel.

I stooped to pick up my hat and noticed that my paperback was lying in the sage along with it. Placing the one on my head — although for some reason it didn't seem to fit as well as it should — and the other in my waistband at the small of my back, I crossed the tracks.

The snow was falling gently, not really amounting to much but giving a clear indication of the temperature as I stumbled forward, hugging myself and wishing I had my horsehide jacket.

The light had come from the Shiloh Saloon. I climbed the concrete steps and pushed open the door. Stepping into the life-giving warmth, I suddenly felt a little dizzy.

"Hey, you all right?"

I tried to speak, but my voice caught in my throat and I just stood there, leaning on the coat tree.

"If you're drunk you're gonna have to get out of here."

Doing my best to appear normal, I turned toward the three men seated on bar stools and the heavyset woman behind the bar and croaked, "Howdy."

The bartender raised a hand to her mouth. "Jesus."

Evidently, I wasn't persuading them of my

normalcy. "Um . . . I could use a little help." I started to lean backward and felt the world slipping away.

Fortunately, two of the men were at my side in less than an instant. "Boy, do you know you're covered with blood?"

I tried to laugh. "Yep, I woke up out there on the tracks about five minutes ago."

"You got hit by a train?"

They sat me in a nearby chair. "No, I was on one."

I could feel the blood that was frozen in my hair and on the side of my head start to thaw.

"You fell off a train?"

I stretched my jaw and heard popping noises. "Well, I had some help."

The oldest of the bunch looked at the bartender. "Get him some whiskey and roll up that rag with some ice for his head."

She gathered up the towel and filled it and then turned back to look at me from the liquor shelf. "Anything particular you like?"

On the high plains, it was a medical certainty that for any ill, whiskey was the remedy. Falling back on the old joke, I croaked, "Wet."

One of the men, a tall, whip-thin cowboy, pried off my hat, tilted my head, and looked at the wound. "You did this falling off?"

"I was walking next to The Western Star — was getting ready to get back on after they fueled and watered her — when somebody hit me."

"The sheriff train?"

"Yes, ma'am."

The older man took the ice pack from the woman and held it against my head. "Somebody must've coldcocked you, because that's the only way I'd hit a big bastard like you."

I knocked back the shot glass full of whiskey and winced.

"You're gonna be all right." She filled me another. "But you need stitches."

I looked around the small room, my eyes still not focusing, maybe from the blow and maybe a little from the whiskey. "I'm feeling a lot better, really."

"Like hell — every time you talk your head bleeds and winks at me." I reached up to touch it, but she pushed my hand away. "Leave it alone. I've got a first-aid kit behind the bar. Let me see what I can do."

As she went to fetch it, the shorter man studied me. "Son, somebody hit you that hard, they were lookin' to kill you."

"Could be."

"Nothing but sheriffs on that train. You a sheriff, then?"

"No, sheriff's deputy."

"You make some enemies?"

"Evidently."

The bartender arrived with the kit and pulled up another chair, turning it around and sitting on the back to give herself enough of a height advantage to work on my head. "Well, he didn't use his fist." I felt a tug, and she held a good-size splinter in front of my face. "Treated, so it must've been a piece of a tie or something. Good thing it's bleeding like that, what with the creosote."

"Can you get it so that it stops?"

She leaned back. "I can tape it up, but I'm not sure it's going to hold."

"You get the bandage on, and I'll wedge my hat down over it to keep some pressure. I need to catch up to that train." I looked at each of them in turn. "Anybody headed west?"

I started to stand, but the tall, skinny cowboy put a hand on my shoulder. "Easy, son. Easy." He glanced back at a long-haired man in a velvet jacket and leather top hat who had been keeping to himself. "Hey, buddy, aren't you headed west?"

The man was smoking and drinking a cup of coffee. "San Francisco."

"Can you give this fella a ride?"

He seemed uninterested. "I don't think so."

I took a deep breath, which cleared my head a little. "The train stops in Wamsutter — I heard the crew talking about it."

He still didn't look at me. "You're a cop?"

"Kind of."

He smiled and pulled at the hair that was below his shoulders. "Yeah, well, man, that shit ain't gonna go over with the bunch I got on that bus."

The tall cowboy looked at him hard. "Mister, this man needs a hand."

"Then you drive him." The hippie threw down the rest of the coffee and stubbed out the cigarette. "Not my problem, man."

He walked past us and left, closing the door behind him. I looked at the others. "Anybody else headed in that direction?"

The cowboy shook his head and looked at his friend. "Your truck don't go that distance, will it, Phil?"

He frowned. "Not in this weather."

I tipped my hat to the cowboys and then to the bartender. "Thank you for your help, ma'am." Then settling the beaver felt back on my head to increase the pressure on the bandages and to hopefully keep it on in the wind, I walked out the door.

It was still blowing snow, and I tripped

down the steps, catching myself on the antenna of a sedan parked at the bottom. I spotted the hippie driver standing by a large silver Challenger bus with purple stripes. He was finishing the last drag on what I assumed was a cigarette but might have been something more potent, before opening the doors. "Hey . . ."

He dropped the cigarette and stamped it out. "Don't do this to me, man."

"Look, it's ninety miles, and I need a ride, and for better or worse, you're it."

He shook his head. "No way, man, not with your being a cop — I mean you could be a narc—"

"I'm a deputy from a tiny sheriff's department a couple hundred miles from here. I don't have jurisdiction."

"Don't care, man." He adjusted the leather top hat. "A pig's a pig to the people on this bus."

I sighed and looked down at him. "You know, a man hit me on the head earlier this evening, and I'm looking to take it out on somebody. I'd just as soon it be the guy that actually hit me, but it could be you." I stood up straight, a hand holding the bifold door closed. "It's ninety miles to Wamsutter; you're going to take me there or I'm taking your keys and driving this bus myself."

He looked around, and I'm not so sure if it was my physical intimidation or the absolute desolation of the Wyoming landscape, but he weakened. "Look, they're all asleep, and with any luck they'll stay asleep until we get to Winterland — but if they do wake up, you're not anything *close* to a cop, you dig?"

"How does he look?"

I readjusted my rear end on the hard wooden bench. "Like he's dying."

Lucian looked reflective. "Well, hell . . . there's hope, then."

"What, that he'll die before they let him out?"

The old, one-legged sheriff lifted his own cup in a toast. "Here's to it." He turned and studied the side of my face. "In case it's slipped your mind, this one is guilty numerous times over, and there is nary a cell in the bottom of the state prison in Rawlins that he doesn't damn well deserve to inhabit until he is dead." He stood and limped to the other side of the marble hallway. "That he wasn't introduced to a good dose of hydrogen cyanide was the judge's mistake and not ours." He glanced up and down the empty hallway. "When do these damn lawyers come to work, anyway?"

I pulled out my pocket watch. "Not till nine, which is why I'm sitting on this rock of a bench."

"What time is it?"

"About five minutes after the last time you asked me that question, and ten after the time before that."

He crossed the hallway and sat again. "Well, aren't we in a good mood." He paused. "Did he say anything?"

"No, he's unconscious."

"Well . . ." He sipped the last of his coffee and crushed the cup in his hand, flapping the lid of an adjacent trash can in order to dispose of it. "You just remember what he did when you start feeling magnanimous."

In the distance I heard a pair of cowboy boots headed our way, and we both looked up to see a lean, handsome individual with curly gray hair peeking out from under a silver-belly cowboy hat. He was holding a white confectionery box tied with a blue ribbon, and his smile broadened as he looked down at us. "You fellas want a donut?"

I stood. "Thanks, but I don't eat donuts."

He smiled. "I thought you might be cops."

"We are." Lucian followed suit and stood. "And the hell with you, I do eat donuts."

He held out a hand to me. "Scott

Snowden."

"Sheriff Walt Longmire, and this is retired sheriff Lucian Connelly — careful when you hand him one — he hasn't had his shots."

He laughed, nodded, and tried to open the door but finally gave up. "Well, I'm glad I brought the pastries."

I got up. "Excuse me for asking, but are you connected to the compassionate release case?"

"Yes, I was brought in by the state."

"Prosecution or defense?"

He smiled the broad smile and opened the box, holding it out to Lucian. "Neither."

Lucian studied the contents and then reached in, picking a powder-coated cream filled. "So whose side are you on?"

"Neither." Snowden pulled out a chocolate frosted and took a bite, chewing as he spoke. "I'm the new judge."

"What the hell happened to Healy?"

"Bonefishing in the Bahamas." The judge swallowed. "Usually they adjust the timing based on the judge's calendar, but the defense was pushing that the case is time sensitive due to the prisoner's condition. In these situations they arrange a transfer on a judge-to-judge basis, and Stu Healy contacted me to hear the case." He cocked his head. "What, you fellas don't like me?"

Lucian studied him. "We like you fine, but we'd developed a working relationship concerning this case with ol' Hang 'Em High over the last few decades, and you'll excuse us if we're damn surprised to see a new face."

He gestured for us to sit, which we did. "Usually this case has been handled by the Board of Parole?"

I leaned back on the bench, which squealed in protest. "Yep."

"But they presented in court by habeas corpus this time."

"Which means?"

"First, let's review what we know: the prisoner was convicted years ago, and he's done decades of time. What that means, legally speaking, is that the case is closed on him. Guilt has been determined and a sentence imposed, and from my understanding of the case, many appeals over the years have been exhausted?"

"Many."

He nodded. "Even though his lawyers have filed for parole every four years, the sentence was an indeterminate one — sentenced to life, as opposed to a minimum or maximum term of actual years, so that he is ineligible for parole without a governor's commutation."

Lucian pulled another donut from the box, which Snowden had put down on the bench next to him. "He damn well better not, or I'll drive up the street to the mansion and shoot him in the ass."

"Well . . ." Snowden paused on that one. "Be that as it may, to simplify, the parole process is administered by the Board of Parole, which is comprised of seven gubernatorial appointees. It is the only body with the jurisdiction to request the governor to consider a compassionate release, unless —"

Protecting Lucian's cholesterol level, I closed the box of donuts. "Unless they file that habeas corpus Great Writ."

"Yes, constitutionally guaranteed and available to any prisoner to present the claim that he is illegally held."

"How can they claim that?" Lucian chewed on his donut. "You just said yourself that he's guilty as homemade sin, case closed."

"There's nothing illegal about keeping an aged, infirm prisoner incarcerated, and there probably isn't any hope legally in getting him released in this manner."

"Then why are his lawyers doing it?"

"I suppose we'll find out this morning." He shrugged, and his voice took on a singsong quality. " 'When the men on the chessboard get up and tell you where to go . . .' "

Lucian turned and looked at me, recognizing a quote when he heard one.

"Grace Slick, Jefferson Airplane."

My old boss glanced back at the judge and then at me again. "Who's Grace Slick, and what the hell does Jefferson's airplane have to do with the case?"

The seats on the bus were almost as luxurious as the ones on The Western Star, and when the driver instructed me to sit on one, it felt like I was sinking into a sofa. I could hear music playing toward the back, but the curtains dividing the front of the bus from the back seemed to indicate that I should mind my own business, so I just sat there watching the night sky pass by the moonroof and thinking about who could've hit me.

It didn't take a genius to figure it had been George McKay, but I was having a hard time understanding why. Sure, I'd had contact with his female companion, but I wouldn't think enough to warrant hitting me over the head with a hunk of wood and leaving me on the tracks to freeze to death — but was the assailant trying to kill me or just get me off the train?

My head hurt, and I was tired, but I knew after receiving such a blow I shouldn't sleep, so I pulled out the Agatha Christie and began reading. After about an hour I'd finished the fifteenth chapter of part two. It was a gift from my father, the ability to read quickly and still retain the details.

I put the paperback down on the plush seat next to me and thought about what Leeland had said about whodunits — he did it, she did it, nobody did it, or they all did it.

I yawned and thought I might take a short nap, even though I knew better. I'd given the driver instructions to exit at Wamsutter, that I'd jump out since the railroad tracks were fairly close to I-80 at that point.

I'd no sooner closed my eyes when I heard the curtain being pulled back. I lifted my head and saw a beautiful woman in a flowing caftan standing there looking at me with an odd blanket printed with stars and planets thrown over her shoulders and rose-colored octagonal sunglasses on her face despite it being the middle of the night.

"Well, hello, cowboy."

"Ma'am."

I started to get up, but she cut me off with a shake of her head. I noticed she was barefoot on the gold shag carpeting. "The bus is moving, so you're not Leon."

"That's the driver?"

"So they tell me." She glanced up front and then out the sunroof above my head. "Where the hell are we?"

"Wyoming."

She stooped a little, raising her tinted glasses, and peered out the darkened windows. "Looks like the moon."

"And about as populated."

"I've never been to Wyoming — what's it known for?"

"Yellowstone National Park, Devils Tower National Monument . . ." She didn't seem impressed, so I added, "We're the first state to give women the vote and the first state to have a female governor."

She clutched the blanket around her as she raised a fist. "Right on."

I stuck out a hand. "Walt Longmire."

She took mine in hers and studied it. "Big hands — lots of scars." She sat down on the sofa beside me. "So, what do you do, Walt Longmire?"

Remembering the conversation I'd had with the driver, I answered, "I'm a cowboy, ma'am."

She pursed her perfectly bowed lips and looked at the bandages that protruded from the underside of my hat. "What happened to your head?"

"Um, a horse."

She nodded. "One of the two regrets in my life." She uncoiled her legs and placed them, crossed at the ankles, over my lap. "So far."

"What's that?"

"I've never ridden a horse." She glanced down at my book. "A cowboy who reads?"

"Yep."

Lowering the sunglasses onto her freckled nose, she studied me. "Isn't that unusual?"

"Not really."

She reached into one of the pockets of the caftan, pulled out a small baggie of marijuana, and went about rolling a joint. "Care to explain?"

"After the cowboys who worked for the big outfits or ranches got cut loose in the fall, they'd find a place in the town to winter up, and one of the things they always took with them was a stack of books to pass the time."

She licked the paper and sealed the joint, sticking it in the corner of her mouth. "Sounds like a nice way to spend the winter." She glanced out the window again. "I'd imagine they are formidable here."

"Can be." She lit the joint with a Scripto Vu Lighter, took a puff, and then held it out to me. "No, thanks."

She shrugged. "Bad for the voice, but it helps me sleep." Her Day-Glo blue eyes changed to green and she leaned forward and looked at me for a long minute. "So, what are you doing on my bus?"

"Your bus?"

"Yeah, my bus."

"Are you famous?"

She cocked her head to one side in disbelief. "You don't know who I am?"

"I'm afraid not; I've been out of the country for a while."

She actually seemed pleased with the idea. "Cool. You going to San Francisco, Walt Longmire?"

"No, ma'am. Wamsutter, just down the road."

"That where you live?"

"No."

"What's there?"

"I'm catching a train."

She took another toke on the joint. "Where's it going?"

"Evanston and then back to Cheyenne."

"Cheyenne, that where you live?"

"No, ma'am."

She lowered her gaze and looked at me. "Then where the hell do you live?"

"A small town called Durant, up near the

Montana border at the base of the Bighorn Mountains."

"Sounds heavenly."

"Where do you live?"

"On this bus — at least it seems like it. We did a free concert in Central Park and now we're headed west for gigs in Hollywood, San Diego, and San Fran."

"Sounds like a lot of work."

"It's just singing, you know, but most of the concerts turn out to be three or four hours."

"That's a lot of singing."

"Yeah." She continued looking at me, and I was struck by the intelligence in her eyes. "So, you got a girl up near the Montana border at the base of the Bighorn Mountains, cowboy?"

"A wife, or she used to be."

"Used to be?"

I reached into the watch pocket of my jeans and pulled the ring out. "I think I'm getting divorced, and she's pregnant."

"That's pretty brave."

"What do you mean?"

"A divorced woman having a child on her own in this society — pretty bold, if you ask me." She took the ring and examined it. "My marriage broke up last year when I started fooling around with my guitarist, but I got a daughter out of it, you know?" I nodded, and her eyes came back to me. "I've kind of sworn off men for a while. . . . But you're cute. Is riding a horse anything like riding a cowboy?"

"So they tell me."

She rubbed her legs back and forth together in my lap and slipped the ring on her finger. "How far is it to Wamsutter?"

"Not very."

She smiled and sat up, letting the blanket fall away, exhaling the smoke gently into my face. "That a challenge?"

We both felt the bus decelerating and then the curved incline as Leon took the exit ramp. "I'm afraid it's a disappointing fact."

She looked out. "Not much here."

"Nope."

She leaned against a pillow and planted her feet firmly back in my lap. "Stay."

"What?"

"I get a feeling for people, and I like you. Stay on the bus and come to San Francisco with us."

"I —"

"The whole scene in the city is so far out, you'll have a blast, I promise."

The bus slowed to a stop, and Leon called, "Hey, cowboy!"

She leaned in closer, holding the joint out

to the side. "Stay."

"I . . . can't."

"Why?"

"I've got a job to do."

"Here? Or up near the Montana border at the base of the Bighorn Mountains?"

I thought about it. "Maybe both."

She stayed like that, looking at me for a bit, and then, sadly, she took her legs away and pulled the blanket back up over her shoulders.

The driver appeared, top hat and all. "Dude, we're here."

I took a deep breath and stood. She reached a hand out to me and then followed us to the exit. Leon threw the lever, opening the door to the excruciating wind.

Tucking my hat down on my swollen head, I stepped out under the cold, partially clear Western sky.

"Hey, Walt Longmire." I turned, and she was standing on the lowest step, the top of her head almost even with my nose, her hand holding my ring out to me. "You're going to want to give this back to her."

"I'm not so sure that she . . ."

As she flipped the butt end of the joint away, we both watched as the wind hooked it left like a major-league curveball. "I am."

When I took the ring, she slipped the

blanket from her shoulders and wrapped it around me, pulling me in close and touching her lips to mine. Seeing the eyes that close was like getting hit with a cattle prod, but after a moment I reacquired speech. "What was the other thing?"

She leaned back in the doorway, the caftan blowing around her knees, and hugged herself in an attempt to stay warm. "Huh?"

"You said there were two things you regretted not doing and one was riding a horse; what was the other?"

"Fucking Jimi Hendrix."

I stood there for a moment more, clutching the spacey blanket around me so that it wouldn't blow away. "Well, come up near the Montana border at the base of the Bighorn Mountains sometime, and I'll help you with the other one." I started to go but then turned back just as Leon began closing the door. "Hey, what did you say your name is?"

She smiled, still pleased that I had no idea who she was. "Grace."

The door closed, the air brakes released, and the big silver Challenger bus pulled up the ramp and back onto the highway, the fumes of diesel and illicit drugs the only indication that it had been there at all.

I turned and walked under the overpass

toward the lights of the town. As a few snowflakes whistled by me, I silently prayed the train was on the tracks ahead.

It was cold enough to slow the blood in your veins, and I held the blanket in close in an attempt to keep from freezing. I thought that if I didn't find the train I was going to have to come up with something better than huddling in the entryway of the Sinclair gas station I had just passed.

Mercifully, as I entered the main part of town I saw the same kind of light that had illuminated the sidetrack in Medicine Bow.

Approaching the train from the rear, I cut toward the road where the barrier arms were lowered and the clanging bells were deafening. As cold as I was, it took me a minute to register what was happening, but fortunately I stopped before getting hit by a train going in the other direction.

It figured that I'd travel for miles in a nice warm bus with a good-looking woman only to be dropped off on the wrong side of the tracks to freeze to death as a hundred and fifty coal cars passed by.

Crouching down, I clutched the blanket and thought about what the woman had said about Martha being brave. I was going to have to make a choice and decide if I wanted to spend the rest of my life with her;

of course, it seemed that she had decided that she didn't want to spend the rest of her life with me, and if that was really the case, then all bets were off and there really wasn't any reason to stick around Wyoming.

Either way, I was going to at least find out who hit me in the head and give them a little of what they deserved before I moved on.

The train finally passed, and I rose up from the street like a derelict and carefully looked both ways. The barriers lifted, and I trudged across, turning right and walking along the embankment that led toward the large red light at the rear of the caboose.

I didn't want to wake anyone up if I didn't have to, so I decided not to climb up the ladder into the passenger cars, and instead continued trudging along until I got to a group of men who were smoking cigarettes and talking. I stopped behind the nearest one. "Hey, you guys been missing anybody since Medicine Bow?"

Joe Holland whirled around, and, looking more than a little surprised to see me, grabbed me, twisted me, and threw me on the ground. Two more men held me down, but I pushed and started to get up — at least until somebody expertly sapped me on the back of my already sore head.

My face hit the ground, and I lay there listening to their voices, feeling like my battered brains were leaking out through my eyes.

"Is that the son of a bitch?"

6

Lucian rested his elbows on the counter of the Luxury Diner and watched as I took an oversize bite of my cheeseburger, my granddaughter strapped in her car seat on the stool between us.

"I don't think you're supposed to be feeding that child French fries."

I ignored him and gave her another. "She likes them."

He shook his head and turning back to the mirror over the milk-shake machine, puzzled over this morning's meeting. "What the hell would they hope to gain by all this rigmarole?"

I thought about it as I chewed, thankful for the extra time it took to swallow so I could think it over. "I just sat through a two-hour meeting, and I have no idea."

He took a bite of his BLT and joined me in chewing more than lunch as we stared at ourselves in the mirror. "They can't win a case like this."

Lola reached for my cheeseburger, so I took another French fry from my plate and gave it to her. "No, they can't."

"So, are they just stupid?"

All three of us chewed some more.

After a while, Lucian raised his coffee mug; the waitress hurried over, the old sheriff's feelings about jiffy service being pretty well known statewide. As she filled his cup, he turned back to me. "Well, if they aren't stupid, then they know something we don't."

"Like what?"

"Well, if I knew that, then we'd know, now wouldn't we?" He leaned down and spoke to Lola in a confidential tone. "Your grandfather isn't so smart, sweet pea."

"The lawyer they had with them . . ."

Lucian stared at me, his dark eyes unblinking over the brim of his mug. "The one who smirked all the way through the meeting?"

"Yep, that one. Where was he from?"

"Hell if I can remember."

I chewed and finally came up with it. "Cody."

"That was it."

Shrugging, I fed Lola another fry. "Well, then, you would think he wouldn't know any more than we do."

He sipped his coffee. "Sure acted like he did."

The front door jangled and two of the three of us turned and watched as Henry, who was so covered with spatters he looked as if he might've stepped out of a Jackson Pollock painting, sat down beside me. "How's the job going?"

He plucked a menu from the holder and studied it. "On the ceiling or me?"

I studied him. "You look a little uneven."

He nodded. "The ceiling is much better."

I daubed a little paint off the sleeve of his sweatshirt and considered it. "Avocado?"

"Silver Blue Sage." He lowered the menu as the waitress approached and smiled at her. "Hello."

She was young, and she melted from his direct look, hardly able to get the word out. "Hi."

"Would it be possible to get a glass of water, please?"

She recovered a little confidence and flipped her blond hair, her eyes still lingering on him. "If I have to swim for it."

He glanced at the three of us in the mirror and spoke to the image. "Vic elected to take a shower and will join us later."

"Did Cady finally go to work?"

"Yes, but not before we all had a long

discussion about the different forms of compassionate release."

"Well now, why do I not like the sound of that?"

"There is good and bad." The girl returned with the water and set it in front of him. "I will have the Caesar salad with chicken, please — balsamic vinaigrette on the side, if you would, and no bread."

Lucian snorted, and I glanced at him. "That's the reason he looks the way he does." I took another bite of my cheeseburger and spoke as I chewed. "And why we look the way we do."

Henry sipped his water. "Many states have expanded their criteria for compassionate release to include terminally and chronically ill inmates."

"And Wyoming is one of them."

"Not yet, but it is a pet project of the governor's wife."

I turned very slowly and looked at him. "You're kidding."

"I wish I were, but the good news is that this expansion has not significantly increased the number of inmates released anywhere. The current statistics indicate that the life expectancy of a prisoner up for compassionate release varies from six to twelve months, but that since the petition can take sixty-five days in court, most die in prison before their cases are even processed." He sipped his water again, obviously parched from painting my daughter's ceilings. "Cady tells me you went to the hospital last night."

"I did."

"You do know they have technology in this town that can tell if a victim has been suffocated with his own pillow." I sipped my tea and fed Lola another fry. "I do not think your daughter would like you feeding your granddaughter French fries."

I turned and looked at him. "She likes them."

He shrugged and continued. "Grounds can also be familial, but since the convicted has no living family members, that is precluded."

I turned to Lucian. "Do we know that?"

He continued eating. "Know what?"

"Does he have any family?"

"Not that I know of, but I ain't no expert on the son of a bitch."

I sighed. "I guess we need to find that out."

"Let the state do that."

I shook my head. "The governor's wife?"

The waitress brought Henry's lunch, and he started to eat. "She is concerned with budget overages, and the Bureau of Prisons, with the release of one hundred prisoners by compassionate release, could save the system $5.8 million — not to mention relieve some overcrowding."

"The governor's wife."

"Yes." He paused, his fork suspended above the romaine. "Releasing a prisoner all relies on good faith, which is a rare commodity these days." Henry took a bite and chewed for a while longer. "The entire process really relies on the opinion of the physician in a highly subjective, case-by-case basis — near death or terminally ill are idiosyncratic terms." He ate some more. "I do not suppose you spoke with the prisoner's doctor?"

"I didn't think he would be at the hospital after midnight."

The Bear nodded. "You might want to start there; it may help ease your mind to know how much longer he thinks the prisoner will live."

"I'll track down the attending physician and find out who his counterpart is in Rawlins." I thought back to the meeting this morning and to our puzzlement as to what the lawyers thought they were going to be able to do.

"Publicity."

I turned to the Cheyenne Nation — he had, as usual, read my mind. "What?"

"I am betting that you are trying to discern what the defense is venturing to gain by this ill-warranted attempt to go to court. People in high places have agendas, Walt, like the rest of us, and they need the press to help them get attention for these agendas; along with the Board of Parole, the governor has plans and more important, the wife of the governor has them as well."

I pulled at the stainless steel handcuffs that were attached to the caboose railing and rattling like the wheels on the rails underneath us. They'd at least been kind enough to allow me to keep the gifted blanket, which was good, considering that as near as I could tell there wasn't any heat in the tail end of the train.

If I leaned my head forward, I could use my free hand to massage the back of it, where the railroad special agent had delivered the second blow in a matter of a couple of hours. I blinked a bunch of times, trying to get my eyes to stop seeing two of everything, the dim light in the caboose not helping, the bare lightbulb overhead having a ghostly flare around it.

"I brought you some water, sir."

Gibbs kneeled in front of me with a couple of paper cups. I took one hand and sipped the water, trying not to gulp it, then gave him back the cup and took the other.

He tipped his white chef's hat back. "They hit you pretty hard, didn' they, Mr. Longmire?"

I handed him back the second cup. "Can I get another, please?"

He stood and went to pour me some more.

I stretched my eyes. "What's going on, Mr. Gibbs?"

He glanced around to make sure we were indeed alone in the caboose. "I'm really not at liberty to repeat what I heard, sir."

"C'mon, Gibbs. Whatever they say, I didn't do it."

His red-rimmed dark eyes focused on mine. "They say there's a man dead."

I leaned back against the batten boards of the caboose and took a deep breath as the rails clicked below us. "What?"

"They found a man on the tracks, dead, with his head stove in."

"That was me, but I wasn't dead — just knocked out."

He glanced around again. "They said it was one of you sheriffs, but they didn't say who, at least not to me."

"Where?"

"Near Fort Fred Steele, about halfway between Walcott and Rawlins."

"No, it was in Medicine Bow — somebody hit me and, to make a long story short, I was lying by the tracks for a while and then I got a ride." I rubbed the back of my head again, trying hard not to feel like a bongo. "And then I attempted to get back on the train till I got hit in the head again." Flexing my jaw, I smiled and concentrated on seeing just one of him, finally bringing his face into singular focus. "Don't worry about me, Mr. Gibbs. I'll be fine. It's all just a big mix-up."

There was a noise behind the old chef, and I looked up to see my boss, a couple of the other sheriffs — Otis Phelps and Bo Brown, to be exact — and the railroad security man. They had entered the car and stood over the two of us, Holland the first to speak. "What're you doing there, Gibbs?"

"I was just giving him some water, Mr. Holland."

"Well, that's enough. Get out of here."

"Yes, sir."

The older man stood slowly and walked around them, leaving us alone in the caboose as I discreetly rattled the cuffs on the steel railing, giving more than a little scrutiny to the two rusted screws that held the thing in place. "Somebody mind telling me what's going on?"

"You were kind of MIA here for a few hours; how about you tell me where you've been?"

I ignored Holland and spoke to my boss. "Sheriff Connelly, do you mind telling me what's going on?"

His eyes didn't meet mine. "Maybe you need to answer the question."

I stared at him. "What?"

"Just answer the question."

I slumped back against the wall. "Look, I understand there was somebody lying by the tracks, but I think that must've been me. I woke up in Medicine Bow, the train had already left, and so I hitched a ride till I got to Wamsutter, where they were refueling. When I tried to get back on, the rail bull here knocked me out with that damn sap, and cuffed me to this railing. Now, will somebody please tell me what's going on?"

"Marv Leeland is dead."

I wasn't sure I'd heard him correctly. "What?"

"They found a man missing an arm is what they said. Marv Leeland was found on the tracks at Fort Fred Steele, shot." When I didn't say anything, Lucian continued.

"Now, where have you been for the last few hours?"

Laughing, I shook my head. "Wait." I looked around at the four of them. "You think I killed him?"

They didn't say anything, just stood there looking down at me.

"You've got to be kidding." I yanked on the cuffs, grabbed the rail, and tried to stand tall. "Where's George McKay?"

"What's McKay got to do with this?"

"He's the one who saw me get off the train, and I'm pretty sure he's the one who hit me with a piece of railroad tie and left me for dead on the ground back in Medicine Bow; whatever happened on this train after that, I had nothing to do with."

"Have you got anybody else who can vouch for you?"

"A whole bar full of people back at the Shiloh Saloon who helped clean me up and get me a ride west so that I could catch up with the train. I was just walking up when Holland here sapped me — and I'm gonna tell you that I'm pretty damn fed up with people hitting me from behind." With that, I gave one strong heave and yanked the railing from the wall, allowing it to slip from the cuffs and land in my hand — I swung it up onto my shoulder with both hands like a baseball bat. "In case you haven't noticed, I don't have my weapon. Did anybody think to check our berth and see if it was there?"

They glanced at one another.

I glared at them and stuck my cuffed wrist out to the railroad man. "Do you want these back?" Uncuffed, I started for the dining car. "Let's go to our suite and then have a word with McKay."

Finally getting to our rooms, I stepped in and reached up to collect our weapons from the upper cabinet. As I handed them to my boss, I thought I caught a whiff of a familiar scent and was now more than a little worried.

He flipped loose the leather strap on my Colt and pulled it from the holster. Dropping the magazine, he sniffed the barrel before turning and looking at the others. "Hasn't been fired."

Holland mumbled, "Doesn't mean a damn thing. We don't know what kind of weapon was used."

"Well, it wasn't mine." I grabbed my horsehide coat, slipped it on, and then knocked on the door of the compartment adjacent. We stood there waiting, and as I started to knock again Kim LeClerc opened the door. She had a sleeping mask on her forehead and was dressed in a full-length bathrobe, which I was surprised did nothing to showcase her impressive bosom.

"You lose your key?" She pushed the mask back a little more and looked at us for a moment before shutting the door in our faces, her voice sounding through the wood panels. "What the hell do you people want?"

"We're looking for Sheriff McKay."

"Well, if you find him tell him to sleep somewhere else — he's not welcome here."

I leaned against the door. "So he's not in there with you?"

"No, he most certainly is not."

"When did you see him last?"

There was noise from inside the berth, and I thought for a moment she might be covering for him. "How the hell should I know?"

"Miss LeClerc, were you awake when we stopped in Medicine Bow?"

She leaned against the jamb and opened the door wide — now with the bedspread wrapped around her — so that we could see that there was no one else inside. "Was that the last stop?"

"Actually, the one before that."

She produced a cigarette from who knew where. Placing it between her lips, she continued to talk, her tobacco- and whiskey-darkened voice reminding me of nightclubs and questionable times. "Who the hell can tell where we are? This train seems to stop every twenty minutes."

"So you haven't seen him since Medicine Bow?"

"I suppose."

"Four hours ago."

"Like I said, I suppose. I've been asleep, you know? It's a thing most normal people do this time of night, Deputy." With that, she closed the door.

I turned to the assembled posse. "After our altercation in the parlor car earlier this evening, I met Sheriff McKay trackside in Medicine Bow when I got off to get some air. The conversation we had led me to believe he was not quite ready to let bygones be bygones. Later, as I was attempting to reenter the train, someone struck me from behind and left me there on the tracks. For obvious reasons, I'm assuming it was Sheriff McKay, and now that he doesn't seem to be around, I am even more assured of that theory."

Holland looked at the others. "Is there anyone that can confirm what you're saying?"

I threw a thumb toward the front of the train. "The engineer and his brakeman up in the locomotive; I went and talked with them."

"Why?"

"I couldn't sleep, and I was curious — I'm funny that way." I leaned in a little, pretty sure that if I put my mind to it I could throw the railroad man through the nearest window in one try. "Look, Holland, if you've got something more to say, then just say it, because we're going to have to search this train from one end to the other, find George McKay, and get some answers."

He stared at me for a moment and then turned and gestured for Phelps and Brown to follow him. "We'll start at the front; the two of you start at the rear and we'll meet back here, but don't you think I'm not going to radio up to the engineer and check your story."

"Knock yourself out — unless you need my help."

"It started with a heart attack, but then we discovered cancer of the pancreas, which is much worse, being one of the more belligerent carcinomas. And this one is one of the more aggressive varieties." The prison doctor, Robertson, crossed his leg, resting a powder-blue-stockinged ankle on his knee and bobbing a loafer. "I don't know how familiar you are with human anatomy. . . ."

"I've never been shot in the pancreas." He'd agreed to talk to me without seeming very happy about it, and from his behavior I was pretty sure he rated me as a somewhat unintelligent, rural gunsel. "If that's what you're asking."

He studied me. "It's a glandular organ behind the stomach. There are a number of different kinds of pancreatic cancer, but his, like about eighty-five percent of the cases, is pancreatic adenocarcinoma, a cancer that affects the portion of the organ that produces digestive enzymes."

I leaned forward on my stool and rested my elbows on my knees. "Were you his regular doctor over at the prison?"

"No, Dr. Howe is his general physician there. They run a clinic on a daily basis, and I come in once a week to follow up on anything that looks more serious. My work is mostly here in Cheyenne." He waited for me to speak, and when I didn't, he continued. "I mean, to be honest, he's been there so long I think everybody just ignored him until he was found on the floor." The young man stood and ran a hand through imaginary hair as he looked out the hospital window toward the rail yard. "Once somebody took a look, though, it was textbook, really — yellowing of the skin and loss of appetite. There really aren't any symptoms in the early stages, so that by the time a diagnosis is made, even in the least severe cases, it's too late and has spread to other parts of the body." He grimaced at me. "He's riddled with it."

I took off my hat and glanced around the lab where I'd tracked the doctor down. "Causes?"

"Smoking, obesity, diabetes, and certain genetic traits. A crapshoot, really, but in his case the diabetes was a factor, that and HIV." He turned to look at me. "Don't be surprised; it is a prison, after all."

I rolled the brim of my hat in my hands. "So what are his prospects?"

"Quite bad, actually. After being diagnosed with this particular strain, only twenty-five percent survive a year, only five percent survive five years — but given how advanced his is, I'd guess he'll be dead in two weeks at the absolute most."

He leaned against a counter and folded his arms. "You're the one who arrested him, I mean, back then?"

"Yep. He's been in Rawlins since 1973."

He pulled out his cell phone, looked at it, and then returned it to his pocket. "I must admit that when you contacted me, I did a little research on you."

I looked at him.

"I've read a number of interviews you've given, and I'm impressed by the philosophical response you have to your chosen occupation and to human nature."

I smiled. "For a sheriff?"

"No, I don't mean it that way at all." He swallowed. "At the risk of getting myself into trouble, you seem to have preserved your humanity, which I would imagine is difficult in your line of work."

"Why would that thought get you in trouble?"

"I'm about to get to that part." He gestured in the patient's general direction. "He's going to die, if not in hours, in days."

I stood, pulled my hat back on, and walked over to the window, my back to him.

He stood up and moved a couple of steps toward me. "You don't think that there might be some mitigating circumstance that —"

"Short of miraculously being discovered innocent?" I continued to look at the rail yard. "No. What we are concerned with here is the appropriate punishment for multiple murders. Capital punishment is an extreme sanction that would perhaps have been suitable for this most extreme of crimes, but we make mistakes, and taking another life due to human error is the worst we can do in a society based on law. And even if we get it right, killing the killer is not going to bring back the victims."

I paused, and I guess he thought I was through, but I wasn't, not by a long shot.

"But if a defendant is judged to be guilty and sentenced to life without parole, he should die in prison. That's the meaning of the sentence. In my experience, a sentence of life without parole allows survivors to move on. I'm sure that the victims' families long ago gave up the thought that anyone would ever voluntarily release him, no matter what the circumstance. Imagine what this would do to them. No. Life in prison without parole means dying in prison, Doctor."

He looked at his loafers. "I'm in the business of keeping people alive, Sheriff, no matter who they are or what they've done."

Seeing we had an irreconcilable difference of perspective and figuring I'd gotten everything I was going to get from him, I turned and walked toward the door. "You and Jean-Paul Sartre tell that to the victims' friends and families, would you?"

"Why the hell would anybody kill Marv

Leeland?"

I adjusted my gun belt over my shoulder as we moved through the parlor car. It felt kind of silly looking for McKay beneath the tables, behind the bar itself, and under the piano, but you never knew. "Maybe he was on to something . . . or someone."

Sheriff Connelly put a hand on my arm in an attempt to slow me down. "What's that supposed to mean?"

I stood at the center of the empty car and looked around. I sighed and looked down at him. "That conversation I had with Leeland in the observation car?"

"Yeah?"

I weighed the thing in my mind; I wasn't sure if I wanted to show all my cards to anybody just yet. "He mentioned something about what you and Sheriff Eldredge were discussing earlier." He shook his head, and I made a decision. I needed at least one other person on my side. "Supposedly, somebody's been cleaning up messes all over the state without jurisdiction."

He thought about it and scrunched his eyebrows together. "You mean that lynching in Albany County?"

"Among other incidents not strictly within the purview of the law." I studied him. "Sheriff, has anything like that happened in our county? Any unexplained homicides of individuals you'd just as well see dead?"

His chestnut eyes narrowed. "What are you asking me?"

"I'm asking if you're involved in this somehow. Leeland was pretty well convinced that it was more than one sheriff — he called it a cabal — and before this goes any further, I want to know if you're involved."

There was a long silence.

"I've only known you well for a few weeks, Sheriff, and even with that limited knowledge, I know you're willing to work outside the law to get things done. So, I'm going to ask you one more time, and if I'm not satisfied with your answer, I'll just do this myself."

His mouth set, and I could see he was thinking about how he was going to respond to his subordinate, or whether he was going to answer at all. "I've had suspicions, but I haven't shared them with anybody —"

"That doesn't answer my question."

His face turned a lively crimson, and he exploded just as I expected he would. "Well, if you'll shut up for a damn minute, I'll answer your damn question." He stood there, then turned and looked straight at me. "No, I don't have anything to do with this, whatever it is."

Satisfied for the moment, I fumbled with my book. "Sheriff Leeland gave me a list of all the unsolved murders that have taken place in the last three years." Finding nothing inside the Agatha Christie, I searched through the rest of my pockets in an attempt to find the piece of paper. "I swear I had it in my . . ." I took a deep breath and settled myself. "Somebody must have taken it, probably the same person who hit me in the head and left me for dead."

Lucian looked a little doubtful. "A list?"

"I had doubts myself when Leeland was telling me about it, but it seems that someone or a collection of someones has been moving around the state, systematically killing who it was they suspected in some very nasty cases. At least, that's how it was relayed to me."

He looked a little incredulous. "And Marv spoke with you about this?"

"He did, and now he's dead."

He shook his head slowly. "Why would he talk to you?"

I studied my new boss. "Because he thought a sheriff or a group of sheriffs were doing this, and I'm not a sheriff. I've only been back in-country for a month, so I'm the only one who couldn't be involved. He needed a fresh set of eyes."

"And now somebody else has that list."

"Yep. I didn't entirely believe him when he was telling me about it, but I'm beginning to now." I rubbed a hand across my face. "Maybe if I'd taken him a little more seriously, he'd still be alive."

"And you think it's McKay?"

"He was the only one trackside in Medicine Bow."

"You think he killed Marv?"

"Well, he sure seems unaccounted for as of late."

He licked his upper lip and looked toward the back of the train. "Let me ask you something: if you'd killed somebody, would you still be on this train?"

I answered honestly. "No."

"Neither would I, but that doesn't mean we won't keep looking, huh?" He moved out ahead of me, shifting his gun belt from his shoulder and slipping it around his middle, where he buckled it up and adjusted the holster with a thumb. "Let's go."

Following his lead, I buckled my Sam Brown around my hips and tried to keep up as we pushed open the door and reentered the dining car where Marv Leeland and I had had our conversation. "I can't think that there would be that many places to hide on a train."

"That's according to how bad you want to disappear. Whoever took the list doesn't want anybody to know about this, and the only reason I can think that they might've let you live was because they thought you were dead and because they were in a big hurry to get back on. You were not the primary target in this deal."

"I didn't think I was."

"Yeah, but if there's anything to this sheriffs' cabal, they know you're alive now and know what Marv knew, and they're gonna want you dead, too."

He took one side and I took the other as we worked our way through the car toward the back. "That's comforting."

"Just don't let anybody get you alone somewhere until we get this sorted out."

"So far, you're the only one I trust."

He pushed open the door and continued on toward the caboose, throwing me a grin over his shoulder as the cold air blasted between us. "If I was in your place in these selfsame circumstances, Deputy, I'm not so sure I'd even do that."

7

The battered planet and stars blanket wrapped around her shoulders, Cady peeked in at the three of us from the kitchen. "Another newspaper called."

I nodded and kept playing grab-the-finger with the diminutive love of my life as Dog watched. "Well, that didn't take long, did it?"

We were sitting on the new red leather sofa and were ignoring the world. "Three more on the answering machine."

I stood and, hoisting Lola up on a hip, carried her to where the good smells were coming from, Dog following closely behind. "This may turn into a real mess before it's all over."

She turned and looked at me. "I guess they're going with the full-court press attack."

I smiled at the play on words. "Who? The governor's wife?"

"It would appear she's holding a press conference about it tomorrow afternoon, and I think you should go."

"To somebody else's press conference?" I occupied my granddaughter with my index finger. "I don't even like going to my own."

"Listen, Dad — and I'm not joking — you make an impression. Just go and stand there against the wall and don't say anything; it'll scare the shit out of everybody, trust me." Cady went back to stirring. "And don't take Uncle Lucian." She added onions. "Take Henry and Vic; they're the only ones on the planet scarier than you."

"Uh huh." Lola gnawed on my finger. "One of the newspapers was there at the hospital taking pictures of him as I was leaving."

She made a face as she added tomatoes to the mixture she'd been sautéing in the frying pan. "Great, that'll look good in the morning edition and get the public on his side. Did they see you?"

"Yep."

"Let me guess — no comment?"

"Good thing Lucian wasn't there or they would've gotten plenty."

"Where are the rest of the musketeers?"

"Checking records to see if they can come up with some of the victims' surviving family members to give a little credence to our cause." I sat Lola on the corner of the island, my arm around her waist.

Cady pulled the blanket more tightly around her shoulders. "Wasn't this all happening right after you and Mom got married? Where was she during all of this?"

I kept Lola in place as Dog sat on my foot. "We were fighting."

"About?"

Lola reached out for Dog's big muzzle and giggled as he licked her hands. "Um . . . nothing really."

She sidled over and bumped me with her hip. "Why did it take so long for you guys to get around to having me, anyway?"

It took me a moment to respond. "I was doing my best; your mother just wasn't cooperating." I thought about the missing member of our little circle and felt a familiar sorrow come over me, as it always did when I thought about being robbed of her company. I also thought about the secrets that had remained between the two of us, and the things that Martha had chosen to share with our daughter and the things she hadn't. I didn't think it was the time or place to reveal them now. "If she were here, she'd say let him go."

Cady returned to the stove. "If she were

here, she'd compliment me on that magnificent, homemade pasta on the counter over here."

I was impressed. "How did you do that?"

"The machine you bought me last Christmas."

There was another pause as I switched directions in the backfield. "Oh, that machine."

"It's all right — I figured Henry picked it out." She stirred the sauce and then offered me a taste. "I'm making so much of the stuff I think I'm going to need a pasta intervention."

I took a spoonful from the ladle, and it was marvelous. "The effect of the Moretti in-laws."

"Probably." She watched me with the cool, nickel-plated eyes I'd given her. "Yeah, if Mom were here, she'd tell you to let it go." She stirred some more. "It's not that he isn't guilty, Daddy, but what are you giving up? A few days, a week?"

"Freedom, I'd be giving him his freedom, something I swore would never happen."

She nodded, unknowingly compressing her lips in an exact imitation of her mother. "You may not have a choice."

I spoke under my breath. "No, but I can gum up the works till he's dead."

"Wow." She turned to look at me, fingering a worn spot in the blanket. "That doesn't sound like you."

"It sounded like the young me, a guy you never met."

She turned her face, looking at me askance. "I'm not so sure I would have wanted to." She reached past me, took Lola, and swiveled away. "You mind setting the table?"

"Not at all." Fetching a stack of plates, I placed them around the dining-room table I'd given her, a hand-me-down from her grandparents, and folded napkins and set them out along with the silverware and glasses. Overwhelmed by a sense of personal history, I stood there for I don't know how long.

Dog began barking, ending my reverie. My three comrades-in-arms came in, looking a little weary, Lucian in the lead, and Henry and Vic following behind. "Something smells good in here."

I pulled a chair out and gestured for the old man to sit. "Perfect timing; dinner is almost on the table."

He waved me off and continued toward the back of the apartment. "I gotta go to the bathroom and wash my hands."

The Bear went toward the new sofa, and

Vic sat in the proffered chair.

I fetched the breadbasket from the kitchen. "The guests have arrived."

She handed me Lola and a bottle of red wine. "Could you open that?"

Handing off the wine to Henry, I placed the bread on the table, around which the whole crew was now seated, and sat in the chair opposite him with Lola, who was practicing the word "doggie." "Find anything?"

Henry pulled a folded piece of paper from his shirt pocket and handed it to me. "The survivors' progeny, listed alphabetically with the corresponding individual noted in the margin."

There were five of them, four of them scattered around the country. Only one was in driving distance: Pine Bluffs, about forty minutes away. "Not much to work with, is it?"

He expertly stripped the foil off the wine bottle with the Laguiole stag horn wine knife I'd never seen him without and threaded the corkscrew into the cork. "No, but it is something."

I looked at the name of the woman in Pine Bluffs. "Marv Leeland's daughter is still around here?"

Pulling the cork in one expert move, he

reached across the table and poured Vic a glass, then me.

Vic sipped her wine. "So it would appear."

Lola reached out and snagged the cork. "Guess I'll drive over there in the morning."

When we found ourselves back at the caboose, Mr. Gibbs was sitting on the little set of stairs that led to the cupola. He was playing his cigar-box guitar and sipping from a pint bottle that I assumed did not contain soda pop. He looked at me. "Can I have my railing back?"

"I think I left it in our cabin." I rubbed my wrist where the handcuffs had been. "Seen anybody since we left, Mr. Gibbs?"

"Nope. Things quieted down after you got brought in here and then busted out." He glanced at my gun belt. "I guess things have changed?"

I shrugged. "For now."

He climbed off his perch, took another sip from the pint, and gestured around the room. "But a number of different men were back here in the caboose earlier in the evening, sir." He glanced at Lucian. "Includin' him."

The sheriff snorted. "I was looking for you."

"When was the last time you saw Mr.

Leeland, Mr. Gibbs?"

"He was back here talking with Mr. McKay."

Sheriff Connelly reached out for Gibbs's bottle. "You mind?"

"Help yourself."

He took a swig and pulled a face. "Jesus, what is that stuff?"

Gibbs smiled. "Homemade."

"Broken home, I'm guessing."

I turned back to the chef. "Tell me about Mr. Leeland and the last time you saw him."

"Well, like I said, he was back here with that big man, and they was arguin', so I left to go perform my duties and when I got back here they was gone."

"What were they arguing about?"

He shook his head. "I try not to get involved in white folks' arguments."

I glanced around. "Is there anywhere to hide in here?"

"Not really — well, there's a few cupboards, a few fifty-gallon drums, and four high bunks, but I'm the only one that uses them."

My eyes settled on a large oak box. "What about that trunk there?"

He stepped over and pulled up the lid, revealing tools, a pair of boots, and coveralls. "I keep these here for when I have to do something on the train and don't want to get my whites dirty."

"And where does that ladder up there go?"

"It's just so you can see out or get on the roof."

I moved toward the back door. "And what's out here?"

"Nothin', Mr. Longmire, jus' a little platform on the end of the train."

"Well, if I were going to throw somebody off a train, I'd throw them off the back." I pulled open the door and stepped out onto a small platform with wrought-iron railings, a gap at the center opening somewhat secured with only a spindly looking chain that swung back and forth in the red light emanating from the back of the caboose.

As I stood there watching the Wyoming countryside recede, I thought about how my laissez-faire attitude about this trip had been altered since I was hit on the head. It was a lot colder out here in the wind, and I pulled my jacket around me, zipped it up, and pulled on my gloves. I was just getting ready to head back in when I looked down and saw a lot of dark stains on the platform. I yanked off a glove and stuck a finger in one, holding it up to my face as Lucian crowded the door behind me.

"What the hell are you doing out there?"

I sniffed at the congealed substance. "Blood, Sheriff Connelly, and a lot of it." I looked at the saturated steps on either side of the platform. "Didn't you say Leeland was shot?"

"That's what the Carbon County deputy said."

I thought about it. "And we stop in Rock Springs and then Evanston, where we turn around and head back?"

"Yep. I imagine we'll pick up Leeland's body in Carbon County and haul it to Cheyenne for a proper autopsy."

Crouching there with Lucian standing beside me, I was face-to-face with the sheriff's holster. At that moment I smelled the same scent that I'd caught when I'd handed him his sidearm back in our cabin.

"Something wrong, Troop?"

"No." I thought about what I was going to do next. I'd played along as a soldier on a train full of generals and all it had gotten me so far was my head beat in — twice. This was going to be a gamble, but I didn't see as I had anything to lose — well, besides my job.

I stood and backed him up into the caboose, closed the door behind us, and pulled my Colt, transferring it to my left hand and letting it hang at my side. "Give me your weapon."

"What?"

"Hand me your weapon, Sheriff."

"Like hell I will." His hand dropped to it. "What is wrong with you, anyway?"

He didn't see it coming, not that anybody would have. I brought a roundhouse punch to the side of his head, which bounced him off the wooden wall. Catching my boss on the rebound, I carefully lowered him to the smooth, gray-painted floor.

Sitting in the far southeastern corner of the state, Pine Bluffs is barely Wyoming; you'd swear you were in Nebraska, which actually happens to border the east side of town. Originally named Rock Ranch, it was renamed by railroad officials for a nearby landmark: a collection of pines on a local hillside, the only trees for a hundred miles.

In the early days, Pine Bluffs wasn't much of a town — more like a tent with a chimney — but that changed when it became the final destination of many of the cattle drives from points south and therefore the largest cattle-shipping juncture on the Union Pacific Railroad. For some reason, it was also known as the best-lighted city of its size in the entire country. That, however, was then — now was a different story.

"Well, it shouldn't be hard to find her." Lucian turned and looked at me pumping gas at the Sinclair service station. "Hell, I thought *our* town was small."

"Would you get Dog out and take him for a short walk while I pay?" I finished up and went inside — I don't generally trust machines of any sort, but especially the ones that take your money. And besides, machines don't answer questions.

A middle-aged woman at the counter took my cash. "I'll need a receipt, if you would, please?" She handed it to me, along with the change. "I'm looking for a woman by the name of Abigail Delahunt, possibly Leeland?"

She peered at me above her glasses. "And who's asking?"

I pulled my badge wallet from my jacket pocket. "Walt Longmire, Absaroka County sheriff."

"She in some kind of trouble?"

I noticed a copy of the *Cheyenne Tribune-Eagle* lying there and saw a picture of the prisoner in the hospital bed in Cheyenne, an oxygen mask covering most of his face.

"No, I'd just like to speak with her." I grabbed a paper and tossed some change on the counter.

"She's dead."

"Oh."

"The whole town took piano lessons from her, but I think she passed about ten years ago." She picked up the money, then placed the heel of a hand on the counter and studied me. "You might want to check her house, but I don't know the exact address. From what I understand, her daughter still gives lessons out of it, but that was a while ago, too, so might be she doesn't either."

I pulled the sheet of paper the Cheyenne Nation had provided from my jacket pocket. "Elm Street?"

"Maybe — right across from the park, I think."

I thanked her and met Lucian and the beast back at the truck. "This damn dog of yours spooked a cottontail and almost dragged this one-legged man to Nebraska."

I rustled the monster's head, pulling an ear. "Sorry, he gets excited."

"You find where this woman lives?"

"She's dead."

"Well, damn it to hell." He glanced around. "Flatland for nothin'."

"His granddaughter might still be there." I shrugged, opening the door so Dog could climb back in.

It wasn't difficult to find the house. An old handwritten sign hung in the window, advertising PIANO LESSONS, PIANIST AVAILABLE FOR WEDDINGS, RECEPTIONS, AND SOCIAL GATHERINGS.

As I pulled to a stop behind a silver Dodge half-ton with Florida plates, the old sheriff adjusted his seat back and pulled his hat over his face. "Having no need for a pianist for a wedding, a reception, and/or a social gathering, I now intend to use this critical juncture in the investigation to take a much-needed nap."

"You slept all the way here."

His voice was muffled under the Stetson. "That was my warm-up nap, not to be confused with my postnap nap, which I will be enjoying when we drive back to Cheyenne."

I said nothing and got out.

It was a small house with an enclosed front porch, a common practice in our part of the world. The yard was overgrown, and the curtains were closed in the front windows.

"Can I help you?" I glanced up at a blondish young woman with a thin nose who was standing in the doorway. "I'm not giving lessons anymore." She was wearing an old-fashioned dress and sandals.

"No? 'Cause I could use a few." I stopped at the base of the stairs and looked up at the woman, who seemed young enough to be Abigail Leeland's daughter. "My name is Walt Longmire. I'm the sheriff of Absaroka County, up in the north-central part of the state, and I was hoping you could help me, Miss . . . ?"

"Delahunt, Pamela Delahunt. Just Pam is fine."

"Pam, I was looking for the previous owner of this house — an Abigail Leeland or maybe Delahunt? I was hoping you might be able to tell me about her."

"My mother, she's dead."

"Oh."

She looked a little confused. "What did you want to know?"

"I'm not sure, actually. Marv Leeland was her father?"

There was a pause, and she pulled back a strand of hair and secured it behind one ear. "My grandfather."

I nodded. "He was the sheriff over in Uinta County a long time ago."

"He died before I was born, so I wouldn't know anything about that."

I stood there looking at her. "All right, then, I'm sorry to bother you."

"He had one arm."

I stopped and looked back at her. "Marv Leeland did, yes."

"There was a piano piece she used to play with one hand, I mean written for a one-handed pianist."

"Piano Concerto for the Right Hand in D Major?"

"Left . . . Left Hand in D Major."

I studied her. "Right you are; Ravel, I believe."

She smiled and hugged herself. "I guess Mom used to play it with him when she was little. She sometimes played it when she was teaching me."

"You're from here?"

She took a moment to respond. "Was, but not anymore."

I gestured toward the sign in her window. "Not too much call for piano teachers here in Pine Bluffs?"

"No. I have a job offer in Jacksonville, Florida. I've already been there once, and now I'm just here picking up the last of my stuff."

"I saw your plates — tired of shoveling snow?"

"Something like that." She hugged herself and fiddled with the latch on the storm door. "Look, I've got things I need to do, so if there isn't anything else . . . ?"

"Okay, well, I'm sorry to have bothered you. Good luck in the Sunshine State."

"Thank you." She closed the door and disappeared as I stood there thinking about normalcy, and how it wasn't as prevalent as you might think. With one last glance, I walked back to my truck and climbed in.

As I sat there going over the conversation in my head, Lucian's muffled voice sounded from under his hat again. "Anything?"

"Maybe."

That got him to push the Open Road back to look at me. "Well?"

"She's not being very forthcoming."

He shook his head. "Does that mean she's not going to be much use, because if it does, why the hell don't you just say she's not going to be of much use?"

"Because it wouldn't be accurate." I pulled on my seat belt and started the truck but just sat there. "I purposely misstated the Ravel piece that Marv Leeland loved so much, Piano Concerto for the Left Hand in D Major, and she corrected me — said she knew the piece from hearing her mother play it; but it's strange for a young woman to be so familiar with an obscure piece when she claimed not to have known the man himself."

He stared at me. "I want you to know, there are times when I have absolutely no idea what the hell you're talking about."

I slipped the truck in gear and pulled out. "I'm thinking that Pamela Leeland-Delahunt might've been closer to the memory of her dead grandfather than it first would appear."

"Damn!" Gibbs stood motionless. "You ain't gonna hit anybody else, are you?"

After reholstering my sidearm, I propped Lucian up and checked his pulse. "He's all right; I just needed to look at his weapon, and I was pretty sure he wasn't going to give it up voluntarily."

The old chef slipped down beside me. "Whatever for?"

Thumbing off the safety strap, I slipped Lucian's antique Smith & Wesson .38 from his worn holster. I held the barrel up to my nose and sniffed, then, thumbing open the cylinder, I looked at the empty chamber. "It's been fired."

I went through my boss's pockets and pulled out a folded piece of paper that looked familiar. "Do you own a sidearm, Mr. Gibbs?"

He backed away. "No, sir."

"I'm not sure what's going on around here tonight, but if I were you, I'd just as soon be armed."

He shook his head. "I'm sorry, Mr. Longmire, but I ain't carrying."

I stuffed Sheriff Connelly's weapon into the back of my gun belt.

Gibbs looked at him and then at me. "Mr. Longmire, sir, now that I think of it, he was talkin' with Mr. Leeland earlier this evening, too, and they was by themselves."

"Can you be more exact about the time?"

"Not really."

"Well, we know it was before Fort Fred Steele, which is where they found Sheriff Leeland, and I'm assuming it was after Medicine Bow." I glanced at Lucian. "He was asleep when I left to go outside, or pretending to be." I looked at Gibbs again. "Where were you when all this activity was going on?"

"I was helping make the beds for all them drunk sheriffs and made a couple of runs back here for supplies."

I gestured toward the bottle in his hand. "And for a drink?" He looked ashamed, and I was sorry I mentioned it. "In those visits you never saw anybody open that back door?"

He returned the bottle to the cupboard. "No, sir."

"Because it looks like somebody butchered a pig out there." I moved toward the door and looked out into the night. "Did Mr.

Holland or any of the sheriffs go out on that back stoop after they heard about Sheriff Leeland?"

"Not that I know of, but I can't be sure, 'cause like I said, I wasn't back here that much."

I nodded. Figuring I had only a certain amount of time before the other search party came looking for us, and knowing this particular scene would be hard to explain, I gently slapped Lucian's face. His eyelids began to flutter, and he grumbled a bit, knocking my hand away. "What the . . ."

"Wake up."

"Hey . . ." His eyes refocused, and he looked at me. "What the hell?"

"You fell."

"The hell I did; you hit me." His hand automatically dropped to his side where he found his holster empty. "And for the sake of self-preservation, it's a good thing you took my gun." He laid a hand beside his jaw where I'd roundhoused him. " 'Cause I damn well sure am going to give you a bit of the same — just as soon as I get my brain unscrambled."

"Lucian, your gun's been fired."

He blinked a couple of times but then focused on me as I crouched there in front of him. "What?"

"Unlike mine, your weapon's been fired." I pulled the revolver from the back of my belt and thumbed open the cylinder to show him the empty chamber. "Care to explain?"

He sat there for a long while, and I was thinking he might be passing out again when he spoke. "You go to hell." He stretched his jaw and gave me another sharp look. "And by the way, in case I haven't mentioned it, you're fired."

I shook the folded piece of paper in my hand and it opened like an accordion. "Okay, but before I throw your ass off this train, maybe you could explain how you had this in your pocket?"

He made a noise in his throat. "Took it off you."

"Why?" He said nothing, so I continued. "You were back here with Marv alone, before he was killed. I know that for a fact; now, why?"

"You think you're the only one he talked to?" He shook his head at me. "He called me up a year ago and said he was passing through and did I want to get together and talk. He said that this shit was going on and that somebody was going to have to do something about this cabal, as he called it — and you called it, too." He gestured toward the piece of paper. "That damn thing fell out of your pocket when they were loading you onto this train like a side of beef, and I figured either way it wasn't good for them to find it on you."

I smiled. "So, you really don't think I'm involved?"

"Oh, hell, no. You've only been back in the lower forty-eight for, what, a month?"

"About that."

He grinned. "On the other hand, I can see how you'd think I might have something to do with all this." He rubbed his head and started to stand but then thought better of it and resettled. "When you got up, back in Medicine Bow, I started wondering if something was going on, so I gathered myself and took off after you."

"You followed me?"

"Yep."

"And?"

"When I got to the outside platform, I saw you and McKay having your little tête-à-tête. When he passed me on his way back inside, he said he was likely to reconfigure your general physiology, and I told him he better bring a posse 'cause it was more likely you'd stick your boot so far up his ass that his breath would smell like Kiwi shoe polish." He ran a tongue around his mouth, as though checking for loose teeth. "Then he climbed on board."

"He got back on the train?"

"He did."

"Well, then, it wasn't him that hit me."

"My thought exactly, unless he turned right around after I left and got off the train again."

I thought about it. "Where did you go next?"

"After I saw you heading for the front of the train, I figured you were just going to check out the locomotive, so I got back on. That's when I saw Marv headed through the dining car and took off after him."

"And?"

"We had a conversation about current goings-on, and then I went back to our cabin."

I nodded, then held the .38 up between us. "Well, that explains everything except for how your gun got fired."

He looked at it, and then his eyes met mine. "Damned if I know."

8

"Fancy digs."

I glanced around the grounds of the Wyoming Historic Governor's Mansion and especially the sunroom. "Yep, it is, but they don't live here."

Vic raised an eyebrow. "They don't?"

"Nope. The official residence is the Wyoming Governor's Mansion — note the lack of the term 'historic' — which was built back in 1976."

"Why do that?"

"This original building is on the National Register of Historic Places, which means you can't change anything without getting permission, so I'm betting the state built the one in 1976 because the governor and his family had, among other things, an affection for modern plumbing." We'd situated ourselves along the back wall of the heavily windowed room as the newspaper, television, and radio station journalists arranged themselves around the empty wicker divan in the center of the crowded room. "How come when I'm around these media folks I always feel like I hear locusts in the background?"

The Cheyenne Nation stood beside me and smiled but said nothing.

A bushy-haired man with a handlebar mustache approached. "Walt Longmire, I didn't think we'd see you here."

I folded my arms.

"Mike Barr of the *Casper Star-Tribune;* I left a message on your daughter's machine."

"I don't know how to operate that thing."

A pencil hovered over his pad. "I was just hoping to get a few words about the compassionate release issue we are discussing here."

"No comment."

"None at all?"

I nodded toward the small wicker sofa, which the TV folks were now light testing. "I'm pretty sure the first lady is going to be making some comments. I'm just here to listen."

The pencil was still over the pad, ready to strike. "Walt, everybody knows you're personally involved with this case, and I'm sure they'd like to hear your side of things."

Vic interrupted. "Is that a pencil?"

"What?"

She glanced at us and then back to him. "Do you see that? I haven't seen a fucking pencil in years."

The newspaperman sighed. "Walt . . ."

"Where do you get that thing sharpened, anyway?" She reached for it, but he closed the notepad and stuck it behind his ear. "Is that a Ticonderoga?" She leaned forward, examining him. "Do you have a little card that says 'Press' that you stick in the hatband of your fedora, too?"

Barr shook his head and moved away. "You three are a bunch of assholes."

I raised my voice so he could hear me as he disappeared into the crowd. "Say, you're not going to lead the story with that, are you? I mean, the *Star-Tribune* is a family paper and all."

Wyoming's first lady entered the room, accompanied by two individuals whom I recognized. Flashbulbs went off and the general thrum of excitement swelled as she smiled and shook hands with members of the fourth estate.

Henry gestured toward Bob Delude and Robert Hall, aka the Bobs, who were the legendary drivers and bodyguards of the governor and his family as well as other high-placed government officials. "I bet they are really pleased to be here."

Despite being a traditional beauty, blond with blue eyes, Carol Fisk was not your usual, decorative politician's wife; she was directly involved in setting policy. A graduate of Bowling Green with a postgraduate degree from Cambridge and a law degree to boot, she was a United States district judge, the first woman in the Equality State to hold the post. As first lady, Carol worked on behalf of a number of causes, including equal pay for women, sorely needed in a state where men with a high-school education earn more than women with college degrees. A big proponent of public education and libraries, she was also a champion of literacy — and I found it very difficult not to admire her, present circumstances notwithstanding.

Her husband, Wally, the gov, was a likable, tough individual with an aviation background who'd made his fortune building cranes and whose greatest skill was getting the fractious facets of state government to work together, sometimes even getting them to think it was their idea.

"Hi, how is everybody?" Ms. Fisk looked around the room. "It's wonderful to see all of you, and I appreciate your coming here to talk about one of my many, many causes."

There was a collective smattering of laughter.

"As most of you know, one of the concerns making me think about the way we implement the compassionate release of inmates in the state is that spending has ballooned and overcrowding in the prison system has become a burden."

One of the TV talking heads interrupted. "So, this is being done primarily for economic reasons?"

She smiled at him. "I'll be taking questions later in the press conference, so if you could please hold your questions until then, I'd appreciate it." She resettled herself and glanced our way, and I was pretty sure we'd just been found out.

"It's difficult to implement overarching legislation concerning compassionate release in that the individual cases vary to a great degree, and because the implementation relies on the criteria of a medical petition where a great deal of inconsistency hinders the process."

One of the Bobs, Robert, spotted us in the back and made a face and a few of the press folks laughed.

"Things have gotten a bit better for prisoners suffering from terminal illnesses thanks to the new prison hospice program, but that cannot replace the comfort of dying with dignity among family and friends." She glanced at the reporter who had interrupted, figuring the smattering of laughter must've had to do with him. "Not to mention the cost to the state." The first lady glanced around, a little bit confused but plowing ahead nonetheless. "And then, obviously, there are the cases where there is no proper medical care available in a prison setting."

Now Bob was looking at Robert, and of course the man couldn't resist fooling around, but this time the governor's wife happened to be looking in his direction. "Is there something wrong with you, Robert?"

He straightened up and cleared his throat, looking like a teenager who'd been caught passing notes. "No, ma'am, sorry."

She looked at the other Bob to see if he was up to something and then faced forward again, looking directly at me. "As I was saying . . . with lots of aging inmates in the system and the poor health of that population in comparison with the general public, compassionate release can go a long way toward alleviating costs. Nevertheless, each case still has to be judged on an individual basis. Which brings me to the one at hand."

I ducked my head and pretended to brush

an imaginary piece of lint from my shirt-front, then listened quietly to the rest of the press conference while studiously avoiding eye contact with either of the Bobs.

After the first lady finished her prepared remarks, there was a flurry of questions, which she answered gracefully before exiting through the double doors that led to the mansion proper.

After a moment, the Bobs were standing in front of me. "You got us in trouble."

"You got yourselves in trouble, and you got me in trouble, too."

Robert shook hands with Vic and Henry and then glanced around. "Sounds like your man is going to walk."

"Maybe."

Bob leaned in. "We can always go into the hospital and take him for the proverbial ride, but I don't think he'd make it to the curb."

At that moment, another man approached, smaller and not wearing a uniform or a gun. "Sheriff Longmire?"

"Yep."

"I'm Mark Rivera, the press secretary to First Lady Fisk. She'd like to speak with you in the library."

Vic smirked. "You're in trouble."

I nodded to the functionary. "Okay."

He gestured toward the door. "Now, please."

I glanced at Vic, Henry, and then the Bobs. "You bet."

The sun was just creeping over the high plains at the rimmed cliffs as I finished my report to Joe Holland in the borrowed railroad office in the tower overlooking the Rock Springs rail yard. "I appreciate this, Deputy. Especially after the rough treatment I've given you recently."

I delicately touched my head and put my hat back on at an angle so that it didn't press directly on the wound. "That's all right, I've been hit harder — earlier tonight, as a matter of fact." I sipped the wretched coffee from the cracked Union Pacific mug he'd provided and then rested it back on the metal desk between us. "What are you planning on doing?"

"We've got an APB out on McKay, but nothing so far. I agree with you that the last place I'd be would be on this train if I'd killed somebody. He must've jumped ship back in Medicine Bow if he's the one that hit you, but I can't imagine how, or exactly when. I mean, we were all standing outside the train, and I can't help but think that somebody would've seen him get back on

— and never mind that from there, where the hell do you go?"

"So, if they found Leeland's body at Fort Fred Steele, and if it is McKay who killed Marv, why hit me? Wouldn't you do the deed and bolt?"

He shook his head. "Damned if I know."

I shrugged. "Anybody else missing?"

"Nope, everybody else on the manifest is still aboard and will stay that way till we get back to Cheyenne."

"House arrest?"

"Train arrest." He frowned at all the paperwork splayed in front of him. "I've got to tell you that I'm not real thrilled with all this."

"Well, I can understand —"

He waved a hand, dismissing my statement. "Aside from what appears to be a probable murder, I've got a whole train full of sheriffs, law-enforcement professionals, who, instead of helping, are second-guessing every move I make."

I stood and walked over to the window that faced the tracks, wiped some of the dust away, and gazed into the flat, yellow morning light. An arched neon-red sign announced HOME OF ROCK SPRINGS COAL, WELCOME.

"Oh, I wouldn't take those sheriffs personally; I think they'd do the same thing to each other."

"Some of them still think you did it."

"Well, they're welcome to prove it in a court of law."

There was a silence. "You mind if I ask you a question?"

"As long as I don't have to incriminate myself."

"You're the man on this train with the least seniority, but you're very good at investigating." He stood and placed his hands in his pockets. "What, exactly, did you do in the service?"

I looked at him and then, just as I turned back toward the window, I could've sworn I saw out of the corner of my eye a '59 Thunderbird convertible make a turn and disappear. Maybe I just wanted to see one. "Marine Corps investigator."

"Ah." He smiled. "Any ideas as to why McKay would've done it?"

I hedged. "None whatsoever — I mean, he's a hothead, but I think that's only because he thought something was going on between me and the blonde he's traveling with. Have you spoken to her?"

He looked at a list lying on the surface of the borrowed desk. "Next."

"Anybody else on that list?"

"Your boss."

"I don't think he did it."

"You second-guessing me, too?"

I turned back to the railroad bull. "No, but I can pretty much vouch for his whereabouts till Medicine Bow and after Wamsutter."

He stared back at me. "Curiously enough, all the excitement happened in the period when you weren't on the train."

"You check my story?"

"Sure did. We can't find the people on the bus you described, but everybody at the Shiloh Saloon says you were there and not in the best of shape." He walked over and looked out the gritty glass with me. "That still doesn't get your boss off the hook, though."

"Give me a motive, and I'll think about it."

I'd been thinking long and hard about whether to share the information that the dead man had relayed to me, but I didn't see any other way of advancing the investigation. "Sheriff Leeland thought he was on to something. Over the past few years, there have been a number of unaccounted-for murders in the state of individuals who have evaded justice. Leeland had a suspicion that it was someone in the sheriffs' association, maybe even a group, what he called a cabal, who have taken the law in their own hands. He suspected they were exchanging murders in each other's counties so that they wouldn't get caught doing it."

Holland stood there, staring at me. "Well, that certainly opens up the motivational aspect of the investigation."

"If there's anything to it, you're going to need to find out which sheriffs have been in office for the last three years, where they've been in the state, and whether that coincides with the people who have been killed." I pulled the piece of paper from my shirt pocket and handed it to him. "Mr. Leeland gave me this list of sheriffs he was suspicious of. You'll notice that Lucian isn't on the list."

He took the paper and studied it. "My God, it's half the sheriffs in Wyoming."

"I know. I think he was hoping to narrow the possibilities on this trip, but it looks as if someone got wind of Leeland's investigation and took things into his own hands."

"Sheriff Leeland shared this with you?"

"Me, and Lucian, and I don't know how many others."

"Neither you nor Lucian is on here." He looked down the list of names. "McKay isn't on here either."

I thought about the fact that my boss's sidearm had been fired, but until I had more to go on, I felt no need to share that information. "No."

He leaned an elbow on the window frame. "You know, it's possible McKay's dead, too, lying out there on the tracks somewhere between here and Medicine Bow."

"Yep."

"And we've still got a killer or two or three on The Western Star." He moved over to the desk and picked up a telephone. "I guess we'd better have somebody check the rails from here to Medicine Bow."

"Yep."

"What are your plans?"

I yawned and glanced down the tracks through the snow flurries — The Western Star appeared to be catching her breath. "I think I'll head back to the dining car and have breakfast. I'm hungry."

He nodded and then spoke into the phone. "Just a second." He turned back to me as I reached the door. "I'll meet you on the train?"

"Sure."

"And if you don't mind sending Miss LeClerc in?"

I pushed open the door and found her sitting on a leather chair. "Howdy."

She looked at me and burst into a fresh set of tears. "I can't believe this is happening to me."

I sat in the chair next to her. "It'll be okay; he just needs to talk to you. Tell the truth, and you'll be fine."

She wiped her eyes and looked at me. "Yeah, that always works, huh?"

"Well, actually, most of the time it does." I tipped my hat back and looked at her. "You mind if I ask you a question?"

"Okay."

"When was the last time you saw McKay?"

She sniffled. "George?"

"Yep, George."

"He was really mad when we got back to the cabin and said a bunch of stuff about you."

"And when was that?"

"I don't know, when we got back to the cabin one time." She sniffed. "Do you really think he did all this?"

"I honestly don't know, but he's gone missing and that makes him a suspect."

"Somebody was killed, they say?"

"Marv Leeland, the sheriff of Uinta County."

"The nice old fella with the one arm?"

"Yep, him."

"Oh, that's a shame."

"That's pretty much how everybody feels about it." I took her hands in mine in an attempt to get her to focus. "What time did George leave your cabin?"

"I don't know. . . ."

"Had the train stopped?"

She thought about it. "Yes, it was stopped."

"And he never came back after that?"

"No."

I thought about the brief conversation we'd had trackside. "Did George ever talk about the other sheriffs, specifically Marv Leeland?"

"Well, he talked a lot about the sheriffs' association; I think he was trying to impress me, you know, to get me in the sack. Wasn't the one-armed fella the head of the sheriffs?"

"Yep. What did George say? Can you remember?"

"Just that he thought he should be the next in line but that there were a couple of older men who were more likely to get it even after he said he'd done a bunch of trips for the association. Fund-raising for their elections, I think."

"How many trips were there?"

"Oh, a half dozen, I think he said."

"Over how long of a period of time?"

"I don't know, at least a year or two — way before me. Before that he said he was focusing on his own election." She smiled. "You've got to remember, I've only known him for a few days."

"Just one more question: are George's things still in your cabin?"

"Yes, why?"

"Did he take anything with him when he left, a bag or something?"

"No." She thought about it. "Well, there was a small case he had."

"Any idea what was in it?"

"No."

"Would you mind if I take a look around your berth? I thought if I could go through his things it might give us an idea of where he went." I smiled at her. "Do you have a key?"

She rifled through her pocketbook and finally produced it, attached to a large brass chain. "Here you go."

"No, you hold on to it. I'm going to go have some breakfast and then, when you're through here, I'll meet you at your cabin. Deal?"

She sniffed once more. "Deal."

"Now, you'd better get in there and tell Mr. Holland everything you know."

"That won't take long." She stood, and I did the same. She placed a hand on my chest. "Thank you."

"No problem." I was just pulling away when, with an amazing amount of strength, she brought my face down to hers, but I wasn't taken by surprise this time and resisted.

She smiled disappointedly. "Can't blame a girl for trying."

She turned away and approached the office door where Holland stood, holding the knob and studying the floor. "Miss LeClerc?"

She straightened her fur and turned, giving me a playful wave. I pulled my hat down, bandages be damned, flipped up the collar of my jacket, and stuffed my hands in my pockets as I bumped open the door and took the metal stairway back down to the huffing Western Star.

As I walked up the tracks toward the dining car, I saw Sheriff Connelly knocking the used tobacco from his pipe by tapping it on the heel of his boot. "How'd it go?"

"He let me walk."

Lucian handed me my paperback. "Gibbs said he found this in the caboose. Thought you might want it."

I took the book and stuffed it in the

pocket of my jacket. "Thanks."

He looked up at the ironclad sky. "Weather's changing," he pronounced as if it were a philosophical statement. "I'd say that if we don't get moving we're gonna get snowed on." He glanced around dismissively at the flurries, but his eyes sharpened. "I mean really snowed on."

"Yep."

"You tell him about my gun?"

"No." I studied him. "Should I have?"

He lit the pipe with a match and puffed to get it going. "I'd say that's up to you."

I smiled down at him. "That's why I didn't." I thought back to the interview and then the postinterview with Kim LeClerc. "But I just spoke to her — she had something interesting to say."

"The chanteuse?"

I shook my head at the nomenclature. "Yep. She intimated to me that George McKay had made a number of trips to different counties over the last couple of years for the sheriffs' association."

Lucian's eyes darkened. "What kinds of trips?"

"Well, he said fund-raising, but I don't think either of us would be inclined to believe that."

He smoked his pipe, unconsciously imitating the steam emanating from the locomotive behind us. "Bringing George McKay in for fund-raising would be like bringing me in for public relations." He then stamped his foot and turned, lifting his good leg up onto the stairs, trailing the prosthetic behind him. "C'mon, I'll buy you breakfast."

"Does that mean I'm back on the payroll?"

He thought about it. "We'll call it probation."

The first lady was sitting on a rolling ladder when I entered the mansion library, cradling an ancient-looking leather tome in her manicured hands. "This is a first edition of the English version of *Les Misérables,* Carleton Publishing, 1862. Do you believe that?"

I looked around at the tiger-striped oak furniture, the wood paneling, Tiffany fixtures, and the oriental carpets. "Maybe we should sell it and raise some money for the care of inmates."

She ignored my comment. "I keep telling Wally that we should take all these books and put them at our place, just to protect them." She glanced around. "But he says this mansion belongs to the people of Wyoming and that the collection needs to remain here." Her eyes came back to me.

"How many of the people of Wyoming do you think have actually read this book?"

"Does starting it count?"

She smiled. "I know you have, Walter. That's one of the things I really like about you — both a man of action and a man of thought."

I walked closer and laid an arm on the brass rail. "Say, you are in politics, aren't you?"

"And you're not?"

I made a face. "I think I've run my last race."

"Gonna let that Basque deputy of yours or that spitfire of an undersheriff handle the county?"

"Maybe."

She studied me for a moment and then looked back at the book in her hands. "I've always loved this novel; it has so much to say about human society, character —"

"Justice."

She smiled again, but it quickly faded. "I'm surprised by you, Walt. I never thought of you as . . . as a vengeful person."

"Pharisaic, I think, is the word you're looking for."

"Maybe." She looked down. "You know, I'm not used to begging for prisoners' lives."

"Is that what you're doing, begging?"

"I don't want to have a grudge match in the papers with you, Walt."

"I haven't said a word to anybody."

"You don't have to. The fact that you're here in Cheyenne speaks volumes." Feeling the grain, she rubbed the palm of her hand over the cover of the book. "Mistranslated from the French, most people think it means 'the miserable' or 'wretched ones,' but I think a better translation would be 'the dispossessed' or 'the outsiders.' "

"Pretty much describes everyone in the book."

"Yes, it does. Especially the police investigator, Javert."

I didn't say anything.

"Pharisaic, isn't that the word you used? Imagine a man so bound by the rule of law that he would rather die than bend even the smallest one."

"All the characters and their motivations are products of their society; that's why it's such a marvelous book — but there's a difference between the story in your hands and ours."

"And what's that?"

"The prisoner in our story is not guilty of stealing a loaf of bread but of taking lives — numerous lives. Now you may think I'm intractable, but I see myself as an instrument of the law, and in my county or in my book, for that matter, there is no slide rule of justice — guilty is guilty."

She replaced one of the greatest novels ever written on the top shelf and lowered the heavy glass that protected the books. "And the difference between you and Javert?"

I held out a hand, which she took. "I can reconcile my devotion to the law and the knowledge that a lawful course can sometimes be immoral."

She walked past me toward a large partners' desk. "And you don't see anything immoral in forcing an aged, weak, terminally ill man to die in prison?"

"It's the law. He was tried, found guilty, and duly sentenced. Why does this come as such a surprise? He was given multiple life sentences — why is it suddenly so difficult to understand that he was condemned to die incarcerated?"

"Walt, I can't help but think that this is something personal." She turned to look at me. "I'm going to advise Wally to commute the sentence."

I took a deep breath and slowly exhaled. "You do as you see fit, Carol, but you weren't there."

■ ■ ■ ■

"This is the best damn biscuits and gravy I've ever had."

Gibbs grinned, refilling Lucian's coffee cup. "I got that recipe from the chef at Gadsby's Tavern on the George Washington, C&O line. They retired the 965 about five years ago, but it was a heck of a galley. Monsieur Henri Lafontaine was the chef, a Creole from down Louisiana way, and he wouldn't use anything but that good andouille sausage. That's what makes the difference."

I paused between bites. "Mr. Gibbs, how long have you been working for the railroad?"

"All of 'em? Since nineteen and thirty-two, but it ain't the same as it used to be. Once upon a time we had class, rolling class, but since they been making all the cuts an' everything — I don't know how much longer there will even be a railroad; pretty soon we'll just be a bus on rails."

Lucian sipped his coffee. "There'll always be railroads as long as Wyoming's got coal, and we got plenty of that."

"Maybe so, but I don't know about these passenger trains, Sheriff." He refilled my cup. "But it ain't just the trains, it's the people."

I nodded. "Taking the current events as an example? I wouldn't judge everybody like these sheriffs, Mr. Gibbs — most of the regular citizenry are better behaved."

"I don't know, Mr. Longmire; every time we run a train, things have been disappearing. These cups you're drinking out of, hats, blankets — somebody even ran off with the meat cleaver outta' the kitchen."

Lucian looked at his watch. "The world ain't what it used to be, that's for sure." He stood. "I'm supposed to go talk to that goof ball Holland." He glanced at me. "Where the hell is he, anyway?"

I nodded toward the back. "He's in the office up in the tower, second floor."

Lucian looked at his leg. "Well, hell."

I got in one more sip of coffee before folding my napkin and placing it over my empty plate. "Which reminds me, I've got an appointment with Miss LeClerc to see if I can find anything in their cabin that might help us figure out where McKay is."

Sheriff Connelly pulled his jacket from the back of his chair as a few of the other sheriffs stumbled in for an early breakfast, and Gibbs went over to pour them coffee. "Holland know about that?"

"I don't care if he does or not. The LeClerc woman says she'll unlock the berth, and I'll have her stand there while I search the place, just to prove there's no monkey business going on."

"What's your take on Holland?"

"A burnout, I'd say. He's been at it too long." I grabbed my own coat and hat. "You know, nobody has taken blood samples from the back of the caboose or photographed what we assume is the crime scene. Nothing."

He moved past me toward the group of sheriffs who had just come in. "I suppose they figure they can just wait till the train gets back to Cheyenne and then let the state crime lab go over it."

He pulled up a chair and sat at the sheriffs' table, and I muttered to myself, "An outdoor crime scene traveling over six hundred miles at sixty miles an hour through inclement weather . . . brother." Slipping my jacket on, I lodged my hat on my head again and walked past the group of sheriffs, who quieted when I approached. I tipped my hat. "Gentlemen."

There wasn't a lot of traffic in the passageways, most of the revelers having decided to sleep in, I supposed. When I got to our cabin I could see that the door next to ours was propped open. "Miss LeClerc?"

Her voice sounded from inside. "Present."

I peeked in and found her lying on the lower bunk in pajamas and a robe. "Planning on a nap?"

"Just plain going back to bed — care to join me?"

Not for the first time, I felt a little uncomfortable in her presence. "I'm afraid I've got work to do."

She shrugged. "You mind if I ask you a question?"

"Shoot."

"You seem sad."

I nodded. "Personal problems."

"With that blonde I saw with you on the platform back in Cheyenne?"

"That would be the one. We're married, or were."

She glanced out the window and bit a fingernail in a provocative manner. "Hell, that's no big deal. I've been married three times."

"She's having my child."

"Oh. How far along?"

"About four months. She came to visit me in Alaska, and things seemed really good then."

"Maybe things'll be good again."

"I'm beginning to doubt it." I took a deep

breath and sighed it out. "So, where's George's case?"

"Upper bunk."

I flipped the latches on the Samsonite. For the moment, I ignored the pink set. I pulled the bag closer to get a clearer view and was in the act of sifting through George Mc-Kay's belongings when I felt a tug at my jeans. I looked down to find Kim LeClerc had unzipped my pants and now had a hand inside. She was looking up at me from crotch height with a lascivious smile. "You don't mind if I check out a few things myself, do you?"

I was about to disengage her from my nether parts when I heard a noise at the doorway. I turned in time to see a familiar blonde standing there taking in the tableau.

9

"Let me explain?"

She said nothing, only looked at me with those big hazel eyes, her hands neatly folded on the table.

"Um, she's a nurse . . . for the state, and I needed to have an examination and I was just turning my head to cough when you showed up."

She smiled faintly and turned her coffee cup in her saucer.

"She works for the railroad and was looking for contraband?"

She smiled again, a little broader this time.

"Actually, she's a singer from Casper with an overly active libido."

She gazed out the window of the dining car, but the smile held.

"I played piano last night and she joined in, and evidently she thought there was a stronger bond between us than I did." I reached out and took her hands in mine:

they were warm and soft. "I've missed you."

She took her hands back and sipped her lukewarm coffee, grimaced, and returned it to the saucer with a soft clip of china. "It's only been a night, but evidently you've kept busy."

"You don't believe my story?"

"Which one?" She shook her head and a lock of hair fell across one eye like always. "Actually, I do. You're so inept with women that I find it hard to believe that you could've possibly initiated that encounter."

"It's true." I grinned and then took a sip of my own coffee just to give the talk a little air.

She glanced around to make sure we were out of earshot. "Walt, it might be none of my business, but what's happening on this train?"

"Nothing." I sighed. "Really." She continued to look at me, and I leaned in. "One of the sheriffs was killed, Martha."

Her eyes widened.

I looked at the surface of the table and the spotless white linen. "His name was Marv Leeland. He was from Uinta County, and he had a theory that there was a group of sheriffs within the association that might've been swapping murders, and now he's dead, which may or may not prove him right." Hoping to change the subject, I fingered my silverware, sipped a little more of my coffee, and studied her. "You know, I'm having a hard time remembering what we fought about back in Cheyenne."

"Your future, among other things."

I took a quick breath and set my cup back down, getting the feeling that I was surrounded by land mines. "Oh, yeah."

"Go back to school, Walt. Use the GI Bill and get a master's and go teach at some college somewhere."

A few sheriffs finished up their breakfasts and ambled out, giving Martha the once-over as they passed. Feeling a heat come into my face, I looked up at them. "Can I help you fellas?" They looked away, and I tried to settle myself. "I think I'm through with classrooms, and if I am as a student, then I certainly shouldn't be there as a teacher."

She glanced up as another group passed, and Wally Finlay tipped a hat to her. She gave a tight smile in return, finally looking back at me. "You're a really good teacher, Walt."

"I'm a really good cop."

The eyes flared a bit. "You're really good at whatever you want to do."

"I want to continue to be your husband."

We both sat there in the silence. "Look, things moved pretty fast up there in Alaska. I wasn't even sure I wanted to get married."

"We are having a baby." I could see Gibbs glancing our way from farther down the car to see if we needed a refill, but I waved him off. "You act like you and the baby won't make me happy."

"What about what will make me happy, Walt?"

I reached into my jeans and pulled out the tiny, antique piece of jewelry. "Look . . ."

"Don't do this again." She stared at the ring like I was pointing a gun at her. "Not again — not here, and not now."

I looked at the promise in my hand and felt like I was floating. "You want to know what I learned in Vietnam? I learned that if you're lucky, I mean really lucky, you find the one thing you want in life and then you go after it; you give up everything else because all the rest of that stuff really doesn't matter."

"Walt . . ." A little extra moisture appeared in her eyes, giving them that glow that killed me. "Please."

"I saw Henry Standing Bear's car out there on the street, and I couldn't believe it was you." I glanced at the flurries galloping by the window, their speed multiplied by the velocity of the train. "Call it simplistic maybe, but I know what I want now."

"You and me and Henry, we all grew up together, but a lot of the times it doesn't have a fairy-tale ending. All those years in Vietnam apart when I sat here waiting for you . . . Walter, it happened way too fast in Alaska. Maybe we're not supposed to be together — maybe we're not meant for each other."

"I don't believe that." I pushed back my chair and kneeled beside the table.

"Oh, God. Please don't, I think I'm going to be sick."

Kneeling there with the ring in my hand, I sighed. "Well, that would certainly rob the moment of the romance I'd intended." I cleared my throat, hoping I'd find my voice there. "Will you stay married to me?"

There was a long pause before she finally spoke. "No."

"No?" I chewed the inside of my cheek.

"I'm afraid that we'll be living quiet lives of regret and desperation, and I just can't face that, not now, not with the baby." She stared at her lap and pulled her hair back out of the way. "You say you've learned things over the last few years; well, I've learned a few things, too."

"And that's why you drove all night to

meet me here?"

Her eyes came up. "I went to Denver because Henry asked me to pick him up at the airport. He's the one who said we should head west and catch you so that you and I could talk. He's meeting me at the train station in Evanston so that you and I can have a few hours."

"Maybe I should marry him?"

"Maybe you should."

I stood and sat back in my chair and tossed the ring onto an empty plate where it rattled and stilled.

We moved to the observation car, where we had the open vista of the high plains to ourselves; I supposed the other sheriffs and their guests weren't interested in the topography between Rock Springs and Evanston.

"We aren't talking."

I glanced over at her. "I didn't figure there was much more to say."

"Tell me about this case."

"That's the last thing I want to talk about."

She settled into the lounger and crossed her arms. "Well, we've got almost two hours to fill."

"I can think of other things we could do."

"No."

"Just for old times' sake?"

She looked out the windows at the rapidly traveling clouds. It was midday, and all I could think was that she probably wished she were somewhere, anywhere, else but here. "I don't think that would be a good idea."

We sat there in silence for a while, both of us thinking about what might come next.

"I don't know, Martha. Maybe I've changed. I never thought I grew up in a sheltered environment." She smiled but said nothing. "I don't mean to sound dramatic, but I've seen a lot of things since I've been gone and not all of them positive." I hesitated a bit. "Nothing specific that I want to talk about, but I always thought that people were good, down deep."

"And now you don't?"

I took a breath, feeling more like crawling under the moving train than continuing the conversation I had started. "Not as much."

She glanced around to make sure none of the sheriffs had wandered in. "And you think this job will help you to recover your faith in humanity?"

"No, not at all, but maybe I can help even the score." I waited a moment and then continued with what sounded even to me like a rationalization. "I was able to do some good in all those places — I guess at a cost, but I think the final results were worth the price."

She reached out and ran her smooth, warm fingers over the scars on my hand. "Worth it to you?"

"To me."

"Then maybe this is something you should do."

"It is." We both turned to find Lucian Connelly standing in the aisleway. "I hope I'm not interrupting." He extended a hand and even went so far as to take off his hat. "Hello, missy."

Martha looked at the hand the way I'd guess Eve had regarded reptiles, but finally took it. "Sheriff."

"What are you two lovebirds doing here?"

"Just talking."

He pulled out the chair beside her and sat on the back. "You're Jack and Mildred Pierson's girl, aren't you?"

"Yes, sir."

I watched him flipping the Rolodex in his head, tracking through her family history in those few, brief seconds. "I've noticed you — hard to miss a pretty young gal such as yourself." She maintained eye contact with him, and I was proud of her. "I was just waiting around to see if you were going to make a mistake by not staying married to this lunkhead here."

She started to stand. "I don't think that's any of your business."

He slipped his hat back on and stared at her. "Oh, yes, it is. You see, I think that feller there has all the makings to be one of the finest lawmen to ever grace the great state of Wyoming. Right now Absaroka County is mine, but someday I'm going to want to hand it off to somebody that's worthy. In the meantime, I need steady, decent, focused deputies, and, missy, from experience I've learned that married men fit the bill much better."

Her mouth hung open in surprise until she finally began shaking her head. "You think I should stay with Walter for the betterment of your department?"

"Well, that would work for me, but I doubt it's a good enough reason for you."

"And what should my own reason be, in your opinion?"

"I've got a feeling he's one of the finest men I've ever met."

She smiled at him. "He's only been on your staff for a couple of weeks."

"Oh, I've had my eye on him a long time."

"Have you, now?"

"Young lady, I'm beginning to think you

might not like me all that much."

She continued studying him. "You might be right, but more important, I don't think what you do for a living is good enough for him."

The sheriff just smiled. "Good enough?"

"Yes."

He looked away and wet his lips with a quick flick of his tongue. "Ma'am, with all due respect, I deal with life and death every day, and the stakes don't get any higher than that." He held his gaze on the snow-covered prairie as it sped by. "Now, you may be right about Walter here being able to do or be anything he wants, but if you're thinking there's something else he could do that would make more of a difference in his lifetime, then I'm going to have to rein you up short." He glanced at me.

She said nothing.

"There's only one higher calling than the law, and he already did two tours of that one." He turned and started toward the door. "I did a few tours myself." He tapped my shoulder as he passed, and I wondered if he'd done me more damage than good. "John Schafer, Albany County, is looking for you. Probably wants you to go with him when he visits his bedbug of a brother in the loony bin in Evanston." He turned and looked at me. "Just go, every new guy does it." Then he looked at Martha. "Think of it as your swan song to law enforcement." He studied me. "It's not like he's asking you to go visit Annie Welsh or anything."

Before I could ask who Annie Welsh was, Martha, in a voice with a little more than an edge to it, interrupted. "I suppose you're used to people doing what you tell them?"

He studied her and then tipped his hat. "Yes, ma'am. I am."

Judge Snowden bit into his sandwich — it was a warm fall day and we had decided to picnic. "They've got me in this apartment about a block from here with a mini refrigerator, so I bought some cold cuts and started making my own lunches." He tipped his light-colored hat back on his head. "Problem is I can't make a sandwich to save my ass." He looked up at me as he picked at a wilted shred of lettuce. "Do you suppose the very last produce trucks in America end up at the grocery stores in Wyoming?"

Even though the Californian made fun of my state, I liked the guy. "It's possible." I glanced at the cottonwood trees surrounding the plaza. It had been a warm fall, even down here in Cheyenne, and the leaves on the cottonwoods were still a brilliant yellow.

"You're out of the case now?"

"So it would appear; judges pale in comparison to governors."

"But you're off it?"

"Figuratively. I'm waiting until your governor or his wife holds another press conference."

"Figuratively enough to advise me on what to do?"

"Oh, I'm always available for advice; there's just usually a consultation fee." I stared at him, and he finally smiled, and not for the first time I thought that he was an exceedingly smart man. "Just kidding."

"Then what should I do?"

He dropped the remains of his unsatisfactory sandwich into a brown paper bag and wiped the corner of his mouth with a folded paper towel. "The hardest thing in the world — nothing. The wheels of justice grind slow but exceedingly fine." He deposited the makeshift napkin in the sack. "Anyway, from the information I've gleaned from the medical advisory board, he'll be dead before he ever sees the light of day."

"So wait it out?"

He bit his lip. "Or risk looking like a vindictive prick in the papers."

"Is that a legal term in California?"

"It ought to be — we have enough of

them." He brushed off a few crumbs from his jeans, straightened his tie, and, shooting the cuffs of his shirt under his blazer, looked around for a wastebasket.

We walked over to one of those green wire trash containers. "You don't strike me as the type to back down." He turned and slam-dunked the garbage into the receptacle. "But you also don't strike me as the kind who goes looking for a fight."

"Maybe I was a couple of decades ago, but I'm not so sure I've got the energy for it anymore." I shook my head as we walked back toward the capitol building. "You ever have a case like this before?"

"I live in Napa; the closest I've ever been to something like this is disputes between wine growers, not that they can't be a ruthless lot."

"Nobody wins?"

He stopped and looked at me. "Pick your battles, Sheriff." He patted my shoulder and directed my attention to a black SUV sitting at the curb with the Bobs standing by the doors. "You may not always win the war, Walt, but it's good to know you fought the battle." He turned and continued toward the capitol building.

I walked to the Bobs with my hands raised. "No need to shoot, boys, I'll go peaceable."

Robert made a gun out of his hand, holding a forefinger on me as Bob went around to the driver's side. "C'mon, we're taking you for a ride."

"Proverbial?"

Bob opened the door. "No, it's a Suburban."

The black leather seats were configured across from each other, and I climbed in and sat so that I faced the two men occupying the back. "No fair; two on one."

Joe Meyer, Cady's landlord and the attorney general, smiled at the other man. "Yeah, four if you count the Bobs."

As we pulled out, I put on my seat belt, slipped off my Ray-Bans, hanging them in my shirt pocket, and looked at the formidable man in the dark suit and bright yellow tie across from me. "Governor Fisk."

He reached a hand out. "Call me Wally."

"Walt." We shook. "Where we headed, Wally?"

"Someplace where we won't get interrupted."

Joe and I made small talk as we swung up Business 25 past the airport and Sloan Lake, then took a left, heading into the Frontier Days Rodeo Grounds at the north end of town. Evidently they were expecting us — the gates were open and the security detail waved the Bobs through into the main arena.

Delude swung the Suburban around as Hall threw an arm over the seat. "You want us to do a few donuts? Good dirt for it."

Joe, more knowledgeable of the Bobs' driving predilections than the governor, suppressed a smile. "Um, that's okay, Bob — just stop here."

Fisk unbuckled and opened the door for himself. He leaned forward. "Take a walk with me, Walt."

I glanced at Joe as I climbed out after the governor and closed the door behind us, watching as the SUV pulled away. "Does this mean we have to walk back?"

He half smiled, kneeled down, and picked up a handful of soil, crumbling the earth between his fingers. "You ever rodeo?"

"Nope, grew up on a working ranch and never saw the attraction."

He stood up. "I used to do some rough-stock riding."

"You look it."

He smiled, patting a bit of a stomach. "Well, back in the day." He took a few steps toward the chutes. "Never anything this extravagant."

I studied the massive grandstand, a little

surreal without the thousands of people filling it.

"Got a box around here?"

He pointed. "I sit right there, among the people." He turned back toward me. "Real easy to get on your high horse these days."

I toed the real estate with my boot. "Is it?"

He studied me for a moment, then dropped the rest of the dirt and sniffed his hand.

"I wonder how much blood, sweat, and tears I sifted through my fingers just now."

"I don't know, but I'm betting there might've been a little bullshit mixed in there as well."

To his credit, he laughed. "I'm inured, considering my occupation. Do you know what I really do for a living, Walt?"

"Run the state?"

"I make deals. That's what governing is — giving a little, getting a little."

I stuffed my hands in the pockets of my jeans and said nothing.

He looked around the arena like it was the ruin of a fallen city. "I liked the competition, I have to admit, but I was young and not quite sure of what it was I wanted to do with my life. Then I met Carol and started figuring things out."

I nodded and threw him a bone. "A woman can do that to your life — raise the stakes."

"You're married, aren't you, Walt?"

"Widowed."

"Oh." He looked at the dirt he'd just dropped. "I suppose I should've known that, huh?"

"No reason."

He took a deep breath and looked around. "You're a highly visible man in the state."

"So are you."

He shook his head. "Oh no, I'm just a lame-duck governor looking to get out of office before I find some way to step on my dick and screw things up."

"How would you do that?"

"I don't know . . . maybe having a highly publicized pissing match with a legendary sheriff over a case that doesn't amount to a hill of beans."

I sighed. "I don't think you have that much to worry about. The honorable Judge Snowden thinks I'll end up looking like a . . . 'a vindictive prick,' I think were the words he used."

"Well, then, he doesn't know Wyoming."

"Maybe, but he knows the law."

Wally turned his head and focused on me with a practiced smile. "The law is the last thing I'm concerned with here."

I tried to smile back, but it wouldn't take, so I just stood there looking at him. "I suppose Joe Meyer told you how I feel about people telling me how to do my job."

"He has, and I've got the same attitude. The question is, whose job is this?"

"Well, it was mine. I'm the one who arrested him."

"Yes, and it was the state and people of Wyoming that found him guilty, sentenced him, and incarcerated him."

"For a multitude of lifetimes."

The governor nodded and walked past me toward the chutes. "You know, a lot of people claim my allegiances are to corporate interests rather than to the people. Well, I could make some sort of overture by commuting a death sentence as my swan song, but since no one is currently awaiting execution and we haven't performed one since 1992, I'm thinking maybe of a life-sentence commutation." He stood with his back to me. "You know, I've got another six months in office, and right now I'm considering a request from your buddy Joe." He turned back to look at me. "Joe seems to think we need to have a special investigator for the attorney general's office."

I breathed a laugh. "Does he now?"

"The position would have jurisdiction over the entire state." He began walking in a circle around me. "Imagine that, statewide jurisdiction; the ability to pick and choose cases from all the dockets in Wyoming."

"I suppose Joe told you what I'd say to this as well."

He placed a hand on my shoulder. "Yes, but I told him I could try and make it worth your while."

"No." I turned to look at him, the two of us squaring off like a couple of old bulls. "I'm afraid you can't."

10

She fiddled with a delicate chain and the ring that hung from it — a small diamond with matching chips in a vintage setting. "Was it a long walk?"

"I had plenty of time to think."

We spoke in low voices in an attempt to not wake up Lola, who had fallen asleep in the Pack 'n Play. She barely fit inside it these days, but it was her comfort zone and she didn't want to give it up. The Greatest Legal Mind of Our Time continued to interrogate me. "I can't believe they dropped you at the rodeo grounds and wouldn't give you a ride back."

"Oh, they would have, but I was making a point and wouldn't get in."

She shook her head. "Hard-ass."

"I guess."

"Special investigator for the attorney general's office, huh?"

I nodded and leaned back on the sofa.

Slipping off my boots. I put my feet up on the coffee table, but Cady looked at them as though they were cow pies, so I lowered them to Dog's back. "I think they made up the position."

"We'd be in the same building."

"They didn't say anything about an office."

"Try and get Joe Meyer's; it's on a corner." She gazed toward the kitchen where Alexia was cooking up something that smelled wonderful. "You have never been susceptible to bribes. I can't believe my landlord would try something like that; he's known you for years."

"I'm not so sure Joe was party to the whole thing — this might've been Fisk's deal."

"Maybe they think they're doing something noble."

"Maybe, but I think it sounded more like a public relations ploy." I slouched further into the sofa, maybe a little more tired than I thought. "I'm still not sure if it's coming more from Wally or Carol — either way, I'm stuck in the middle."

"I'm sorry, Daddy." She got up and crossed over to sit beside me. "Why don't you just say the hell with it and go home?"

"Hey, Al, she's trying to get rid of me now

that she got her furniture moved."

Alexia yelled back. "I don't think so, Sheriff — if she could, she would move you in here along with the sofa."

Cady waited a moment and then rested her head on my shoulder. "Part of me wishes you might take them up on it, for me and for Lola's sake." She sighed. "I'm not going to say it hasn't been nice to have you around. I get lonely, Dad."

I reached a hand out to my widowed daughter. "I'm sorry, honey."

"I don't think my life is going to be as easy as yours and Mom's."

I sighed and stared at the ring she wore around her neck. "You don't want that, anyway."

"What?"

"Your old man roaming around down here with nothing to do." I looked at Dog, his muzzle next to Lola. "At the moment, I've got a job, but in case you haven't noticed, I'm rapidly approaching an age where I don't have to have one."

She was silent for a moment. "What would you do?"

"I don't know, maybe nothing."

"Oh, I don't think that's a good idea."

"You don't think I'm capable?"

She grunted a laugh. "I know you're not."

Wiping her hands on a dish towel, Alexia came in from the kitchen. "Miss Cady, the enchilada casserole will be done in a half hour."

"Thank you, Alexia. Are you heading home?"

"*Sí,* Miss Cady; with the little one asleep there really isn't anything more for me to do, and I have promised Ricardo and his amigo that I would make them dinner."

My daughter sat forward and turned to look at her. "I'm sorry, you shouldn't have stayed here cooking for us if you had to go home and cook again."

"I don't mind, Ricardo *es un chico muy bueno.*"

I leaned my head back on the sofa to look at her. "The other fellow, Coulter, how do he and Ricardo know each other?"

"He met him at a club in Denver where he was playing his guitar, and they became friends." She said nothing more, but by the look on her face, I could tell she had some doubts about her son's amigo.

"You don't like him?"

She shrugged. "I don't know; he does not talk about himself at all." She put her hand on her chest. "Not much heart, I don't think."

"Alexia, do you want to take tomorrow

off? I mean we've got a ton of people around who can —"

"No, no. They're young men, and they won't want me there too much, I am sure."

"Then we'll see you tomorrow?"

"*Sí,* in the morning."

"Big Al." I raised a hand, and she shook it, smiling at my nickname for her. "Thanks for taking care of everybody."

After she left, I made a pronouncement. "I like her."

"You like her because she's a great cook."

"I like her because she cares for the two of you in my absence."

The Greatest Legal Mind of Our Time stretched her back and got up, looking in the playpen as Dog raised his head before collapsing again. "I think Lola sleeps better when Dog is around."

"I know I do." I waited a moment before adding, "You can't have Dog."

She gave me a look and started toward the kitchen. "I'm checking on the enchilada casserole — sometimes the preheat doesn't work right; do you want anything?"

"The enchilada casserole."

"Well, you're going to have to wait another thirty minutes for that." She came back, lifted my hat, and kissed the top of my head. "You could take a shower before the posse gets back."

"Where did they go?"

"To get a bottle of wine, and some bourbon for Lucian."

"Who's going to watch Lola?"

Her head reappeared in the doorway. "I am, with Dog's help. Go take a shower."

"The last time I saw you was Johnston Atoll." We shook, and I glanced down at the calluses on his powerful, deeply tanned hands. "What have you been doing since then?"

"Picking grapes."

"Where?"

He leaned against his father's T-bird and laughed, crossed his arms, stretching the blue chambray shirt at the seams. "France, where else?"

I studied his face; there were a few more wrinkles than I remembered. "Good to hear you laugh."

"I have reacquired the ability, along with a number of others."

"Welcome home."

He glanced around at the Evanston rail yard, his dark eyes finally settling on Martha, who smiled at him as she quickly climbed into the passenger seat to escape the freezing wind. "Is that what this is?"

"I had a little trouble recognizing it myself." I joined him in leaning on the car. "Home is home, though it be homely." I reached out and flipped the collar of his shirt. "Don't you have a coat?"

He shrugged. "I did not need one in France — I did not need a lot of things."

"Thanks for bringing her." I lowered my voice so that Martha couldn't hear me, although the engine was running, which certainly masked the conversation. "I asked her to stay married to me."

He looked down at his scuffed chukka boots. "What did she say?"

"No."

"Perhaps it is for the best." He sighed. "Trees teach us patience, but grass teaches us persistence."

"And what did grapes teach you?"

"Wine, which assists with both."

"Where are you headed?"

"The real home." He studied me for a long moment. "Where are you headed?"

I had to be honest with somebody and figured it might as well be my best friend. "I'm not sure — it's complicated. I didn't seem to be assimilating like I hoped I would, so I took this job a couple of weeks ago thinking it would help; deputy for Lucian Connelly, the sheriff — you remember him?"

The Cheyenne Nation turned his head, letting the cold wind push his hair from his face. "I seem to, tough but fair as I recall." He unfolded his arms and pointed at the Colt semi-automatic on my hip. "Those things get heavy, so I put mine down." He started off in the opposite direction toward Front Street. "Come on."

Instinctively, I fell in behind him. "Where are we going?"

"I am going to buy a jacket."

I caught up and walked with him. "What, the cold finally get to you?"

"Not really, but it would appear we need to talk." We went through a chain-link gate and onto the sidewalk. "Why is it complicated?"

"A man was killed — a sheriff."

He raised an eyebrow as he pulled open a glass door. "And why is this a complication for you?"

"I knew him, or at least I got to know him before he was killed." I followed the Bear into a Western wear store to the tinkling of a bell attached to the door. "Someone shot him and threw him off the train . . . I think."

He pursed his lips as he walked toward a hat rack, pulled off a black flat brim with a beaded band, and nestled it onto his head.

"How do I look?"
"Like Billy Jack, only a lot bigger."
He looked at himself in a full-length mirror. "Who is Billy Jack?"
"An Indian, Green Beret, hapkido expert who beats the shit out of bikers and sheriffs."
"An Indian protagonist?"
"A half-breed."
"I like him already — at least half of him." He pulled a fake-fleece-lined jean jacket from another rack and tried wedging it on one arm, but it was far too small. "Does he look like an Indian?"
"Who?"
"This Billy Jack."
"Not particularly."
He shrugged. "I have not had a lot of time for popular culture lately."
"It's 1972, times are changing."
As he peeled the thing off, a clerk appeared, my gun belt making her a little nervous. Henry handed her the jacket. "Do you have this in an XXL?"
The middle-aged woman with bangs and cat's-eye glasses nodded and started to move away but not before adding, "I'm afraid you're not allowed to try on the hats."
He smiled and cocked his head. "How else can you tell if they fit?"

"We've had problems with Indians with head lice."

She scurried away with the jacket, and the Cheyenne Nation turned to look at me, the hat still solidly on his head, the flat brim underlying his statement. "You were saying something? About times changing?"

Lying there on the sofa, I was uneasy, and I didn't know why.

I'd finally fallen asleep about two hours ago, but now I was awake again, staring at the ceiling with a feeling I couldn't classify, a sense of foreboding that could mean something important or just that the enchilada casserole wasn't sitting well.

Reaching over, I picked up my pocket watch from the coffee table — 12:45 a.m., three-quarters of the way through what most people believe is the witching hour. The term really applies to the hour bracketed by three and four in the morning, earning its nickname because there are no Catholic Church services then, so the demons are at their strongest. Since I wasn't particularly a believer in any witching hour, I got up and got a drink of water.

Downing a glass, I looked out at the partly cloudy skies, the moon feathering its way through the night sky. As I filled myself another from the tap, I looked down and caught a glimpse of a glowing ember like that of a smoldering cigarette in the alley below. Leaning back a bit, I could see a vehicle and waited until the cigarette glowed again.

It could be anything or anybody.

It wasn't like my daughter owned the alley.

Returning to the living room, I got dressed, grabbed my jacket and hat, and made my way outside.

I couldn't use the front entrance to the apartment because the stairs led directly to the car that was idling outside, and I didn't want to use the other as it was through Cady's room, where she and Lola were sleeping with Dog.

So I carefully opened the door to the balcony/deck and shimmied down the supports, all the while thinking that I wasn't getting any younger.

I finally reached the corner of the carriage house and stood there for a moment to catch my breath. When I was satisfied I wasn't going to die, I set out around the other side, quietly opening and closing the gate behind me as I crossed the attorney general's backyard. I turned the corner but pulled up short when I saw someone standing in my way. The man was pushing a shopping cart and appeared to be homeless.

"Hi."

"Hi." He gestured over his shoulder. "There's a car out there in my alley, and I'm waitin' for him to move." He looked around and then added, "I didn't want you to think I was trespassing or loitering or something."

"Okay."

"You a sheriff?"

"I am."

"Saw your truck." He scratched a face full of rusty beard and then stuck a hand out to me. "Peter Lowery."

I took the risk and shook the hand. "Good to meet you, Peter."

He looked up at Cady's apartment. "You live up there?"

I thought about how much personal information I wanted to share with the homeless guy who lived in the alley. "Yep."

He shuffled a bit, and I noticed that, along with the wool stocking cap that barely contained all the hair, he must've been wearing about seven layers of clothes. "Your daughter, she's nice. Granddaughter, too?"

"Yep." So much for keeping things to myself.

I guess he could read my unease. "I don't

mean any harm; it's my neighborhood, too."

"Where do you live?"

He seemed surprised by the question. "Huh?"

"You said it's your neighborhood — where do you live?"

"Oh, well, I sometimes sleep over near the power pole beside that gardening shed across the alley." He pulled at the gray wool cap that had seen better days. "I'm not drugged or psycho or anything. I just like living a free life, you know?"

"Sure." I stepped around him and looked at the car that was still idling in the alley. "Ever seen that car before?"

"Nope, so I thought I'd wait here till it moved on."

"How long has it been here?"

"Seventeen minutes thirty-six seconds."

I smiled. "That's pretty exact."

He pointed at a black plastic watch on his wrist, which obviously kept time to the second. "Time's important."

I nodded. "Yep, it is. Do you mind waiting here until I get over there? I'd like to surprise whoever it is."

"Sure, sure. But I can follow you, if you want. You know, give you some backup?"

"That's okay, I think I can handle it."

He seemed disappointed. "Okay."

I smiled again, hoping there was no ill will, and then moved around him toward the alley, where a sedan with Wyoming County 1 plates was parked with the motor running. I could see that somebody was smoking with his head leaning back on the seat so that he could look through the top of the windshield at Cady's apartment.

Glancing back at Peter and indicating to him that he should stay put, I quietly crossed into the alley, crouched down around the back of the Buick, and continued up the passenger side, where I yanked open the door and jumped in.

"Jesus!?" Mike Barr, the *Casper Star-Tribune*'s Cheyenne correspondent, dropped his cigar in his lap and began frantically brushing it off onto the floor mat. "Shit . . . you scared the hell out of me."

I slammed the door shut. "What are you doing, Mike?"

He clutched his shirtfront. "Trying to not have a heart attack. Walt, for God's sake . . ."

I pressed a hand against the dash. "What are you doing watching my daughter's apartment?"

"Looking for you." He calmed down a bit and sighed. "I've called and left messages, stuck my card on her door — I've tried everything."

"You should have been around this afternoon when I could've used a ride."

"Up at the rodeo grounds?" He nodded. "Yeah, one of the security guys called me. You know, you're not the first one he's taken up there to intimidate."

"I'm heartbroken."

"So, how'd that go?"

I glared at him. "What do you want, Mike?"

"What do you think I want?" He turned in the seat and spotted his cigar on the floor mat. "Look, all the press is pretty much lining up with Fisk and his wife, and I can't help but think that you've got your side of the story."

"To tell." I rolled my window down, the stale cigar smoke getting to me.

"Exactly."

"To you."

He grinned. "Why not?"

"No thanks."

He puffed on the cigar to try to get it going again and draped his wrist over the steering wheel as wisps of smoke drifted out the partially open window. "I could be a really good friend to you, Walt, at a time when you need it."

"I've got a lot of friends."

"Maybe not enough." I started to get out,

but he stopped me with what he said next. "You've got a daughter who works in this town; always handy to be on the good side of the press."

I stared at him for a long while and then pulled the handle and stepped out. I closed the car door firmly behind me and then spoke through the open window. "Get the hell out of here, Mike. If it had been Henry Standing Bear and not me who had come down here, he would've broken your neck before he knew who you were."

"Take good care of her."

"I will."

"And try not to get head lice."

"I will not."

I stood, leaving him in the Thunderbird's driver's seat, and walked around to where she stood, having gotten out of the car to talk to me. She took in the environs of the Evanston rail yard, where the skiff of snow had mixed with coal dust to make a peppered landscape. "It's not exactly the airport in Casablanca."

"No, it's not."

"You want to buy a ring?"

"Stop it."

I put my arms around her and pulled her in close. She didn't resist, but maybe she just wanted to keep warm. "What am I gonna do?"

"Walt . . ."

"I've been without you for six of the crappiest years of my life, so I'm thinking I'm due a change."

She leaned back and looked up at me. "You'll be fine."

I snorted a laugh, amused at my own misery. "Nope — of all the things I'll be, *fine* isn't one of them."

She glanced past me toward the huffing train. "You need to go, and so do we."

I opened the passenger door, feeling the blast of heat from inside drift past us. "I'll be back home in two days."

"There's no need; there's nothing to talk about."

"The baby?"

She pulled away, and I let her. "I've got to go."

"Like I said, I'll be there in two days."

She looked straight ahead and didn't say anything, so I closed the door.

The Cheyenne Nation slipped the big bird down into gear, pulled through the open chain-link fence onto Front Street, and drove my heart away.

I felt a slap on my back. "Well, how did that go, Troop?"

I stood there and watched the car before it disappeared behind a few buildings and even listened to the sound of the engine as the cold crept into my bones and solidified. "You say one more thing to me and I'm gonna knock the living shit out of you."

Figuring I needed to get my suitcase packed up so that I could get the hell out of there, I turned and walked toward the train. I'd had enough drama to last me a lifetime. I was close enough to get to Salt Lake City, and from there I could light out for the territories. Anybody who tried to stop me was going to be taking his life in his ill-advised hands.

I got to our cabin and pushed open the door. I grabbed my things and shoved them back into my duffel, not bothering to fold.

"Don't do it, Mr. Longmire, sir."

I turned to look at Mr. Gibbs. "What?"

"It didn't look as though that went well, sir. I understand you're really upset right now, but that ain't no time to be making decisions in your life."

I stared at my boots. "I don't know where I'm going, Mr. Gibbs, and I don't know what I'm going to do."

"Can you live without her?"

I turned back to him. "No, I don't think I can."

"Then get her back."

"She doesn't want me."

"She just like the rest of us; she don't know what she wants, but worse than that, she don't think you know what you want."

"I've told her."

"Hell, told . . . you go get that sweet, young thing and you *show* her." He cleared his throat. "You say you can't live without her, then you better go get her, 'cause near as I can tell, you ain't an easy man to kill. You just come back from the war, didn't you?"

"Yes, Mr. Gibbs."

"On these trains, there's a lot that come back in boxes, but you made it." He clutched his fists together. "There was a woman I fell in love with in Chicago back in them dirty thirties, but I wanted to get out and get my musical career goin'. I thought I could live without her, but they wasn't no way I could live without my music."

"How did that work out?"

"I'm seventy-two years old, and I done think I was half right."

I smiled. "Which half?"

"Unpack your stuff, ride this train back to Cheyenne, and hitch a ride out to where she is and show her you can't live without her." With that pronouncement he turned and walked away.

My eyes dropped to the duffel, and I nudged it with my boot as I thought about what Gibbs had said. Finally I reached down and picked it up. My passport was on top, along with the Agatha Christie, and I heard Leeland's voice echoing in my head — *he did it, she did it, they all did it, or nobody did it.*

I zipped the duffel up, slipped it onto my shoulder, and then closed the door behind me. I ran into Lucian smoking his pipe on the steps.

He moved aside as I stepped down the stairs and then onto the train bed below. I looked up at him and reached out in an attempt to hand him my star, but he made no move to take it. "Thanks for giving me a try, Lucian. I honestly appreciate it."

He just stood there, looking at it and me. "Where you headed, and what are you gonna do?"

I stood there for a moment and then forcefully placed the star in his hand, before walking away. "Nowhere and nothing."

He called after me. "Well, there ain't no hurry about nowhere and nothing — they're always out there waitin'."

I paused, feeling the cold flow up from

the ground through my boots, and was pretty sure I was going to be cold for a long time. I turned the collar up on my horsehide jacket and started off. "I'll send you a post-card."

11

"He must have gone straight to the office and written this shit up to make the deadline last night." Vic lowered the paper and looked at the Bear and me. "What time was it?"

"Right after midnight." I sipped my coffee, took a final bite of my prebreakfast toast, slipped Dog a crust, and eyed my compatriots across the kitchen table. "Does he call me a vindictive prick?"

She studied the article. "Did you really threaten him with Henry?"

I looked out the kitchen window at the barely perceptible dawn, the serrated band of apricot-colored horizon reflecting off the taller buildings downtown. "Vaguely."

Henry joined the conversation. "In what sense?"

"I told him you'd have probably broken his neck, on purpose or not."

He nodded. "A safe presumption." He

took the paper from Vic.

There was a thumping noise from the living room and the party grew by one. "I wish you sons-a-bitches would learn to keep your voices down." Lucian stomped into the kitchen, wearing nothing but boxers, a tank top, and his ubiquitous Stetson Open Road hat, his cane in his right hand. "What the hell's going on in here?" He poured himself a cup of coffee and turned to look at us.

"Old man, I'd appreciate it if you'd put on some clothes and your leg, not necessarily in that order, before my daughter and granddaughter wake up."

He sipped his coffee, finally focusing his bloodshot eyes on me. "Can't find it."

"Your leg?"

He nodded toward the beast under the table. "I think that critter ran off with it." He took another sip and watched as Henry read the article. "What's with the paper?"

Vic gestured toward me. "Your protégé has taken to threatening reporters."

Using the back of one of the chairs to balance himself, the old sheriff hopped over and sat at the table with us, reaching down and petting Dog to show there were no hard feelings. "Well, there's hope for him yet, isn't there, you big bastard?"

I nodded toward the backyard. "Mike Barr

was here last night staking the place out."

He sipped his coffee some more. "Well, you ain't exactly hard to find these days."

"I guess he wanted a scoop; I think he figured he could get something out of me if he was on my side." Henry tossed the paper to the center of the table on top of a bowl of fruit. "The *Star-Tribune* didn't do us any favors."

His finger sprang up and then thumped the table. "You know, it would do the people of this state well to realize that not everybody we go up against is either innocent or well meaning."

Someone started knocking at the door, and all of us turned toward it before looking at one another.

Lucian grimaced. "Who in the hell is that this time of morning?"

"I'm betting it's the fourth estate."

Lucian made a move. "I'll talk to 'em."

Henry got up, stopping the old sheriff with a hand, and moved toward the door. Whoever it was knocked again. "I will get this." We listened as he crossed the living room. He snatched the door open and leaned forward with intent, causing whoever it was to stumble backward. "Can I help you?"

"Um, is this the residence of Cady Longmire?"

The Cheyenne Nation's voice was low and sharp. "There is a child in this house — do you know what time it is?"

Lucian picked up the paper and glanced at it before turning it toward me. The headline read: LONG ARM OF THE LAW REACHES INTO THE PAST WITH A VENGEANCE.

Pulling the handle of my duffel farther up onto my shoulder, I braved the wind and walked the length of town. I was about to take the cutoff toward the highway when a cream-colored sedan with whitewall tires pulled up to the curb beside me. "You look like you need a lift."

I stared at the familiar face that appeared in the driver's side window of the Plymouth Belvedere and recognized John Schafer.

"Where you headed?" I nodded in the direction of the highway. "Giving it up, huh?"

I stared down at my boots as a few flurries swept past. "I don't think I'm cut out to be a lawman."

He nodded. "Maybe I can make you a better deal."

"Than the law?"

"Than hitching."

I stuffed my fists into my jacket pockets.

"How 'bout I give you this car?" I didn't say anything, so he climbed out. "I know we got off on the wrong foot, but I need somebody to go over to the state hospital with me."

I shook my head.

"Listen, I've been visiting my brother in that place every month since he was convicted, and I've never gone alone."

"Why?"

He snorted. "You ever been?"

"No."

He gestured toward the car. "My parents went out and bought this boat for Ed when he went off to college; damn thing's got only about six thousand miles on it." He looked at me, his larger eye holding me in check. "I gotta get rid of the thing 'cause the place where I keep it is getting torn down. I don't want it, never wanted it — too many memories — and Lord knows my brother doesn't need it."

I nodded but still didn't say anything.

"You seem like a stand-up guy, so here's the deal. You come with me to visit my brother and then give me a ride back to The Western Star, and I'll sign the pink slip over to you. When you get wherever you're going, you can just send me whatever you think the thing is worth." He stood there studying me for a long while. He gestured toward the idling monstrosity. "One hour's work for a car?" He ran a hand over the glossy surface of the front fender. "She's underpowered with the slant six, but she's in fine shape. And hell, she's better than walking, wherever you're going."

I had to admit he had a point.

The cold was likely to worsen as the day progressed, and maybe I'd catch a ride, but maybe I wouldn't. The Belvedere wasn't my idea of a dream car, but it had a heater, and beggars should avoid being choosers on I-80 in the winter.

"One hour?"

He nodded and then started toward the Plymouth.

I walked around the long hood. "One hour."

Schafer climbed in, and I glanced around once more, weighing my options one last time before I pulled the handle and got in, tossing my duffel into the back. He pulled out, continuing down the street past the turnoff for the highway, and then took a sweeping left turn. After a few minutes the town seemed to break up, giving way to a pastoral landscape.

We drove in silence until we reached the hospital's main gate, the only impediment in both directions as far as I could see.

"I promised my family that I'd visit him for as long as he lived." He rolled down the window. A young man in a security uniform, who looked to be about twelve, lowered his head and smiled in at us. "How are you, John?"

"I'm good, Brian, how are you?" The young man glanced inside. "This is Deputy Longmire, and he's with me."

"Can I see some ID, Deputy?"

I took out my billfold and handed it to him with my driver's license inside. He examined it and made a notation and then handed my wallet back. "Thank you, sir."

Schafer drove toward a large, square brick building that looked about a hundred years old and pulled across the street underneath a copse of leafless cottonwoods. "A national historic building now — used to call it just the Insane Asylum back then before a devastating fire on September 11, 1917. At that point, they renamed it the Hospital for the Insane, the word 'asylum' having gone out of favor. When they built the Hall for the Criminally Insane in 1935, they called the wings Absaroka and Carbon in hopes that people from those counties might provide a little extra for the inmates around the holidays, but that worked only for a couple of years."

He pointed. "That one's the women's building — looks all alone out there, but there are tunnels that hardly anybody knows about that connect most all of the buildings; they're still used to bring food and patients back and forth." He gestured toward I-80. "On the other side of the highway is the cemetery, but most of the markers just have dates and patient numbers on 'em. You should hear the stories. . . ." His voice trailed off.

I thought about the individuals who had been shunned by society, forgotten even by their own families, and a slight shudder ran through me that had nothing to do with the cold. "Can I ask you a question?"

"Sure."

"Who is Annie Welsh?"

He studied me. "Somebody been telling you stories out of school?"

"Lucian mentioned her."

He sighed and gestured toward the building. "Probably the most dangerous prisoner in the criminal wing. Farm wife out of Goshen County, up and killed her three children one day with a butcher knife, killed her husband when he came home, and then went over to the next farm and killed another couple with the same knife."

"Insane?"

"I'll say. All the way through the trial, all she'd do was repeat the same thing over and over — *I didn't mean to do it.*" He turned to look at me again, before pulling the handle on his door. "Not to worry, she's locked up good and tight."

He got out, and when I followed suit, he tossed the keys over. "All yours."

"I haven't done anything yet."

He ignored me and crossed the street to where a large, overweight man in a white shirt and black slacks stood at the top of the steps with his arms folded. "John."

"Bernard."

"Bad Day at Black Rock."

Sheriff Schafer stopped at the bottom of the steps and looked up at the heavyset man. "You don't say."

"I do. We had a two-man unlock with him this morning, trying to get him to come out for breakfast and exercise."

"So everybody got some exercise?"

"Not funny. The new guy ended up damn near getting an eye torn out."

"Ed always was touchy on the subject of eyes."

The man didn't say anything more but simply turned and entered the building. Schafer glanced back at me. "C'mon."

We walked through a general reception area and then a steel door that opened into a hallway that led to a smaller room, bare except for an empty desk and six chairs lined against the green, two-tone walls. There was a window looking into another office where a woman was typing on a Selectric. "How many guards are there?"

Schafer eyed me again. "Two."

"Only two for both wings?"

"There was only one till '57 when the new warden requested another." He sighed. "Everybody in these wards knows they have to look after themselves, more or less."

We waited until the heavyset guy returned. Ignoring Schafer, he looked at me. "Got any weapons, pocketknife or such?"

I pulled the stag-handled knife from my jeans and then took my .45, still in the holster, out of the duffel, handing both to him.

He passed my things through the window to someone I couldn't see and then turned back to us. "We got a protocol, and as long as you follow it, we won't have any trouble."

Once he'd outlined the rules, we followed him through another security door and down a hall until we came to a steel-grated opening that he unlocked, then locked again once we'd passed through. "Welcome to the tomb, Deputy Longmire."

As he lumbered down the steps, I noticed the walls turned to concrete, which gave way to slip-formed stone, giving an indication of just how old the building was. The tired fluorescents were buzzing and blinking and giving off a strange bluish light. All I could think was that Schafer was right: an hour in this place was more than plenty.

There was a dark hallway to the right of the stairs, which I assumed was part of the tunnel system that ran between the buildings, where every twenty feet or so a protected lightbulb gave out with a feeble yellow pool.

At the next steel grate a man was sitting at a desk. He nodded to the turnkey and the sheriff in turn and then looked at me, and I noticed when he turned his head that his eye was completely covered with a bandage. "Just so you guys know, I've got a patient over in Carbon that I have to escort for meds in five minutes."

Bernard nodded, and the man stood and unlocked the gate, allowing us to continue into a hallway, where we stood, looking at a row of doors on either side — heavy, iron doors with paint that had chipped through the years, a color catalogue of the history of the place.

Each cell had a number above the door, a thick knob that stuck out at about eye level, where a small barrier could be slid aside to provide visual access, and a lower, larger door that worked the same way, which I assumed was used to pass food in and out.

"I hope you're not claustrophobic." There were two folding chairs leaning against the wall, and the guard handed one to each of us, pausing to glance at Schafer. "You know the rules."

"Yes I do, Barnyard."

The man turned and walked away.

Schafer saw me looking at him with a raised eyebrow and explained, "Doesn't like sheriffs — ran against Marv Leeland twice."

"Oh."

"I guess now he'll get another shot at the job." He turned and approached the nearest door, reached out a hand, and gently rapped his knuckles against the rough surface. "Ed, I know you heard us coming."

First there was nothing, but then a voice echoed from inside. "Hey, hey . . . who you got with you this time?"

"A deputy friend of mine from up in Absaroka County."

"I knew a girl there once."

"Ed."

There was a silence. "Hey, hey, what's

your name?"
"Walt Longmire."
There was a noise from down the hall, and Bernard appeared alongside us again. "Schafer, I got a code with the new guy and could use your help."
The sheriff looked at the door and then at me. "I'm here so often that they've decided I'm part-time help. I'll be right back — don't do anything. Don't talk to him, but especially, don't open that slat. You hear me?"
"Yep."
As he walked off, I thought about how long an hour could be. I was still holding one of the chairs, so I unfolded it and sat down.
There was some shuffling inside, and then the prisoner whispered, "You still there?"
I didn't answer.
"I know you're there 'cause I can hear you breathing." He shuffled closer, and I could tell he was right on the other side of the door. "I know he told you not to talk to me, but just listen, okay?"
I waited.
"Would you open that slat so that I can see your face?"
I still said nothing.
"I know he told you to not open it, but I

can't stand talking to someone and not knowing what they look like." After a few seconds, his voice sounded against the metal door again. "I got too much imagination, that's the problem, see?"

Involuntarily, I grunted.

He laughed. "I need you to look at me just to make sure I'm still here. . . . Just slide that slat aside, would you?"

"They told me not to."

"Hey, hey . . . I've got only so much time, but you need to listen to me, because if you don't, more people are going to get killed."

"What do you mean?"

"Open the slat."

"No."

There was a pause. "My brother. Hey, hey . . . look, I know I'm crazy, but I'm not the only one."

"I don't know what you're talking about."

"You gotta listen to me. . . . Please open the slat; I need someone to see me so that I know I'm still here."

I found myself leaning forward and slowly sliding the larger grate to the side where I could see the haunted eyes, one larger than the other.

"I wasn't the one that killed those girls."

I sat there silently, thinking about what the man had just said.

"Did you hear me? I didn't kill a one of those girls."

There was some yelling and noise coming from the tunnel outside the cage that connected the two halls, and I stood, looking into the darkness.

"I'm tellin' ya, mister, my brother arrested me, but I'm not the killer. I was on a date with that girl the night she was killed, but so was John."

There was more noise, so I began walking when I noticed that the cage door was hanging open. Leaning to one side, I could see the tunnel but not as far as the first lightbulb. Taking a few steps, I eased past the doors against the far wall as somebody threw himself against it. I pushed the cage gate the rest of the way open and stepped through, peering down the tunnel where I could see that the lightbulbs were on until about halfway and after that, there was nothing but darkness.

I stood there for a moment and then thought that I could see something moving in the shadows. "Schafer?"

Whatever it was that was moving, it stopped.

I glanced back toward criminal row, but nothing had changed there. I took another step toward the tunnel and listened, feeling a stillness in my hands and a coolness coming over my face the way it always did.

Something moved in the hallway again and a lightbulb exploded, leaving only two between the darkness and me.

I slowly zipped up the front of my jacket, figuring a layer of horsehide would be a wise precaution, and then slipped on my gloves, pulling them tight across my knuckles.

It was strange that Schafer and Bernard would both leave me here, but I figured whoever it was that was knocking out the lights was up to no good.

I stepped into the middle of the opening, stood up straight to a full six and a half feet, and spread my arms out a little to make an even larger impression. "Whoever you are, maybe you better step into the light so that I can see you."

Someone whimpered.

"I don't want to hurt you, but I don't intend to be hurt myself."

Someone edged into the light just a bit, and I could make out a figure in a long light-colored smock or dress, with some kind of tiny pattern in the fabric, a curled-up crippled hand twisting and untwisting the cotton up near the shoulder.

I raised a hand. "Stop right there."

Whoever it was ceased moving; whoever it

was, they were tall and incredibly thin.

"Are you one of the patients here?"

Nothing.

"Can I help you?"

More nothing.

I took a step farther into the tunnel. "Look, I don't work here, so I'm not sure who you are or what you need. I'm just trying to be helpful until the regular staff arrives."

I could see in the half shadows that behind the hair the patient was female.

"Miss?"

She studied me. Her eyes were dark, the pupils dense with hardly any reflection in them, and her lip sagged a little on one side. She began keening like a dog, but higher pitched, like a siren. Her chest swelled and her breath gave out, but she sucked in savagely and started again, almost pitch perfect to where she had left off.

"Miss?"

She took a step forward, and I could see her face plainly now. There were dark circles under her eyes and a pointed chin that was thrust out at me as she continued to emit a sound that wavered between a scream and an aria.

I took another step closer. "Miss?"

She jerked back and looked straight at me,

the dark eyes focused as she spoke in a high voice. "I didn't mean to do it."

It was about then that I saw the knife.

12

"Press conference — this afternoon at four thirty."

"Late for a Friday." The Bear nodded, looking down at the alley like a peregrine falcon and then leaning on the railing. "Just enough time to make the announcement and answer a few questions."

Vic joined him. "But not too many."

"And then run out the door." He shook his head. "Flight being the better part of valor in politics."

Sitting in the rocking chair, which I had positioned in a pool of sunshine, I leaned back and rocked a bit, Lola sleeping soundly on my chest. "Why do you suppose they don't want me there?"

"Because you might be right." He turned and looked at me. "In my limited experience with politicians, I have learned that you do not have to be right all the time, but that it is absolutely essential to never appear wrong."

"I think I'll do what they want and skip it. My being there will just throw more kerosene on the fire."

Vic pushed off the railing, stuck a hand on her hip, and studied me. "Do you mind if I ask how the hell this change of mind happened?"

I stared at the redwood planks on the deck where Dog lay snoozing. "I think I'm letting my pride get in the way of doing my job." I glanced up, cupping a hand on Lola's back as I repositioned myself. "This is not within the strict purview of my job description."

She shook her head. "And your purview is?"

"Law enforcement on a county level. Heck, I'm not even in my county."

She glanced at Henry in disbelief and then back at me. "You were asked to be here and testify in a parole hearing for an inmate who isn't able to travel and, as it turns out, isn't capable of even participating in the hearing."

"So why don't I just go home?"

"Um, because you've been trying to keep him locked up for decades?"

Alexia called out to us from the kitchen

window. "Sheriff, would you, Miss Vic, and Mr. Bear like some iced tea?"

It was tempting, but I was getting antsy. "No, thanks, Alexia. I think we're going to go out for lunch." I stood and moved toward the door with Dog following. "Do you want to put Lola in her crib?"

She appeared in the doorway, pushed open the screen, and took her from me. "Would you like me to wake Mr. Lucian?"

"No, this is his midmorning nap, not to be confused with his early afternoon nap, or his late afternoon nap." She nodded and disappeared with Dog following, and I turned to the dynamic duo. "And then there were three."

The Bear started down the steps as Vic and I followed. "He seems to be sleeping a lot lately."

My undersheriff shrugged. "Well, he's like a thousand years old."

We turned the corner and continued our descent. "Have you heard anything from the home office?"

"I spoke with Saizarbitoria, and he says nobody's set fire to the county, if that's what you mean."

I half smiled as we crossed the alley and approached my truck from the rear. "Maybe we'll all just head north tomorrow and try not to make this into something about me."

Vic looked past me. "What the fuck?"

Henry followed her gaze to my windshield, which looked as though someone had fired a mortar through it.

I unlocked the door, pulled it open, and watched as a cascade of tiny safety-glass chips fell out onto the ground. I glanced around, looking to see what might've fallen through the windshield. The culprit was nestled on the floorboard next to the transfer case shifter. Reaching in, I grabbed the thing and held it up as the Cheyenne Nation opened the passenger side and Vic crowded my shoulder, both of them looking at the item in my hand.

Vic summed it up. "It's a rock."

"Yep, it is." About the size of a softball, it was in fact a river rock, marbled in complexion with an explosion of glass dust stuck on one side where it had gone through my windshield. Ignoring the safety hazard, I wiped it off with my glove. Someone had left me a message in heavy, black Magic Marker:

BACK OFF!!!!

I held it out for Henry to read.

"Evidently they thought that smashing the windshield was not exclamation enough."

■ ■ ■ ■

Her shoulders had swayed just a bit as if that arm was disconnected from her body, and that's probably why I noticed the knife at all. There were people talking, their voices echoing off the stone walls, but they sounded far away, unlike her voice, which resonated in my head.

I slowly stepped to the middle of the hallway, giving myself room to move if I needed to. "Ma'am."

"I didn't mean to do it."

"Is your name Annie?" She didn't say anything but lowered her head a bit so that she was looking at me through the tangle of hair. "They said your name is Annie."

I thought I could hear more noises behind her, closer this time. She turned her head a bit but never took her eyes off me. I figured the best thing was to keep the conversation going, even if it was a little one-sided. "Have you seen Bernard or Sheriff Schafer? They were here a few minutes ago and said they would be right back."

"I didn't mean to do it."

"I know, Annie — they told me." I raised my hands just to show her I didn't mean any harm. "Sometimes we do things that we feel sorry about afterward. I've done things I wish I hadn't done, honest."

Her eyes unfocused as she looked up at the last remaining lightbulb, and I thought that I might be getting through to her. It was in that instant that she moved, rattlesnake fast, and swung the knife straight for the bulb; I jumped back as it shattered, leaving us there in the dark.

I heard a noise again and I was sure she was closer, but with the limited light behind me I could only guess where. It was probably slipping on the damp, smooth concrete floor that saved me.

She thrust the butcher knife past my abdomen as I fell against the far wall and scrambled backward as she advanced, swinging it at me again.

I could hear the sound of the blade as it sliced the air. Retreating to the cage door, I stumbled through and reached for the gate, but she was too fast and slashed at the chain link, the sparks flying off as I yanked my hand away.

I stumbled for the next gate and had just closed my hands on it when I felt something catch and rip down my back, but I ignored it and swung the gate shut. The lock cylinder was turned so that it was open, and I didn't have a key, but lodged my boot against the bottom as she threw herself against it with a scream that sounded like a hyena.

At maybe a hundred pounds, she bounced off the thing a few times, and then screamed again. She stood there on the other side, breathing hard and looking at me.

"Annie, you need to stop this."

She lunged at the gate again, this time noticing that it bowed out in the middle, then lowered her head to look at my boot, just on the other side.

"Oh, hell."

I yanked my foot away as she dropped to the ground and jammed the knife through the chain link, barely missing my toes. Grabbing the top of the gate, I held it shut with one hand as she stood and pushed the knife through the middle, missing the front of my jacket by inches.

I thought I'd hit on a method of holding her at bay when she feinted to the bottom and then swung at my fingers at the top again. The knife scraped across my knuckles, and I was forced to yank my hand away just as she threw herself into the partially open gate.

I unzipped my horsehide jacket and slipped it off, draping it from my left hand. I backed away as she approached again. "Annie, I don't want to hurt you, but I will."

Swinging the jacket, I wrapped it around my arm and got ready to make a move on a woman less than half my size. I figured if I got my wrapped arm between us, I'd just use all the training I'd had at USC against those thousand-pound blocking sleds.

It might kill her, but I didn't figure I had any choice.

"Annie?"

We both heard the voice behind me, but I didn't dare turn.

"Annie, you need to not hurt him." She stood still. "You don't want to hurt anybody, Annie. I know that — you didn't mean to do it before, right?"

She turned. "I . . ."

"Did you?"

Her head shifted like the carriage on a typewriter, stuttering, starting, and then still.

He continued talking, his voice muffled from behind the heavy door. "You need to stop attacking this man."

Her eyes came back to me before looking down at the knife, which she regarded as if she'd never seen it before. She dropped it and then looked up as it rattled onto the floor. "I didn't mean to do it."

She leaned against the wall and then slowly slid down to the floor, her hands in front of her in a supplicating position overtop of her folded legs, almost as if a valve had opened and the air had left her.

Taking a step forward, I toed the blade, spun the handle around, and picked it up. She stared at the floor and ignored me as I stood and backed away, stuffing the knife in my belt and looking at the still open trap in the heavy door where I saw a battered, scabbed pair of hands clutched together in a prayer.

"It's a rock."

"As the head of the Wyoming Department of Criminal Investigation's lab, is that your expert opinion?"

"Pretty much." T. J. Sherwin held exhibit A out to me. "It's a river rock, if that helps — from, say, a river. I can call up the state geologist and get a second opinion, but I think he's going to agree with me that it's a rock."

I turned and looked at Henry and then at Vic, who was covering her face to keep from laughing. "You know, that's the problem with modern law enforcement, rampant smart-ass-ism." I turned back to look at T.J., still holding the clue. "What can you tell me about the writing?"

She studied it. "It's English, and I think a

black marker was used."

"Not permanent?"

Unable to hold back, Vic joined in. "What is these days?"

T.J. shrugged, her head dropping to one side in disbelief. "What do you want from me, Walt? Rocks don't make for good fingerprinting, and even if we got a marginal print, it's going to be a needle in a haystack." She looked at the softball-size stone again. "You want a handwriting analysis on two words in block print?"

"I don't suppose you've seen anything like this before?"

She snapped a finger and pointed it at me. "Oh yeah, now that you mention it, there's a serial windshield smasher that's been running around the state doing just this type of dastardly deed." She gestured with the sample. "And this, this right here is the one piece of evidence that we needed to put together a lineup. We were thinking of calling in Duane 'The Rock' Johnson, or maybe Kid Rock? How about Chris Rock or Rock Hudson?"

"He's dead."

"See? We're narrowing the field already."

Vic grunted. "Rocky Marciano, Rocky Colavito, Rocky Bleier . . ."

I dismissed her with a glance. "You're not

helping."

T.J. handed the rock back to me. "No, there have been no other cases such as this — it's groundbreaking, actually."

"Not funny."

She shrugged again and walked us down the hallway toward the front offices and the main entrance of the converted supermarket that served as DCI headquarters. "You're under a lot of pressure lately."

"A little."

"I read the article in today's paper." She suddenly smiled. "Did you really threaten to kick Mike Barr's ass?"

"Not in so many words." I glanced at the Bear, who had headed for the parking lot and was now leaning on the Bullet's grille guard, his face turned toward the sun like an Aztec's. "I think I actually threatened him with the Cheyenne Nation."

She glanced around as we crossed the reception area to the door. She opened it and looked out at the gorgeous day. "I'm sorry, Walt. Realistically, there just isn't anything I can do."

I clutched my rock and gave the head of Wyoming's DCI a one-armed hug just to show there were no hard feelings. "I'll see you around."

She pointed at the evidence. "If I hear

anything, I'll let you know." She smiled. "I'll call Vic's cell phone."

I waved her away. "Go back to your lab and smell some more toxic fumes."

When we got to the Bullet, the Bear had finished worshipping the sun and was sweeping more glass from the passenger-side seat. "Where to now?"

I opened the back door and let Vic in. "I'm thinking the scene of the crime." I brushed a few more shards off my seat. "And then the windshield replacement shop on Old Lincoln Highway."

I pulled into the alley behind Cady's and parked as both Vic and the Cheyenne Nation gave me a questioning look. "I need to see a neighbor."

I shut the door behind me and, cradling the rock, walked over to the yard that was adjacent to the carriage house, but the three rather uninviting garage doors that faced the street were closed.

The garden shed was one of those prefabricated metal buildings that had seen better days, as had the property on which it stood. It sat next to a power pole on a little L-shaped portion of land, a weed-festooned tract that I was betting neither landowner knew that they possessed and consequently one that no one cared for.

There was a wooden fence that reached to about chest height, but a few slats were loose, which could allow a person to slip through. There was a shopping cart parked on the other side, so I was pretty sure the occupant was home. "Hey, Peter?"

There was no answer.

"Peter, I know you're in there, because your shopping cart is out here."

After a moment, the homeless guy appeared; he wouldn't make eye contact with me. "I don't know nothin' about your windshield."

Vic laughed, and I glanced at the Bear, who smiled and held an eyebrow in abeyance. "Well, seeing as how I didn't ask you about my windshield and yet you just volunteered the subject, I believe you might indeed know something about it."

He looked puzzled. "Huh?"

I gestured behind me at the shattered glass. "Because you knew something happened to my windshield."

He continued to peer at me from around the corner of the tiny building. "You're trying to trick me."

Vic shook her head. "We don't have to, dumb ass, you already tricked yourself."

"I don't understand."

She sighed, and I decided to start over. "Hey, Peter, do you know how a rock went through my windshield?"

He glanced around to make sure that no one would overhear. "Um, maybe it fell off something."

I tipped my hat back and rested my forehead on one of my arms. "Come over here to the fence."

"No."

I raised my face and looked at him and gestured toward the Cheyenne Nation, now standing beside me. "I'm tired and don't want to climb over this fence, so if you don't, I'm going to send him after you." I then gestured toward Vic. "Or have her shoot you."

Slowly, the vagrant came around the tin building and drew closer. "Um, it was a dude."

"Had you ever seen him before?"

"No."

"He was just standing here in the alley?"

"Yeah."

"Did he have a car?"

"Yeah."

"I don't suppose you got the license number, type of car?"

"Not really."

Desperate, I threw out another question.

"Color?"
"He was white."
"I meant the car."
"Black."
"Okay then, what did he look like?"
"Like a dude . . ."
"He was driving, so he was older than sixteen?"
"Yeah."
I sighed again. "A lot older than sixteen?"
"No."
"Twenties?"
"Maybe."
I glanced at Henry. "Do you mind taking over? This is wearing me out."
He caught the man by the front of his shirt and pulled him to the fence, his face now about four inches from Henry's. "What did he look like?"
The words came tumbling out. "Blond, he was blond and buff — you know, like a bodybuilder. . . . T-shirt and jeans with a leather jacket. It was an SUV, black, definitely black."
The Bear turned to look at me, and I nodded, at which point he released his grip and Peter backed away, running into the shed. "I'm calling the police."
"If I thought you had a phone, I'd take that threat more seriously."

■ ■ ■ ■

I watched as they secured Annie Welsh on a gurney and hauled her away. "You almost got me killed."

"Sorry about that."

John Schafer leaned against the wall and lit a cigarette. "There was an uproar in the mess, we had to close it off, and I guess she got around us. She's got a knack for it."

I handed him the blade. "What about the knife?"

"She's got a knack for that, too." He examined it and then handed it to Bernard. "Seen that one before?"

The guard studied it. "Nope, but I don't frequent the kitchen, and I'm assuming that's where it came from."

"Might be something you ought to know."

Schafer turned and walked through the cage toward the stairwell. "You coming?"

I started after him and then stopped to look back at the cell behind me and at the set of hands still folded in the small opening. I walked back over to the door and kneeled down, taking one of the hands in my own. "Thank you."

There was no answer, but after a brief squeeze of my hand, I watched as he withdrew both into the cell. I stood and remained there for a moment before turning and walking past Schafer, leaving a hole in the trail of cigarette smoke that occupied the dank hallway. "Let's go."

Collecting my things at the reception area, I went out to the Plymouth and leaned my back against my ticket to freedom. I could see the asylum graveyard across the highway, but I was no longer worried about the individuals buried under the stark numbered cobblestones; rather, about those who were buried alive in the catacombs of the hospital.

"I'll drive to the train station and you can drop me off." Schafer patted the roof of the sedan. "Then she's all yours."

I tossed him the keys and, dropping my duffel into the back, opened the door and climbed in.

Schafer started the beast, turned the wheel, and navigated to the exit. He studied me from the corner of his eye and finally spoke as we drove through the gate. "Sorry about that."

"No big deal."

He nodded. "Didn't get to spend much time with my brother . . . but I guess you did."

I was silent.

"What'd he have to say?"

I placed a hand on the dash and looked out the window at the town of Evanston. "We didn't have a lot of time to talk."

"How's he doin'?"

I turned and rested an arm on the back of the seat, giving him a nice, lengthy look. "How do you think he's doing?"

Schafer studied me for a moment more and then burst out laughing, barely keeping the car on the road as he wiped the tears from his eyes. "I was just wondering if his story had gotten any more believable, and — hey, hey, hey — I guess I got my answer, huh?" He chuckled a bit more as he cut across the road and swung into the depot parking lot where The Western Star sat waiting.

We both got out, but he hadn't noticed that I was carrying the duffel in my left hand.

"Here you go." He tossed the keys toward me, and I caught them with my right. "I filled her up before I got you, so she's full of gas and ready to go."

I stood there for a moment and then looked at the great steam engine working its breath up for the long pull back across Wyoming. I tossed the keys in the air once, caught them, and then casually slung them onto the top of the car. As they slid toward Schafer, I threw my duffel onto my shoulder and began walking toward the train. "Won't be needing them."

He called after me. "Hey, hey, hey . . . you don't want the Plymouth?"

I didn't answer and continued down the side of the train toward the sleeper cars.

"Are we going to have the pleasure of your company after all?"

I looked back and could see John Saunders, the engineer, hanging an elbow from the cab window and looking down at me.

"Until Cheyenne. For another six and a half hours, I'm guessing."

He glanced at his wristwatch and looked doubtful. "We don't get moving, and it might be longer than that; there's a front comin' in, and if it hits before we get to Elk Mountain, we're going to be spending a cold night on the tracks."

I nodded and kept going, noticing that most of the sheriffs I passed were still hungover. I finally found the one I was looking for standing on the steps to our sleeper car, as if he hadn't moved since I'd left.

He was stuffing the bowl of his pipe but paused to cock an eyebrow at me. "Change your mind?"

I stopped, set my shoulders, and looked

up at him. "Do you like mysteries, Lucian?"

He struck a match on the surface of the Pullman, lit the old briarwood pipe, and looked down at me, the flame highlighting his face with an infernal glow. "No, I do not."

"Neither do I." I looked up and down the tracks. "You gotta promise me something."

"What's that?"

"Don't hold back information pertinent to a case and leave me in the dark again, ever."

Smiling broadly, he puffed the pipe until it caught and then blew out the match and tossed it into the cinder bed of the rails. "You bet."

I had a feeling, and not for the first time, that I'd just made a deal with the devil.

"Why are we in fucking Nebraska?"

"Pine Bluffs, Wyoming — if you please."

"Looks like fucking Nebraska."

"The young woman who was living at Leeland's daughter's address was here. She said she was his granddaughter."

The Bear unbuckled the seat belt of the Mitsubishi rental car we'd gotten in Cheyenne as a temporary replacement for my disabled truck as I made the turn and pulled up in front of the small house, its driveway empty. "Why would she throw a rock through your windshield?"

"That's not why we're here — we're here to see if she would testify to the fact that she suffered because of her grandfather's murder. I don't like being pushed."

Henry climbed out the passenger side as I lowered the windows a little bit for Dog, cut the engine, and reached back to flip the seat forward so Vic could escape the clown car.

As we approached the front of the place, I noticed that the piano lessons sign wasn't in the window any longer. "I guess she's out of business." Both Vic and the Bear looked at me. "There was a sign in the window."

He cruised past me and approached the front of the house, knocking on the frame of the screen door before casually opening the thing and trying the knob. Only an expert would've noticed how casually he placed his shoulder against the jamb and leveraged the locked door open with a little brute force.

He nodded and waved for us to follow.

Vic and I entered and glanced around at the empty living room.

Henry walked toward what appeared to be the kitchen and looked at the empty rolls of packing tape, a broken pair of scissors, and a collection of odd newspapers. There were a few unused boxes stacked against the wall and a couple of tattered towels on the floor, a layer of dust coating everything.

I went in the other direction past the bathroom, where the plastic curtain lay in the tub along with a broken curtain rod. There were two bedrooms in the back, one with a couple of loose pieces of wood on the floor, which could've been used to support a mattress in a frame.

"What were you hoping to find?"

I turned to see Vic standing in the doorway. "Her."

Henry squeezed past and walked to the single window in the back, stooping a little to look outside. "Hmm . . ."

"What?"

"Dead crabgrass."

I stepped over to the light switch and flipped it on but nothing happened. "Can I ask you something?"

"About the crabgrass?"

"No." I was about to ask when I heard a noise from out front. "Was that Dog?"

Vic glanced over her shoulder. "I think so."

I'd just begun moving back toward the front of the house when I heard the front door opening. I stopped and gestured for

Vic and Henry to step back and clear the view. I leaned in and could see the shadow of someone passing along the living room wall.

Whoever it was didn't say anything, and I was getting a funny feeling about the whole thing when one of the floorboards in the bedroom creaked under my boot.

I was just about to speak when a 12-gauge round traveled through the partition beside me, blowing a sizable hole in the wallboard. Throwing myself to the side, I snatched the Colt from my holster and looked back to see that Henry had flattened himself on the floor with fluttering pieces of Sheetrock floating in the air around him. Vic already had her weapon out as I switched to the other side and leveled my .45 from a crouched position, just as another round went through the wall where I'd been standing.

Henry stayed where he was, and I was about to throw a few rounds back when I took a chance. "Absaroka County Sheriff's Department, hold your fire!"

There was a long pause and then a very shaky male voice responded. "Who?"

The adrenaline was still coursing through me like an electric service line. "Absaroka County Sheriff's Department, damn it, and

I'm the Absaroka County sheriff!"

"Oh, shit. Why didn't you identify yourselves?"

"Why didn't you identify yourself, especially before you started shooting? Who the hell are you, anyway?"

"Officer Louis Mittenbueller, Pine Bluffs Police Department."

"Hold your fire, Mittenbueller." I watched as Vic helped the Bear up. "I'm not kidding. If you fire that howitzer one more time, I've got an undersheriff here who is going to start shooting back."

"Right."

I could see his shadow again as I stepped into the hallway and, with Henry following, moved into the back side of the living room, where a young man with a shaved head in black BDUs held a Remington shotgun at port arms. "Sorry about that, sir."

I reholstered the Colt and leaned into him. "Whatever happened to knock and announce?"

"What?"

"Announcing your authority to the premises and then waiting a reasonable time before entering."

He nodded. "Well, we got a phone call; somebody said there were two individuals, a white man and woman, and . . ." He glanced at Henry. "And a native, and that they had broken into a house. . . ."

Vic shook her head. "I'm in uniform, you douche."

"When did you get the call? We've been here only about three minutes."

He stood up a little straighter. "About two minutes ago — we're in the top five percentile in response time nationwide."

"What's your percentile on shooting people?" I sighed. "Sorry. It's all right, our fault, too. We were kind of cowboying it." I gestured toward the road. "I'm usually driving my unit, but somebody threw a rock through the windshield. We're looking for the woman who used to live here —"

"Mrs. Leeland-Delahunt?" He made a face. "I don't think she could lift a rock even when she was alive."

"You knew Abigail Leeland?"

"Leeland-Delahunt. Sure, I took piano lessons from her growing up, but she died."

"We're looking for the current resident, Pamela Delahunt."

"Mrs. Leeland-Delahunt's daughter?" He looked somewhat confused and then volunteered, "Well, you're in luck — she's down at our office."

13

"Who threatened you?"

Pamela Delahunt sat in one of the Pine Bluffs Police Department office chairs, a hand over her face. "I thought I should report it, but now I just want to get out of here, okay?"

Her truck was parked out front with a horse trailer packed with her belongings attached. "I understand, but whoever is doing this shouldn't get away with it."

She shook her head. "It's not my problem anymore."

"Maybe not, but it's still mine." She took her hand away, and I could see that she'd been crying. "Just tell me what happened."

"After you came by, there were phone calls. Mostly they were just silent hangups, but then they started saying things like I should keep my mouth shut, that if I wasn't careful I'd be sorry." She clutched her hands in her lap. "What are they talking about?"

"What else did he say?"

"Oh, that I'd better stick to piano lessons." She laughed, a hollow sort of sound, and wiped her eyes.

"So, it was a man's voice?"

"Yes."

"Young or old?"

She thought about it. "In between, maybe."

I glanced up at Vic and Henry, but none of us had any ideas. "Did he have an accent, anything about his voice that was distinctive?"

"Maybe a twang? He was angry."

"Was it a landline or a cell phone — was there any static?"

"I don't remember."

I sighed and leaned back in the chair, which let out a high-pitched squeal. "I'm afraid I may have gotten you into trouble by coming over here. I'm fighting a very public battle so that the man who killed your grandfather stays in prison."

"He told you what?"

I leaned against the upper bunk and, looking out the window, felt the shift as the train began pulling out from Evanston in the same direction as the east-traveling snow. It was almost as if the storm front had wedged itself under the back side of the steel wheels and was rolling them forward against their volition. "That he wasn't the one who killed those girls."

Lucian fidgeted for a moment, unsure as to where to go with this information. He huffed a breath from his mouth in frustration. "You talked to him alone?"

"There was an incident in the cafeteria, and Schafer went to help take care of that."

Lucian pushed his hat back on his head, a little confounded. "So, the brother says he's innocent?"

"That's what he said."

Lucian thought about it. "They all say that."

"He says he killed the guard in Rawlins, but that it was self-defense."

He nodded and then took a step out into the hallway to make sure no one was listening before coming back in and closing the door. "Anything else?"

"John Schafer was pushing hard to get rid of me — offered me a car."

"Well, you were pretty hip on leaving."

I turned around and looked at him. "Lucian, if somebody is trying to put together a syndicate of sheriffs that go around solving each other's problems by murdering suspects, we're looking for a killer."

"Every one of these sheriffs has killed men, so that ain't exactly going to thin the herd."

"Maybe not, but it's a start."

"Just talk."

"Dangerous talk." He looked shaken but not completely convinced. "Lucian, we've got one man dead and another one missing, and a man in prison who says he's innocent. Now I'm not sure these two series of crimes are connected, but I'm not ruling anything out. If you've got another scenario, I'll be glad to entertain it."

His eyes sharpened, and those dark brows furrowed over the walnut eyes. "So, what do you want to do?"

"A full-blown investigation will have to wait until we get off this train, but in the meantime we could take a look in his compartment."

"Schafer's?"

"Yep."

"For what?"

"I don't know." I sighed and leaned an elbow on the bunk again. "You need to go find him and keep him busy for a while, and in the meantime, if you could ask Mr. Gibbs to come here, I'll get him to open Schafer's compartment and I'll take a look around. I'm not sure how this all fits together, but there's something we're missing."

"Alrighty." He started to go but then turned back. "Be careful; if what you're saying is true, there's more than one of 'em in on this — and if it is Schafer, he's bound to know you've got suspicions." He moved to go again but then stopped and added, "Welcome back."

"I'm not sure I'm all the way back."

"Well, you let me know when you get there, and I'll think about cutting you a check." He turned and walked away.

When he was gone, I pulled my M1911A1 from my duffel, dropped the magazine to check the loads, and then slapped it back between the grips. It was the one I'd carried in Vietnam, on Johnston Atoll, and in Alaska. When I started, Lucian had offered me a standard-barrel-length .38 from the department locker, but I'd grown used to the weight of the large-frame semiautomatic and had felt naked in its absence. It had been a calculated risk bringing the Colt home with me from Southeast Asia — servicemen were not allowed to keep their weapons — but the sidearm had become a part of me. I weighed it in my hand and couldn't help but think about what Henry had said about it getting heavier and how I wasn't so sure I was gripping the thing as much as it was holding on to me.

There was a movement in the doorway, and I turned, carefully slipping the Colt behind my back.

"I heard you and Sheriff Connelly just now."

I waited for her to continue.

"Look, I don't mean to threaten you." She glanced up and down the hall behind her just as Lucian had. "But if you don't help me, I'm going to tell everyone what you're up to."

"Well, for someone who doesn't want to threaten me, that was pretty good."

"I need your help." LeClerc sidled in and closed the door behind her.

"Um, given our most recent interaction, I'd just as soon you left that open."

"I haven't been completely honest with you." She leaned against the door. "Look, I know we didn't get off to a good start." She stood there for a moment and then lowered her voice. "I have a reason to be on this train, too." She whispered. "My sister was one of the girls who were killed."

My eyes met hers from under the brim of my hat, and I lowered my voice, too. "Go on."

She studied me, weighing how much she could trust me. "My little sister, Melanie, was strangled to death, and these sons-a-bitches haven't done anything to bring the bastard that did it to justice." She closed her fingers into fists. "Her name was Melanie Wheeler, and she's dead because of those men."

"That your real name, Wheeler?"

"Yes."

I nodded. "Why were you with George McKay?"

"I couldn't get close to Schafer, and I thought McKay could help me."

"Help you what?"

"Find the man who killed my sister."

"Ed Schafer appears to be at the top of that list."

"You spoke with him, and you know he didn't do it."

I sighed. "And what about McKay?"

She gestured in futility. "He took a powder."

I broke a smile, just wide enough to let her know I wasn't buying it. "You honestly don't know what happened to him?"

"No."

"How much did he know about you?"

"I told him about my sister, and he said he'd help."

"With privileges?"

Her jaw stiffened. "Not all of us are as big

as a refrigerator with a head — we have to find other ways of getting what we need." I stared at her but said nothing, and she made a move to leave. "Sorry to have bothered you, Deputy, I guess I misjudged."

I threw out a hand and held the door shut as she looked up at me, tears in her eyes. "Schafer's brother was tried and convicted, but I know he wasn't the one who killed my little sister."

"How do you know?" Her glance dropped to my side where the big Colt hung in my hand, and I watched as her eyes widened. I slipped my sidearm into the back of my waistband and kept a hand on the door. "How do you know that?"

She wiped the tears away with the back of a hand and then adjusted the extravagant pile of blond hair on top of her head, confirming my suspicion that it was a wig. "Because I saw Melanie after her date with Ed."

I stood with Pamela Delahunt as she made the final preparations for the twenty-five-hour drive. I glanced back at the horse trailer in the flat light of the afternoon, the horizontal beams striking the raised surface of the ridged metal and the edges of furniture that stuck out the openings. "I wonder if anybody's ever hauled a horse in one of these things?"

She laughed at the old Wyoming joke.

"You're not going to do it all at once, I hope?"

"No, I'll take a couple of breaks along the way."

I nodded. "I'm sorry I caused this trouble for you."

"Oh, I may have caused some of it myself." She nodded, biting her lip and placing a foot onto the running board. "Was he a good guy?"

I leaned against the side of her truck and studied her. "Your grandfather?"

"Yeah."

I glanced back at Vic and Henry, leaning on the fender of the rental car parked just behind Pamela's trailer. "Yep, he was one of the best."

"My mother hardly ever talked about him."

"Sometimes that's the way people deal with the pain of losing a loved one." I could feel her wanting to get on the road. "Well, we're holding you up."

Her head dropped, but she leaned in closer. "I never got to meet him, you know? I was born in '83." She took a breath. "He died in 1972."

"Yep."

"So, this man, he killed my grandfather?"

"Yes."

"You're sure of it?"

"Yes, but that's not your problem." I leaned in a little closer myself. "He would've wanted you to get in this truck and get on with your life." Helping her along, I opened the door and held it for her. "So, come on, let's get you on the road."

Reluctantly, she climbed in, and I closed it behind her.

She laid an arm on the sill and studied the road ahead. "Thank you."

I laughed. "For what?"

"For caring." She pulled the truck in gear with a flourish and backed the trailer directly into our rented Mitsubishi. Vic and Henry leapt out of the way just before the trailer smashed the grille, hood, and one of the headlights with a thundering crunch. After that, the only sound was a slight tinkling as shards of broken glass dropped on the pavement.

Pamela was alarmed as she turned and looked at me, then glanced in the side mirror at the destruction behind us. "Oh, my God."

"I believe Florida is in the other direction."

She burst out crying, and I reached in and gripped her shoulder, doing everything I could to keep from laughing, until Henry and Vic joined me at the window.

Vic, of course, was the first to speak. "Fuck it, it's a rental."

Still sniffling, Pamela wiped her nose with the back of her hand as I pulled a handkerchief from my inside pocket and handed it to her. "Here, you can mail it back to me."

Nodding, she pulled the gear lever into first and inched out and away.

Vic and Henry joined me in the street, Vic following the horse trailer for a few steps, then turning to look at me, her arms crossed. "You don't think she's involved?"

"Nope."

She glanced over her shoulder as the truck and trailer made a turn, heading for the highway. "I hope you're right."

I breathed a laugh. "This just keeps getting better and better."

"The thing is, I was supposed to go out on a blind date with John that night, but I just had a funny feeling and begged off." She started crying again and looked at me with tears on her cheeks. "And the next morning they found her in the park near the railroad tracks in Laramie."

"That doesn't necessarily mean that John did it."

"Well, if he didn't, then who else?" She stared at me. "What did he tell you?"

"Who, Ed?"

"Yes."

"It was a somewhat limited conversation through a steel door." I gestured toward the hallway where she'd obviously been listening. "You heard the conversation between Lucian and me, so you know as much as we do."

"Do I?"

I pushed my hat back on my head and studied her. "What's that supposed to mean?"

"Did he say something about my sister?"

"No."

"You're sure?"

"He didn't mention any of the women by name." She seemed disappointed, and I was sure it was hard to believe that someone you loved could have something like that done to them and then simply be forgotten like yesterday's news. "I'm sorry."

There was a knock, and she jumped. Mr. Gibbs opened the door and stuck his head inside and then immediately retreated. "Sorry, Mr. Longmire, I didn't know Miss LeClerc was in there with you. . . ."

I called out to him. "It's okay. You can open the door, Mr. Gibbs."

"Yes, sir." He did and widened his eyes at me in a conspiratorial fashion. "Um . . . Sheriff Connelly asked me to assist you?"

I glanced at Kim. "You'll excuse me?"

She looked at Gibbs and then at me. "Sure, I guess."

I joined Gibbs in the hallway and followed him toward the front of the train. In the space between cars, I placed a hand on his shoulder and asked in a low voice, "I'm assuming that Sheriff Connelly has told you what's going on?"

He didn't look at me. "I don't want to know, Mr. Longmire. I have enough trouble remembering which doors I locked and which ones I unlocked." He stepped into the next car, turned to the door of the first cabin on the left, and knocked. "Sheriff Schafer?"

"I think Lucian is keeping him busy somewhere else."

He ignored me and knocked again before slipping a hand down to pull out a prodigious key ring. He unlocked the door, then quietly continued past me down the hallway until he disappeared. As the train rumbled on, the door threatened to shut, so I stuck a hand out and held it, slowly pushing it open.

The room was neat and orderly, with a medium-size valise sitting on the lower bunk along with a long coat and a pistol case. After a quick run through the cabinets and closet, I picked up the case, ascertaining that it was empty. I slid the coat aside and looked at the valise, noticing that the latch was locked.

I crouched there with my thumb on the metallic wheels. Now came the tricky part — birth dates were common, but Schafer didn't strike me as the type. There were a few dates he'd mentioned back at the hospital, but it was the cataclysmic fire that stuck in my head — maybe it had stuck in his, too.

I thumbed the numbers 9, 11, and 17 and watched as the latches popped free.

On the top was a small container of mustache wax.

Shaking my head, I pulled a sweater from the suitcase and pushed some other items of clothing aside. It was beginning to dawn on me just how stupid this might be, when I noticed some newspaper clippings in the lid pocket and pulled a few out.

Holding one up, I began reading. *Following a tip, a half-dozen Rawlins police officers surrounded the rear of the Pioneer Café on November 6 at 1 P.M. where they found the deceased. The exact circumstance of the death is yet to be determined, but it appears the young woman was strangled. . . .*

I leafed through the clippings and read another one.

Pauline Davenport was discovered by WYDOT, November 8, in a barrow ditch adjacent to the parking lot on the south side of Green River, her neck having been broken. . . .

And another.

The victim, Lisa Pell, had been strangled and left in an abandoned vehicle. . . .

Another.

Francine Harrison.

Yet another.

Elaine Lenz.

And even another.

The Laramie native and University of Wyoming student was found strangled Saturday night near Optimist Park after her brother said that she hadn't returned from a date the previous evening. . . .

I glanced at the name — Melanie Wheeler.

Wheeler was enrolled at the School for Geology and was scheduled to graduate in the spring, and as near as police can tell, she was killed on the day before. . . . I glanced at the date at the top of the clipping — 1965, November 4. It was November 3 today; I thought about it — the same day Melanie Wheeler was killed, seven years ago.

There really wasn't a great deal more, other than a few quotes from the family and neighbors on what a fine young woman she'd been. There were a half dozen in all, young women who had been strangled in locations trailing across the I-80 corridor from Cheyenne all the way to Evanston in a six-year period.

I checked the rest and noticed that the dates the bodies were found were all in early to mid-November. I carefully folded the clippings, replacing them in the lid of the case before closing it and latching it shut. I placed the coat and the pistol case back as they'd been and then glanced around the room to check my work before exiting. I closed the door behind me just as two men turned the corner, the knob still in my hand.

I smiled at Sheriffs Tillman and Brown. "Can't seem to get my key to work."

Tillman, the Sheridan County man, was the first to speak. "Probably not, seein' as how that's not your room."

Remembering that the different cars were named for Wyoming mountain ranges, I glanced around. "Isn't this Bighorn?"

Brown shook his head. "Wind River."

"Oh. No wonder."

Pretending to palm my key back in my pocket, I looked at the two of them as Brown leaned against the wood-paneled wall. "We heard you were calling it quits."

I nodded. "Changed my mind, I guess."

Tillman's eyes narrowed. "What did that — visiting with John Schafer's crazy brother?"

I held the smile. "Maybe so."

"Ed tell you that he's innocent?"

Pulling my hand from my pocket, I shifted, just to give me a clear grab on my sidearm if I needed it. "He might've mentioned something about that."

The man with the thin face nodded and studied me. "Just don't want you getting the idea that you're the only one he's dumped that load of horseshit on."

I studied him back. "What makes you so sure that it's horseshit?"

Tillman glanced toward Brown with a knowing look and then turned back to me. "Girls were dying, six of 'em to be exact, and that all stopped when they locked that crazy son of a bitch up a year ago." He leaned in to me. "Look, you need to figure out which team you're playing on and get suited up. You got me?"

I didn't say anything, mostly because I knew if I spoke again and I didn't like his response, chances were I'd use his buddy to club him into unconsciousness and then throw the two of them off the train.

Not necessarily needing to go in that direction, I started past them. "Excuse me."

Brown gave room, but Tillman left a shoulder square in the passageway.

"I said, excuse me."

He looked up at me and then smirked before stepping aside, cocking his head as he watched me pass.

I made the corner and then realized I was at the front of the train and there really wasn't anywhere to go. I thought about turning back but didn't want to give the two sheriffs the satisfaction, so I just stood there thinking about what I knew, what I didn't, and — more important — who it was I trusted.

It was possible that Schafer was innocent and just kept the clippings from his brother's murders as a penance, but I had to be sure that there were no connections between the two cases. Marv Leeland was dead and George McKay was missing and possibly dead, too, unless McKay was the guilty party, in which case all I was doing was chasing my tail.

Why would McKay kill Leeland? There wasn't any rational motivation unless he was involved in the sheriffs' cabal, and who knew if there was anything to that?

In the short amount of time I'd spent with McKay, he'd struck me as a party-line guy unlikely to break ranks, so why would anyone kill him? It was even harder to come up with a motivation for murdering Marv Leeland — everyone loved the man. But maybe he was coming too close to breaking up the cabal, as he had called it. In a matter of hours we'd be stopping to pick up his body, and if I could talk the majority of the sheriffs into it, maybe they would allow me to examine it to see if I could glean any clues.

Looking up through the glass in the forward end of the accordion-like passageway, I could see that the next car was the tender for the engine, and I had to smile at the thought that Tillman and Brown had watched me attempt to leave this way.

Then another thought crossed my mind as I felt the cold through the grimy window's thick glass: if there was nothing except the tender and the engine ahead, why had the two of them come from that direction?

14

"I called the commandant, and we've got Highway Patrolmen in Nebraska, Missouri, Illinois, Kentucky, Tennessee, Georgia, and Florida watching out for Mrs. Delahunt; if we were guarding her any closer she'd have a police escort."

I leaned on the counter of the rental car company. "Thanks, Jim." He hung up, and I handed the receiver back to the nice, clean-cut young man.

"Umm . . ." He hung it up and looked at me. "I don't think I can rent you another car until I talk with my supervisor."

I shifted my weight. "And where's your supervisor?"

"Lunch."

"Then can somebody give us a ride over to the windshield repair place on Old Lincoln Highway?"

"That's against company policy; besides, I'm the only one here."

"So, that's a no." He smiled and nodded, and I gave up and joined Vic, Henry, and Dog in the lot.

The man who had towed the Mitsubishi wiped his hands off on a red cotton rag that he'd pulled from his back pocket and handed me a clipboard. "I don't suppose you'd like to give us a ride over to Old Lincoln Highway?"

He shrugged. "It's against company policy."

"Right." I turned to the Bear. "You wanna call us a cab?"

"I already did." He gestured toward the red four-door Jeep pulling up beside us, which missed my foot by inches. She stopped and rolled the window down. "What did you do?"

I glanced at the Terror, the Cheyenne Nation, and then back to the Greatest Legal Mind of Our Time. "What makes you think it was us?"

Dog, knowing a good deal when he saw one, jumped up in her window, and she massaged his ears. "It's always you, Dad." She had a point — she always did. It was something she got from her mother, along with an unerring bullshit meter.

We circled around. Dog climbed into the space behind the rear seats, and Vic and I climbed into the back, which meant Henry got the front, along with the third degree. "The Bear will explain."

"It is a long story."

"Well, I've got to get back to work, so just tell me what I need to know." Tossing today's *Tribune-Eagle* in Henry's lap, she wheeled out of the parking lot. "But before you get started, you'd better take a look at this."

The Cheyenne Nation unfolded the paper and grunted.

I sat up straighter. "What now?"

He glanced back at me. "It would appear that we are not alone in our responsibility for Pamela Leeland-Delahunt's difficulties. She apparently wrote a letter — an open letter — to the court, the world at large, and, more important, Governor and Carol Fisk, in favor of keeping the prisoner incarcerated no matter what his physical condition."

"Let me see."

"It is a very convincing letter." He held it away and began reading aloud. " 'I never met my grandfather, but there is a piece of music that reminds me of the loss of him every day. . . .' "

I slid a hand across the sooty condensate on

the surface of the window and looked out of the spot I had cleared before it could ice up again; the only way I saw to go forward was a ladder on the left that led up and over the tender car toward the locomotive; at least that's where I hoped it led.

Cranking my hat down, I flipped up the collar on my jacket and pulled on my gloves, even going so far as to take the gold buckaroo scarf that my mother had given to me from an inside pocket. I tied it around the lower part of my face, looking for all the world like a train robber. It was well below freezing outside and, with the train moving, it was going to feel a lot colder than that.

Once I was prepared, I pushed the door open and stepped onto the grating that divided the two cars, but there was nothing I could see that was of interest.

Reaching out to grasp the ladder's rail, I hoisted myself up and climbed until the hurricane rush of air struck me at the top and I started seriously wondering what the heck I was doing.

Starting over the top, I was glad to see that the handrails continued the whole way, even if there appeared to be a large box in the middle that I was going to have to scramble over.

Crawling on my hands and knees, I held

my head down in an attempt to prevent both my hat and myself from disappearing over the side as the high plains rushed by. The topography wouldn't change much until we got to the bluffs of the Green River near Rock Springs; here, the partially snow-covered landscape looked like the beginnings of the Arctic Circle.

By the time I got to the engine, I was covered in a fine sheet of ice that crackled and fell off as I dropped my legs over the side of the tender and climbed down. I was just feeling pretty good about the whole thing when I felt someone pull my .45 from the back of my jeans and place a hand on my shoulder. He shouted over the thunder of the locomotive and the rattle of the rails. "Stick 'em up!"

When I got to the steel grating I turned with my hands up, only to find John Saunders with a smile and my sidearm.

"This was about to fall out of your pants, so I grabbed it!" He studied me, taking in the scarf over my face, and then motioned toward the naturally heated cab. "C'mon!"

I followed him into the nerve center of the big steam locomotive where it must've been ninety degrees. I pulled my collar down along with the scarf and looked at both of them.

Roback stared at me. "Jesus, where'd he come from?"

"Over the top — can you believe it?"

"What the hell for?"

I turned toward the engineer. "Were there two sheriffs up here recently?"

Saunders glanced at his buddy and then back to me. "There hasn't been anybody here but us since we left Evanston. Why?"

I thought about where the two men could've gone but couldn't come up with anywhere else; maybe they had only stepped forward to talk privately in the space between cars. "I saw two men coming from this direction and made an assumption, something I shouldn't have done." I'd started to step forward when my boot landed on something and my foot skittered out from under me.

Saunders bent and picked up a very large box-end wrench and handed it to Roback. "You don't secure that thing, we're going to lose it or worse."

The brakeman slipped the two-foot wrench under his bench seat. "That pre-valve keeps loosening, and I get tired of dragging the toolbox out. Don't worry, I'll keep it under here."

Saunders turned back to me. "Well, it must've been something mighty important for you to make the trip like you did." He studied me. "If you don't mind my askin', and even if you do, Deputy, what's goin' on back there?"

"We've got one man murdered and another missing."

"I know we're supposed to stop somewhere near Fort Fred Steele to pick up a body, but nobody said anything about him being murdered."

"Well, it's yet to be verified."

"And one missing?"

"Yep."

He glanced at the frozen terrain screaming by. "You got a man missing — he's not on this train."

"My thoughts exactly."

He eyed me. "That's a hell of a state of things on a train full of sheriffs."

I peeled my gloves off and thrust them toward the engine's gigantic boiler. "Have you guys heard or seen anything out of the ordinary on the trip?"

"You mean other than what you've already mentioned? Nope." Saunders glanced at Roback. "You?"

"Nope. How could I? I've been here with you the whole time."

The engineer turned back to me. "I'll be just as happy when this little excursion is over, though, I'll tell ya."

I nodded. "Only a couple of hours to go, huh?"

"Maybe."

I pulled my hands back and flexed some movement into them. "Oh, now why do I not like the sound of that?"

He shrugged and stuck his hand out the window like a kid in a car. "The snow is already pilin' up on Elk Mountain, and if we don't get through there before the rails fill up, we might be there till spring."

"Great." I studied the rear of the cab and the tender, which was already coated with ice. "Is there any other way back?"

"Nope."

I slipped my gloves on and tugged my hat down again. "So, you guys have to climb over that thing every time you want to get in touch with the rest of the train?"

"No." He reached over and plucked a mic from a radio set above. "We've got a radio system that runs to every car."

"Of course you do." I pulled the scarf up over my face. "Well, keep up the speed, I'd just as soon not spend the night on Elk Mountain."

"We're doing a strong eighty — any faster than that in this weather and we're liable to derail."

"Don't do that, either." Checking to make sure I shoved the Colt deep in the back of my jeans, I hoisted myself onto the ladder and started up, comforted by the fact that I wasn't bucking a headwind this time around.

At the top of the tender, I looked down at the segmented Pullman cars and felt like I was looking at the different parts of my life. I wasn't sure of what I was doing, but I was pretty sure I knew why, and the cupola of the caboose looked to be a long way away.

Vic crossed her arms and leaned back on Cady's kitchen counter. "You seem restless."

"I am."

She nodded to herself. "Let's go shoot somebody."

"You think that'll make me feel better?"

"Works for me."

I turned and glanced at my mentor, granddaughter, and guardian, all asleep in the living room. "Those three seem to be hitting it off."

"That's because they all share napping as a favorite hobby. Personally, I like a little more action."

Henry came in from the porch and pulled out a chair. "What are you two plotting?"

"Muscular with blond hair."

Vic turned to look at me. "What?"

"Our homeless friend, he said the guy who threw the rock through my window was muscular and blond. Who have we met that matches that description?" They both looked at me blankly. "Would you describe that Coulter fellow who was with Alexia's nephew as muscular and blond?" I looked around. "Speaking of Alexia, where is she?"

"Cady says she did not show up today, but that yesterday she had mentioned something about her nephew." He studied Vic and then me. "You are circling the wagons?"

I stared at the big Indian. "That phrase, coming from you, is inordinately unsettling."

"Would you like to call her?" Vic pointed at the utility. "There's a phone with a cord but it is nonrotary — do you need me to push the buttons for you?"

"Thanks, but no thanks." Just to show her, I dialed the number from the address book on the counter; it rang, but there was no answer. I hung up, noted the Mendez address, and decided to go for a drive. "I'm making a house call."

"You want company?"

"Well, I usually prefer to do my wild-goose

chasing solo."

She ignored me and started toward the door. "I'm going with you."

"You coming, Henry?"

He looked at me, dark eyes sparking. "If you are right and something is on, I will do better to stay here."

I nodded and headed down to the Bullet. I looked for Peter Lowery, but he didn't seem to be around.

Vic leaned forward. "Nice windshield."

"It's remarkably clean, isn't it?"

Vic put the address into her magic phone, and we discussed the case as I headed south on Business 25, then looped over the railroad tracks and under the interstate. Taking a right onto Fox Farm Road just before it turned, I drove into a quasi-residential neighborhood where there were a few rundown houses overlooking the highway.

"So, if I get on that road it'll take me to Philadelphia?"

"In twenty-four hours." I cast an eye her way. "Missing home?"

She made a face. "That patrolman in Pine Bluffs, Mittenbueller . . . he reminded me of Michael in some odd way."

My breath caught a little in my throat as I thought about her murdered brother, and how gentle she'd been with the Pine Bluffs patrolman who'd almost killed me. I reached out and squeezed her hand, but she turned away.

There were no numbers on the small houses, but I recognized Alexia's white Chevrolet in one of the driveways, so I parked behind it and we got out. There was a low chain-link fence, but I didn't see any dogs, so I let us in. As I passed the Chevy, I placed a hand on the hood out of habit, but it held no trace of warmth.

Marching up to the door like a census taker, with Vic close behind, I gave a smart rap on the storm door, and we stood there and waited.

I knocked a few more times and then wished I'd brought Henry along so that we could've done a proper Reservation search warrant. Glancing up and down the road, I turned to Vic and was about to open the door when a Cheyenne Police unit turned the corner and slowed upon seeing my truck, emblazoned with the Absaroka County Sheriff's Department stars.

Attempting to seem nonchalant, I waved, but he stopped and his window went down. He was young, with the ubiquitous aviator sunglasses. "How you doin', Sheriff?"

"I'm good, how 'bout you?"

"What are you up to?"

"Breaking into this house," I said, following the best, if not the official, policy.

He nodded. "Can I help?"

I smiled. "Might lend some credibility to the act."

He parked, and the smartly uniformed officer joined us on the small porch. "Nico Severini."

"Walt Longmire, and this is my undersheriff, Victoria Moretti."

He nodded to her and then looked back at me. "You've been in the papers a lot lately." He then added in a loud voice, "We got a call about some noise."

"Really?"

He looked at me with more than a note of incredulity and then lowered his voice for a response. "No." He reached past me and knocked on the interior door. "Cheyenne Police Department — hello?" I watched him turn the knob, the door opening just a bit. "Hmm . . ." He spoke loudly again. "The door seems to be ajar, which I find suspicious; how 'bout you?"

Vic answered loudly. "Absolutely, Officer."

I pushed open the door.

"You going in?"

"Anything to get out of the Campbell Soup Playhouse." We all unsnapped and withdrew our weapons as I pushed the door the rest of the way open. "Hello?"

There was no answer. I glanced around the front room, where nothing seemed amiss. "Alexia?" There was still no answer, so I stepped inside, sweeping the corners and advancing toward the narrow hallway that I guessed would lead past the kitchen and through the house, shotgun style. It was also empty, as were the bathroom and two bedrooms. The storm door in the back was closed, but I moved down the hall and looked through the glass toward the edge of the hillside and the highway beyond. I turned to Vic and Severini and stated the more than obvious. "There's no one here."

Vic glanced around. "But her car's out front."

Severini rested his hand on his sidearm. "Who lives here?"

"My granddaughter's nanny."

"Well, I can see how that would be an emergency. . . ."

"She didn't show up for work and didn't call — she always calls."

"Anywhere else she might be, any other numbers we can phone — friends, relatives?"

"She's got a nephew, a Ricardo Mendez, who lives here, but I don't know his cell number or even where he works. She also mentioned a David Coulter, a friend of his, but I know even less about him."

"Do you have somebody you can call?"

"I can call my daughter — she works with the attorney general."

He smirked. "Well, might lend some credibility to the act."

"They're slowing the train to pick up Marv Leeland's body."

Attempting to clear my head, I sat up in my bunk and looked at Lucian, standing in the doorway of our compartment in his battered B-3 flight jacket. "How long have I been out?"

"Couple of hours."

I swung my legs onto the floor and scrubbed my face with my hands. "Why didn't you wake me up?"

"I just did."

"I mean earlier."

He gestured toward the darkening landscape through the window. "What, you wanted to see the scenery? The damn train's been runnin' at a good eighty miles an hour, so there hasn't been anybody getting on or off — and there haven't been any big breaks in the case, as near as I can tell."

I stood and steadied myself. "Well, then, how come you didn't take a nap?"

"I napped in a booth in the dining car." He gestured toward the rear and started off with me in tow. "They say they're gonna need some help loading the casket in, and you'd be amazed how many bad backs suddenly pop up at a time like this."

"I bet." I locked the door to the cabin. "And nothing else has happened?"

"There aren't any more dead sheriffs, if that's what you're asking."

"That's a relief." I stooped and glanced out the windows at the blowing snow.

"If you're looking at the weather, it's shitty, with a chance of shittier."

"Are we going to make Elk Mountain?"

Just then the train slowed substantially, and I threw out a hand to steady myself.

"We might make it there, but I'm not so sure we'll make it over."

As we moved through the dining car, I could see Gibbs along with some of the other kitchen personnel putting things away in the galley, and he joined us on the far end, wiping his hands on an apron. "I put some food in the refrigerator for you, Mr. Longmire. The sheriff here said you were asleep, but I thought you might get hungry before the night is over."

"Thanks, Mr. Gibbs." He followed us. "You should hang on to every scrap of food you've got, just in case we get snowed in up on the pass."

"Oh, we got plenty of food, there's no worry in that."

We walked through the last connection between the dining car and the caboose, the real bite of the storm blowing between the cracks and through the gaps in the moving metal floor. Inside the caboose, my greatest hits were assembled — the security guy, Joe Holland, and Sheriffs Inda, Brown, Tillman, and Phelps.

Tillman smoked a cigarette between clenched teeth. "Have a nice nap, this time in your own cabin?"

I nodded. "Goes with a clear conscience."

We all bundled ourselves up as the train continued to slow. Brown, who was closest to the door, pulled at his hat as the train ground to an agonizingly slow stop. "Let's go, the engineer says we've got only fifteen minutes. If we don't get him on here in that amount of time we're going to be chasing a train in a snowstorm while carrying a pine box."

Four of us followed him, waiting as Gibbs, the only brains in the outfit, reached out and unhooked the chain that ran across the back railing.

Lucian stayed behind on the platform.

A late-fifties Cadillac hearse from a Carbon County mortuary was backed up to the crossing, where the arms were down blocking the road; the Caddy blinked red along with the lights and the accompanying Klaxons screamed a warning.

Stomping across the snow, embedding the cinders and ash into our footsteps, we stood at the back of the hearse while an attendant and the Carbon County sheriff opened the door. The wind was blowing hard, the snow sticking to the side of my face. The other men hesitated, so I stepped up and took hold of one of the cheap, metal handles on the side and started pulling. "C'mon, let's go. It's cold out here, and the train is going to leave without us if we don't hustle."

They all looked a bit shocked, but it jarred them into motion. Without looking back, I started walking toward the train. I was certainly an expert at carrying bodies, and in that moment I began to wonder if the stench of death was really what was chasing everything I cared about away from me.

When we reached the platform Lucian and Gibbs did the best they could dragging the oblong box into the caboose, but weren't making much headway. I quickly climbed the side steps, grabbed the two front handles, and pulled Marv Leeland into the train for his last ride.

By the time I got the coffin situated, the others had gotten back on, and no sooner had they done so than the steel wheels began to roll toward Elk Mountain.

I'd started to stand when somebody pushed me hard against the wall of the caboose. Catching myself, I whirled around to find John Schafer spitting with rage.

"You tried to search my room?"

Rearing up to my full height, I looked down at him, and his hand automatically slipped to his side. "Yep, I searched your room and found all those nifty little trophies from the newspapers you've got tucked away in your suitcase — and if you go to pull that revolver at your side, I'm going to push the thing down your ever-loving throat and pull the trigger till I hear it click."

He had the good sense to believe me, because his arm went slack. "I keep those clippings to remind me of what my brother did, and why I did what I had to do." He puffed himself up for more and pointed a finger at the coffin. "I still think you had something to do with this man's death, if not the disappearance of George McKay." He didn't sound all that convinced, but threw in a bit more to make it stick. "I need a drink, but if you touch that coffin while

I'm gone, I'll see you hang, tough guy."

They filed out after giving me hard looks, but I'd had hard looks thrown at me before and had found they bounced off pretty easily.

I stretched my neck muscles and tried to unclench my jaw, but the pain in the back of my head wasn't giving up, and I was beginning to think that my unconscious was hammering out a message in Morse code to the frontal lobe.

Gibbs and Sheriff Connelly were still standing there, sadly studying the cheap pine box. Lucian shook his head, unzipped his fleece-lined flight jacket, and pulled out his flask. "Well, boy, I am here to tell you that you sure haven't been making friends and influencing people on this trip —"

"Sheriff Connelly."

"I mean, if you've got anybody on your side on this train other than me and Gibbs here —"

"Sheriff Connelly."

He gestured toward the coffin. "Excluding obvious company —"

"Lucian."

He finally stopped and cocked his head at me. "What, what, for God's sake?"

I kneeled down and ran a hand across the wet, rough grain of the wooden planks where the snow was melting and then pushed my hat back and stared at the two of them. "How much did Marv Leeland weigh?"

As we walked out of the house, I stopped and stood there on the porch, that niggling feeling running up and down my spine.

Vic glanced back at me. "Do you smell what I smell?"

I went back in the house, stood in the living room, and sniffed. It was faint, but there was a metallic smell that grew stronger as I approached the hallway and the back door. The button on the latch was broken, and I pushed the door wide, stepped onto the concrete stoop, and looked around.

There was a picnic table that had seen better days and an open space next door where a gigantic billboard sat, crouched on the hill above the interstate highway, advertising Brian Scott's morning radio show on K2.

There was a breeze coming from the west, and I walked in that direction. It was a smell I'd encountered many times before and not a pleasant one. There was a low chain-link fence between me and the weedy field where the billboard stood, through which I could see a blue tarp rolled up in the weeds at the base of the sign.

Vic and the Cheyenne patrolman hopped the fence and followed me as I walked toward the sign with the face of the voice of Wyoming looking down at me, a hand over his mouth, almost as if he were surprised to find me there.

The tarp had been expertly tied with a nylon rope, the kind that was used for clotheslines, but the outline was unmistakable, even without the blood seeping from one end.

I kneeled down by the body and measured the size against the dimensions in my head as Vic stood a step away. "It's not her, but it's somebody."

Severini's voice sounded over my shoulder. "You'd better not touch anything."

I slipped my knife from my back pocket. "I'm cutting this one piece of rope just so I can see the face."

"I wouldn't do that — we can get DCI over here in a matter of minutes."

"I'm here now — and I need to know who this is." Vic stepped between us, and he didn't say anything more. I unlocked the blade and slipped it under the loop nearest the head. The tarp flapped in the breeze, and I reached into my coat pockets for my gloves, putting them on and carefully drawing the plastic away.

It was Ricardo, Alexia's nephew. Pulling the tarp back a bit more, I could see where his throat had been viciously cut almost halfway through.

I replaced the tarp over his face. "He's the nephew of the woman I'm looking for." I reached a hand out to Vic. "Can I borrow your phone again?"

She handed it over, and I dialed Cady's house number. Henry picked up after two rings. "Longmire residence."

"It's me. Have you heard or seen anything from Alexia?"

"No, we thought you were going to her house."

"I did, and found her nephew. Somebody killed him."

There was a brief pause. "No sign of her?"

"No."

"What do you want us to do?"

"Stay there with my granddaughter, and I'll call Cady. Something is going on."

The line went dead, and I dialed Cady's number at work. "Wyoming attorney general's office."

"This is Sheriff Walt Longmire. I'd like to speak to my daughter, Cady Longmire."

"Just a moment, please."

She put me on hold and then the phone rang.

And rang.

And rang.

"Hello, this is Cady Longmire . . ."

"Cady."

The recording continued unabated. "I'm not available to answer your call right now. . . ."

I hung up and hit redial, and the same woman answered. "Wyoming attorney —"

"Hey, it's Walt Longmire again. Cady's not in her office."

The woman sounded slightly annoyed. "Okay."

"Can you look around and see if you can find her?"

"Mr. Longmire," she began, in a tone of voice that made it clear that she had far better things to do than anything I requested.

"Sheriff Longmire."

"I'm sure she's just stepped away from her desk, or maybe she's gone out to lunch. Is this an emergency?"

"Ma'am, I am kneeling over a dead body about two miles from your office, and I need to talk to my daughter right now."

That got her attention. "Um, yes, yes, sir. I'll see if I can find her. Will you hold?"

"Yep."

As I waited, I watched Severini talking into his body mic. Then he called over to me, "DCI and the Mystery Mobile will be here in a few minutes." He nodded toward the body. "Did you know him?"

Vic and I shared a glance. "Yes, well, I met him once." My eyes went back to the tarp. "He played guitar."

"Sheriff Longmire?"

I turned the phone back to my ear. "Yep?"

"It's just as I thought; she's out to lunch."

"Where?"

"Well, I really couldn't say," she quickly added. "One of my coworkers who was at the front desk said she left with a nice young man — a David Coulter?"

15

Looking for a hammer and a chisel in the toolbox underneath the cot, the first thing I noticed was that Gibbs's spare boots and coveralls weren't in there.

I found the tools, which looked as if they might've been left over from the transcontinental railway days, but I decided not to say anything about the missing clothing. I nudged the toolbox over a little and sat on it as I wedged the business end of the wood-handled chisel between the lid and the coffin itself, gently tapping the edge of the tool inward with the hammer.

"What in the hell do you suppose you're gonna find in there?"

I glanced up at my boss. "Like I said before — how much do you think Marv Leeland weighed?"

"Hell if I know, one sixty or so, give or take?"

I looked at the cook. "Mr. Gibbs, you tried

to move this box; did it feel like it weighed a hundred and sixty pounds?"

He didn't answer right away. "Maybe it's the box, sir."

I shook my head and hammered the chisel, using it to gradually pry the top open. "The track repair crew said they found a man missing an arm on the side of the tracks near Fort Fred Steele, right?"

Lucian nodded. "Yeah."

I popped the lid up enough to where I could get my fingers underneath and then yanked.

We weren't rewarded with a body per se, but rather something I'd seen entirely too much of in the last few years, and we all looked down at the heavy-duty, rubberized black fabric with the carry loops and single zipper: an HRP, a human remains pouch, a body bag. I guess the U.S. government had a surplus.

For a moment I felt like I was falling backward, when really I was frozen in place, and even though I was aware of everything in the caboose, I couldn't move.

"Mr. Longmire, sir?"

Lucian's voice called from far away. "Walt?"

"They used to use cotton mattress covers. . . ."

Sheriff Connelly looked at me strangely. "Come again?"

"In the old days, they used to use mattress covers, but they decided that they needed something that was leakproof. We used 'em for carrying and storing everything when I was . . . when I was over there — ammo, rations, medical supplies."

Lucian looked me in the eye. "You all right?"

I took a deep breath. "Yep. I'm okay. Sorry."

"You're sure you're all right."

I nodded. "The crew said they found a man missing an arm, not a one-armed man." I leaned over and unzipped the bag, plainly revealing the bloodied face of Sheriff George McKay. "Even with an entire limb missing, he'd easily outweigh Leeland."

Lucian kneeled down across from me. "What in the holy hell?"

I glanced up at Gibbs. "The amount of blood on the platform of the caboose and the missing cleaver from your kitchen — somebody hacked McKay's arm off so we'd think it was Leeland."

Gibbs kneeled with us. "But why kill Sheriff McKay?"

"I don't know, but I intend to find out." I unzipped the bag a bit more. "I don't think cutting off his arm killed him, so I want to know what did."

Lucian pulled his side of the rubberized canvas back, revealing McKay's chest, where there was more blood. "Well, I want to know that, too, but I also want to know what the hell happened to Marv Leeland."

The dead man's clothes were blood soaked and frozen, but I was able to pull them apart enough to confirm that McKay had been shot. I leaned back, sat on the toolbox behind me, and looked at my boss. "I'm willing to bet that that's a .38 slug in him, and that it matches your weapon. Somebody used your gun, Sheriff Connelly."

He made a face. "How? We locked our damn door every time we left the cabin."

We both turned and looked at Gibbs.

He shook his head. "I'm gettin' forgetful, but any of the porters could've opened that door; we all have passkeys."

"Anybody else?"

"No." He thought about it. "Well, Mr. Holland, he's got one."

Lucian snorted. "He's the one that hit you over the head."

"That doesn't mean he's our killer — anybody could've stolen a key. We've got a means and opportunity, but what's the motive? I can't figure any reason Holland would kill either Leeland or McKay."

"What say we go talk to him?" Sheriff Connelly thought about it, pulling at his lip before he spoke again. "We'll want him alone, which means it would be easier if we got him back here, but if he knows we've yanked the lid off this box he might not be so open to the idea." Lucian turned and looked at Gibbs.

He stood and backed away, holding his hands out in supplication. "Sheriff, I told Mr. Longmire I'd just as soon not be involved. Mr. Holland, he's the head security man on this line, and he can have me fired with a word."

I glanced at the door and the train beyond. "That's all right; I've got an alternative plan. Mr. Gibbs, would you be so kind as to call on Miss LeClerc in her cabin and tell her I'd like to speak with her?"

He glanced at the open coffin. "Here?"

"I'll catch her before she gets to the caboose."

He thought about it. "Yes, sir, I can do that."

As he started to go, I called after him. "And if you would, please don't mention anything about what we've done and seen here."

He nodded. "I have no intention, sir."

He ducked through the doorway, and the cold blast of air swept past us as I turned to Lucian. "What's your bet?"

"Holland, he seems to have one sideways and he had access to and knowledge of everything on this train."

"John Schafer?"

"What would he have to gain?"

"Marv Leeland?"

"What about him? He's out there alongside the tracks getting covered up with snow."

"Habeas corpus."

"Habeas kiss my ass." He gestured toward the open box. "It's a miracle that they found McKay, and the only reason they did was because he got dumped near a crossing and there was a maintenance crew working that portion of the line." He studied me.

I stooped and zipped up the body bag and placed the lid back on the pine box. "Help me put this thing back together — I don't think there's any reason to expose everybody else to this."

He lifted the other end and aligned it as I began tapping the nails back in place. When I finished, I tossed the tools in the box and started toward the front of the train. "You wait here, and I'll intercept Kim before she gets this far and get her to lure Holland this way."

He pulled his Liberty revolver and thumbed open the cylinder, checking the load again. "I sure do hope you're right about all this."

"Me, too." I stopped at the door. "Somebody's desperate, first attempting to put it off on Leeland, then McKay, me, and now you. I think we'd better be careful who it is we trust." I pushed open the door and, brushing off the snow, battled my way into the dining car. I glanced at the outline of the missing meat cleaver in the adjoining kitchen and thought of the gruesome job that had been done to McKay.

It took a special kind of man to do a thing like that.

I'd just reached up to touch the spot when I saw LeClerc coming from the other end and gestured for her to cut through the galley.

I met her in the kitchen, where no one was likely to interrupt us. "Sheriff McKay is dead."

Her eyes widened.

"They found him on the tracks near Fort Fred Steele."

"I thought that . . . that was Sheriff Leeland."

"No, turns out it was McKay. I saw him myself — he's in a coffin in the back."

She swooned, catching herself with a hand on the counter. "Oh, my God."

I put a hand at her back, not wanting to suggest intimacy but at the same time unwilling to let her fall onto the greasy floor. "I need your help."

Her eyes came up to mine. "How could I help?"

"I need to get Holland back in the caboose alone, where I can talk to him, and you're the only one I think can get that job done."

"Holland?" She nodded, catching her breath. "You think he did it?"

"I'm not sure, but I want to talk to him." I glanced around. "Do you know where he is?"

"He's in the parlor car with a few of the other sheriffs — they're all drinking."

"Tell him you want to meet him in the caboose — I don't care why or how, just get him back there."

She swept her fingers under her eyes and straightened her jacket. "That, I can do." She started to go but then stopped at the other end of the kitchen to look at me. "It's funny that on a train full of sheriffs, a deputy is the one who's going to catch the killer."

"We'll see." As she left, I returned to the caboose to find Lucian alone. "Gibbs isn't playing?"

"I don't hardly think so, and I don't blame him."

I glanced out the window and could see that we'd definitely slowed to a crawl. "You want to get out of here, too?"

He leaned against the stairs leading to the cupola, tucked his weapon under his arm, and looked out the window with me. "Nope, but I'd be interested to know your plan — just get him back here and beat the truth out of him?"

"Marine Corps procedure; sometimes there's nothing but straight ahead."

"Just like this train?"

I took a position behind the caboose door and waited, listening to the frozen wind. "Just like."

"There's nothing on this Coulter character, and to be honest, I'd be more at ease if there was."

I nodded at the phone. "Me, too."

There was a hopeful pause from the attorney general. "Look, it could be nothing. . . ."

"The nanny is missing, and her nephew is rolled up in a tarp underneath a billboard on the side of I-80."

He waited another moment before continuing. "I know, I know. Walt, we're doing everything we can. Every police officer in Wyoming is out looking for this bastard and your daughter. We're doing everything we can and more. We'll find them. There's no way he'll do anything to her, because if he does he knows we'll put him through a meat grinder and feed him to the black-footed ferrets."

I took a deep breath and swallowed all the words that had no business being said. "You'll keep me in the loop?"

"Absolutely. Call this number?"

"Yep, it's Henry's cell." The phone went dead in my hand, and I passed it back to the Cheyenne Nation. "Nothing."

He rocked my granddaughter back and forth in his arms as Vic looked on. "What do you want to do?"

"Find Cady."

"And in lieu of that?"

Vic cupped her chin in her palm. "How 'bout we go out and drive at a high rate of speed and get our hands on somebody?"

"It has to be the right somebody."

She nodded, saying nothing more.

Cady's home phone rang, and I picked it up, stretching the cord to its max. "Yep?"

"Is this the Longmire residence?"

The voice was unfamiliar, and I was quick to respond. "Walt Longmire speaking."

"Sheriff Longmire, this is Dave Walker from the *Denver Post,* and I was wondering if you'd care to comment on the release of the prisoner. . . ."

I hung up the phone.

The Bear studied me. "More about the impending release?"

"Yep."

"Should be sometime tonight."

"I don't care."

He nodded but didn't say any more. I leaned against the counter and looked around. "If I hadn't been so absorbed with all that, I might've seen this coming."

Vic spoke quietly. "You think it's Bidarte?"

"Who else could it be?"

Henry turned to look at me. "Alexia Mendez?"

I shook my head. "I find it extremely difficult to believe that she is involved with people who would kill her own nephew, or kidnap my daughter, for that matter."

Vic's voice was sharp. "If it actually was her nephew, or her name is Alexia Mendez." I turned to look at her, and her eyes had narrowed. "We actually know very little about her, her nephew, and obviously the

Coulter guy, if that's really his name."

"You think this has been a setup all along?"

"It's possible." She reached over and stroked Lola's head. "After Michael, I don't discount any possibilities."

I thought about how myopic I'd been in the last week. It wasn't like I could be on the lookout at all times, but Lucian had been right: as long as Bidarte was out there and there was a contract on my head, we were all just tin bears, ripe for the plinking. I thought about Michael — my son-in-law and Vic's brother — who had been the first victim of the hit man's revenge.

And now he had my daughter.

I should never have allowed this situation to go this far. I had no reason to think that the man was through — and I had no one to blame but myself.

Standing there looking through the window at the almost nonexistent skyline of the state capital, I made a promise to myself that I would get my daughter back whatever it took. At that moment, my eyes fell upon the metal shed in the hinterland between the buildings and the city property — and something just clicked.

I pushed myself away from the counter, stormed past Lucian, who was sleeping on the sofa, and slammed the door open, crossing the deck in about two steps and launching myself down the stairway toward the alley.

I could hear Vic and Henry yelling something at Lucian to wake up, take Lola, and stand guard as they thundered down the steps in an attempt to catch up.

I'd already made the street and had run across. Leaping over the chain-link fence and landing amid the frozen weeds and grass tufts, I banged into the tin shed and, barely fitting, slid between the brick wall and the outbuilding. The set of sliding doors were closed on the other side, but I ripped them open, revealing an inordinately clean, level space with plywood counters on three sides, along with a padded stool that was pushed to the center of the room.

Covering the walls was writing in a neat and precise hand, carefully notating in black marker all of our arrivals and departures in the last week, down to the second.

I stood there in the center, turning in a circle, as Vic and Henry stumbled in behind me.

"Motherfucker."

Toward the back of the hut was a perfect hole cut in the tin with a circular cover that looked to be about the size of a 35mm camera lens. I turned to look at the Bear, who rumbled, "You should have let me kill him."

"Is it me, or is the train slowing down again?"

Sheriff Connelly glanced out the window. "Yep, we are. It's possible they've given up on trying to outrun the storm or that they got word from up the line that the pass at Elk Mountain is already closed. Either way, it ain't good."

I glanced through the window toward the next car. "Here he comes."

As soon as Holland came through the door, I pinned him against the wall with my forearm under his chin and my free hand wedging his sidearm into its holster. "Don't move, don't even breathe, or I'll pitch you through that back door. If you survive the fall, you'll freeze to death before you get to the next town."

His eyes were bulging, but he nodded.

"You see that box there on the floor?" He did his best to look tough, but when I leaned in a little and began lifting him off the floor, he quickly nodded. "Who's in it?"

He gripped my arm with his free hand in an attempt to get me to loosen my hold, which I did. He choked and coughed and then spoke in a rasping voice. "Marv Leeland; didn't you get the memo?"

"I've got another question, wise guy: do you know how Leeland was killed?"

"I suspect it had something to do with being thrown off a train."

"Did you get a formal report from the Carbon County deputies?"

"No, they said they'd file it with their paperwork and send it to Cheyenne."

"I suspect that the body in that box was shot with Lucian's revolver, and since I don't think he did it, I'm figuring somebody was in our cabin and borrowed his sidearm to do the deed. Why didn't you and Schafer want us opening that box?"

He swallowed hard and coughed. "It's evidence, damn it."

"Maybe so, but it's not Marv Leeland."

"Who the hell else could a one-armed man be?"

"George McKay." His eyes widened. "Somebody shot him and then cut off his arm to make us think it was Leeland; now, who could've possibly wanted to do that?"

He struggled to get the words out. "I'm telling you, I don't know."

"Who else could've had a key to open our cabin, Holland?"

He gargled the words out in a rush. "Hell,

practically all of us have passkeys to open up every door in this train as a safety precaution. Including your buddy the cook!"

I stood there holding him a moment more but then slowly lowered his heels to the floor as I considered what he said. After all, Gibbs had been opening doors for me. "Why would he do it?"

He rubbed his neck. "I found out from the personnel director that Gibbs had an uncle who was hanged by vigilantes here in Wyoming earlier this year and made the transfer to this line only a month ago. Now, I grant you that it's a slender thread, but it's better than any motivation you can hang on me."

Lucian blew out the words in a single breath. "He would've had access to any part of the train, and it would've been easy for him to get that meat cleaver."

"Why don't we have a word with him?" Holland looked around. "Where the hell is he, anyway?"

"He didn't want to be back here for this."

"Well, I can understand that." He glanced around. "He couldn't have gone far. Let's go find him."

I reached over and slipped the .357 from his holster, tucking it in my belt. "Sounds good, but I'll keep this in the meantime."

He shrugged. "Doesn't matter — with the amount of charges I'm going to level on you, the only train you'll ever ride will be the one to Leavenworth."

There was a sudden lurch, and it appeared that we were slowly gaining velocity again. Whatever it was that had slowed us down must've been straightened out, and I just hoped I'd have enough time to get the job done.

I pushed Holland forward and followed him into the small bit of space between the cars as Sheriff Connelly brought up the rear. "Just so I'm straight with the plan, we're gonna work our way forward, beating the shit out of everyone until we get to the engineer?"

I yelled over the sound of the windblown snow and the clanking rails as our speed increased. "We might beat the shit out of him, too, if I'm not satisfied."

Moving through the dining car, Lucian waved at Phelps, Finlay, and Hanna as we made our way forward to the bar car, where a few more sheriffs, including Tillman and Brown, were seated.

The two looked up as we passed but didn't move. As we walked through the sleeper cars, Holland looked out the window. "Man-O-Manischewitz, John sure has this sucker wound out."

"I was thinking the same thing. Should we be going this fast?"

Holland shrugged. "He knows what he's doing."

When we'd entered the farthest sleeper car, we finally found Gibbs, who was returning from the other direction, but stopped a good way down the hall when he saw us.

Holland spoke loudly enough to be heard above the sound of the engine. "Mr. Gibbs, I need to speak with you."

He paused for a moment and then came toward us at a slow pace. "Yes, sir, Mr. Holland?"

The security man leaned against the wall in an attempt to steady himself, the train seeming to rock on the rails with a bit more vigor. "Gibbs, do you happen to have an uncle by the name of Merion Gibbs?"

He looked at the floor. "I did, sir."

"You did?"

"Yes, sir. He's dead."

Holland took a somewhat superior tone. "And how did he die, Mr. Gibbs?"

"He was hung, sir. Here in Albany County." He looked sad. "From what I understand it, he killed a woman and there was something like a lynching."

"And even with that, you transferred to this line so you could come here?"

At this, he smiled. "Seems strange, don't it?" He turned and looked out the window, the only illumination coming from the train itself as the series of rectangular lights brightened the fleeing snowflakes. "He used to send me postcards about what a nice place it was, and I put in my papers so that I could see it." His eyes met mine. "But with all due respect, there really ain't nothin' here."

I smiled, and when no one else said anything, I dismissed the poor man. "Thank you, Mr. Gibbs. Are we keeping you from something?"

"Yes, sir, I thought I might go make some sandwiches and coffee — it looks like we might be in for a long night."

Letting him pass, I watched as he rounded the corner and then I turned back to Holland. "Satisfied?"

"I take it you believe him?"

"I do." I turned to Lucian as we jostled against the walls. "Is it me, or does every dirty deal in this thing seem to be pointing back to Schafer and Albany County?"

Lucian pulled the beaded tobacco pouch from his back pocket and the pipe from his shirt and began filling the bowl. "Seems like it could bear some scrutiny, but I think there might be something more important on the agenda right now."

"Such as?"

"Well, in my years in the Army Air Corps, I got pretty good at estimating ground speed, and I've gotta tell you that unless I miss my guess . . ." He stooped and studied the landscape a little more intently than we had. "I believe this train is running at close to a hundred miles an hour."

"You're sure it was Peter Lowery?"

"That's the name he gave me."

"Well, that's probably not his real name, but I'll give it a shot." Agent Mike McGroder tapped a few keys on the computer he had borrowed from the Wyoming attorney general's office. "I've got a Peter David Lowery in Cleveland for armed robbery and a couple of domestics, but he's doing a three spot."

"What does he look like?"

"Black."

"Nope."

He scrolled down. "Peter Lowery here in Cheyenne, but he's sixty-three years old. . . . Walt, I've got over ten in Wyoming alone. No way to narrow the search?"

"Nothing I can think of. What about David Coulter?"

The AIC typed in the name and hit a few keys and made a helpless gesture with both hands. "Over a thousand in the U.S. — you've got to give me something more to go on."

"He had a Southern accent, west-southern, maybe Texas?" I thought about it. "He was military; he said army, and I said Hooah, and there was a flicker in his eyes, which leads me to believe that he could've been more than just a regular GI." I thought about it. "We're looking for a soldier, army elite, Rangers, Special Forces, Green Beret, Airborne . . . possibly Afghanistan over Iraq because of drug connections, maybe look for a dishonorable discharge and any kind of association with Mexico, or Bidarte." McGroder began typing. "His first name will be David simply because it's easy to remember, but the last isn't likely to be Coulter."

"Something close?"

"Probably not."

"This might take a while."

"What about Bidarte?"

The Fed gestured toward the screen again. "Yeah, well . . . his name lights up all over the place."

"Do you have a current location for him?"

"Not really, but I can check with the guys

over in State and see if they've got something. He really doesn't fit into any of the profiles, or maybe it's that he fits into too many." I watched as he typed on the keyboard. "Hello . . ."

"Find something?"

"Well, it looks like there was an altercation with a local drug lord named Miguel Morales in an area of Chihuahua called Las Bandejas near Área Natural Protegida Médanos de Samalayuca, a nature preserve south of Juárez. Looks as if it might've been your buddy Bidarte — at least it was someone who was allegedly responsible for cutting the throats of six fellows down there on Highway 45."

"That would be his MO."

"Well, the Morales character is known for his particular form of punishment, *El Guiso,* or The Stew — he douses his victims in diesel fuel and burns them alive in sealed oil barrels." He looked at me. "And this is the guy Bidarte is wiping out."

Standing, I walked over to the window.

"Walt, there's no way they could've gotten Cady out of the country that quickly. We'll find her. Kidnapping across state lines, murder, extortion . . . I'm afraid Mr. Bidarte has incurred the wrath of the Department of Justice, and we have long arms."

"I appreciate that."

"If he has her, they're probably sitting in a hotel room watching pay-per-view here in Cheyenne."

I stared out the window. "I hope you're right."

"Just in case I'm not, I'll also get in touch with the Policía Federale Ministerial, the investigative arm of Mexico's Federal Police, and our Border Patrol; I know a guy down there who is one tough old hombre, kind of like you."

"Thank you, Mike, and thanks for coming up." I glanced around at the all-but-empty room. "Have you got a place to stay?"

He laughed as he escorted me from the borrowed office. "I'm the federal government; I've always got a place to stay."

I walked through the skeleton crew, attempting not to make eye contact, and took the elevator to street level.

Outside the state capitol, I placed a hand on the railing in front of one of the statues that represented Wyoming's history. I just stood there, but my chest was heavy and each breath felt like I was shoveling air. My eyes drifted to the overcast sky and then to the profile of the pioneer woman, her face fearless and resolute.

Tears came then, tracing the lines in my

face. I'm not sure how long I stood there, but by the time I stumbled into my truck, my face was dry.

I climbed in, closed the door behind me, and sat there staring at the yellow traffic lights that blinked down West Twenty-fourth Street. My first thought was that I needed to get back to Cady's in case anybody called, but then I remembered that I had Henry's cell phone in my coat pocket. I pulled the thing out and pressed a few buttons, calling the apartment only twelve blocks away.

"Hello."

I stumbled. "Sorry, I'm not used to you answering the phone that way."

"Anything?"

"No. You?"

"No. Vic is on the deck, and I am patrolling the perimeter while your Dog is sleeping at the foot of your granddaughter's crib and Lucian is sleeping in a straight-back chair in her doorway with a cocked .38 revolver in his lap. I am not sure which is more dangerous."

"Don't make any sudden noises."

"I do not intend to. Where are you?"

"On my way back. Mike's doing some legwork in their systems, but there isn't anything we can do until he finds something to move on."

"Agreed."

"See you in a few." I deposited the phone in my inside jacket pocket as I hit the starter. For reasons I couldn't explain, I pulled out and headed south toward the Union Pacific roundhouse.

I drove onto the overpass to look down at the big steam engine. There wasn't any traffic, so I pulled over and got out, walking across the lanes to study the gleaming black of the thing through the wrought-iron fencing.

As I stood there, I became aware of the sound of a vehicle approaching and turned around to see a dark Suburban or maybe a Yukon slowing, probably on seeing my sheriff's unit.

Thinking it might be the Bobs, I started to wave, but once I got a better look I didn't raise my arm.

The windows were heavily tinted, and as near as I could tell, the vehicle didn't have any plates on the front. It dawned on me that it might be McGroder, having followed me, just checking to make sure I wasn't going to jump from the bridge, but he would have stopped, and the SUV kept moving, if slowly.

I pushed off the barricade and watched it

pass by my truck, unable to see anything inside except some dark shadows. Now I could see there were no plates on the back, either. They had slowed to a stop and were now sitting at the apex of the overpass about fifty yards away.

Maybe they thought I was in trouble.

Maybe they thought I needed help.

Maybe I'd find out.

I unholstered my Colt and started walking toward them but suddenly found myself running across the three lanes. I was only ten yards from the vehicle when they hit the accelerator and pulled quickly away, leaving me standing there in the middle of the road, a long way from anything.

16

Holland crammed himself in the doorway with the mic dangling in his hand as the car swayed and slapped against the rails. "Security to engineer, you copy?" There was no response. "Saunders, it's Holland." He tried again. "Roback, pick up. Everything all right up there?"

Lucian looked past us out the frost-scarred door at the tender and shuddered. "No other way up to the engine than that, huh?"

I stood at the doorway and looked out the window at the fuel car now covered with snow and, worse yet, ice. "Not that I know of, and it wasn't much fun when I did it earlier in comparatively mild weather and at a much slower speed."

Holland turned to look at us. "Now I'm worried. I don't think there's anybody up there."

"Oh, there's somebody up there, and if

it's who I think it is, this isn't going to be easy."

"Wait, you know who's up there?"

I avoided the question with one of my own. "You think the crew jumped off a little while back when we slowed down?"

"Or got pushed." He gestured with the mic. "Nobody's picking up. Now, if there was an emergency or something going on, there's two of them up there and one of them should be answering."

I zipped my jacket up tighter and pulled out my scarf, tying it around my face as I'd done before.

"What the hell do you think you're doing?"

"Somebody's got to climb over that tender and into the cab."

"I'm the head of security, and this train is my responsibility."

"You're not dressed for it; besides, do you know how to stop this thing?"

He appeared to be at a loss. "In theory."

"Well, I do."

He suddenly looked suspicious. "How is that?"

"The engineer showed me." I tugged on my gloves and handed Holland his sidearm. "Here, you're off the hook."

He stared at me and then out the window.

"You'll never make it — there's got to be more than an inch of ice on that tender; the heat from the engine must be melting the snow just long enough for the wind to turn it into ice."

"If you've got a better idea, I'd love to hear it."

He glanced at Lucian. "Hell with you, I've got only one leg."

I started to push past the security man when he stuck out a hand. "Not to add insult to injury, but at this speed it won't be long before we'll be coming up on the curve at Walcott Junction."

Sheriff Connelly slowly fell back against the wall. "Oh, hell."

As I glanced back at Holland, my voice was muffled by the scarf over my face. "And?"

"We'll never make it at this speed, and when this thing derails, we're all dead." He shuffled his feet and glanced toward the front. "Also, that loco's not in shape to withstand this kind of speed for an extended period of time. If that boiler blows, it's going to unleash over 23,000 gallons of scalding water and steam, not to mention more than 6,000 gallons of no. 5 fuel oil."

"So, what should I hope for?"

"Well, with a derailment you'll have a few

agonizing moments, but if the boiler blows you'll never know what hit you."

Turning the lever, I put a shoulder into the door and watched the thick coating of ice shatter and explode as it hit the grating and disappeared under the train. I just hoped the next thing under the train wasn't going to be me. "God hates a coward."

The vacuum slammed the door closed behind me, so I turned and grabbed on to the tender's railing. The ice on the ladder broke apart as I lifted myself up and climbed toward the top of the fuel car, barely able to see through the blistering wind.

The train swung and bucked like a rodeo bull, and I lost my footing and clung there, my gloved hands slowly sliding down the glazed rails.

Kicking my boots against the stair treads, I was able to dislodge enough snow to get traction and started up once more. I'd just made it to the top when I almost lost my footing again, but hung on. From that vantage point, I could see that the tender looked like a glacier.

Ducking my head back down, I cursed and then reached over with my right hand, grabbing the rail that stretched across, using my left fist to break away chunks the size of dinner plates, a few of which flipped up and flew back at me, exploding on contact and almost taking me off the tender with them.

I slid forward, pounding my fist to clear the way like an icebreaker. I was about halfway across and thought that if I could get as far as the fill spout, I could rest a few seconds before climbing over it, but the train made a major shift. All I could think in that split second was that we'd reached the curve at Walcott Junction and were going to explode like a 500,000-pound grenade.

My left hand was numb from bashing ice, so I hung on with my right like a grappling hook. One leg fell over the side, and I could feel another railing underneath. I lodged my foot for purchase, reached back, and took hold of the fill spout, and slowly pulled myself on top. There was nothing ahead except snowflakes illuminated by the lights on the front of the locomotive that parted to make way for the train, seeming to want to avoid it.

I lay there thinking about whether I wanted to die and came to the conclusion that, no, I didn't want to quite yet.

I'd made it to the front edge despite my hand and some vertigo, and could see that the heat from the engine had turned the snow there to a smothering slush. I tried to peer into the cab, but the snowmelt blew up in my face. Carefully feeling for the stairs, I pivoted, found a tread, and lowered myself down until I found another.

The train swayed again, only to buck the other way. I felt my boot slip and I fell backward, breaking my watch in the process.

The Colt slipped from the back of my jeans along with *Murder on the Orient Express* as I landed on the metal flooring. My head crashed with a soft, melonlike thump that left stars flashing in my eyes like heavy artillery, and all I could hear was the roar of the big locomotive as it threatened to blow apart at the seams.

I lay there for a second stretching my face. Somebody was whistling "This Train." When I opened my eyes, I found the business end of a Model 60 .38 Special stuck against the numb, frozen skin of my forehead.

"Hello, Deputy — it had to be you."

Sitting in the chair in the living room of Cady's apartment, I stared into the night and tried to slow the whistling express of every thought I'd had in the last day, but I felt like the chair I was sitting in was falling backward faster than I could think.

What was I going to do? What could I do? I hadn't been at this much of a loss since Martha had died, and the feeling of coming unraveled wasn't helping one bit. I remembered my father telling me that you knew you were a man when everything went bad and suddenly all eyes were on you for help. All eyes were on me now, and I had no idea what to do.

There was a noise, and I turned to see Henry quietly closing the door to Lola's room. "She asleep?"

"I am amazed that between Lucian snoring and Dog snoring, your granddaughter can sleep at all."

"How about you?"

He sat on the sofa and studied me. "I do not sleep nights like this one."

"I figured." I heard the refrigerator kick on in the kitchen and looked around at the wonderful job my daughter had done in fixing the place up. "I'll die without her, Henry."

"I know."

"What am I going to do?"

"We will get her back."

"How?"

"We will find who took her, and we will find her, and we will get her back — no matter what it takes."

I stared at my lap and nodded, but I didn't seem to convince him.

"You need to look back to the man you once were — the portion of yourself that you have kept locked away for a very long time — because that is the man we need now."

I glanced up at him.

"I will tell you something I have never told you, something that will give you the heart you need for what is ahead." He leaned forward, and I could see the glimmer of the floor lamp reflecting in his dark eyes. "I am a very dangerous man, but you are far more dangerous than I. I have only given a sliver of my heart away, whereas you have given so much; you must go after and retrieve that which will make it whole."

"I —"

"Do not interrupt. There is one more thing which makes you absolutely dangerous — you have nothing to lose."

I glanced toward Lola's door.

"That is mine to protect, and you must trust in my ability to take care of her while you do what needs to be done. It will be contrary to many of the things you have come to believe, but you must cast them aside and become the furious warrior I know you to be."

I nodded; there was nothing to be said.

"I will leave you to these thoughts and your memories of that younger man. If you search long enough you will find him — or better yet, he will find you." He stood, placing a hand on my shoulder and squeezing until it hurt, then he let go and disappeared into the room where the sliver of his heart lay.

I stood and walked to the front door, opened it, and looked at Victoria Moretti's silhouette. She was leaning on one of the railings with a blanket wrapped around her. "Do you guys ever shut up?"

I stepped out and joined her. "All quiet on the western front?"

"It gets much colder, and I'm shooting somebody just so I can come inside."

"Seen anybody to shoot?"

"No, which is why I'm still out here."

"Go inside and get some sleep."

She nodded and started to go but then stopped. "He's right, you know."

"What's that?"

"We're going to have to kill him." She walked on, and I listened as the door quietly closed behind me.

I don't know how long I stood there looking at the alley, and I wasn't even aware of pulling the Colt .45 semiautomatic from the small of my back and holding it up in the mild glow of the streetlights. The metal gleamed, reflections racing up and down the slide mechanism, and the stag grips undulating with the ridges of the elk antlers, almost as if the weapon were breathing.

I leaned forward and placed it carefully on the railing, not trusting having it in my hand at that moment.

I thought about my wife, and then I thought about my daughter.

Picking the 1911A1 up again, I punched the button and dropped the magazine in my other hand and then pulled the slide, launching a round into the air and catching it. Then I sat on the railing and began thumbing each round, lining them up like soldiers on the flat surface of the redwood.

I pulled the tattered old buckaroo scarf from my jacket pocket and spread it out.

With my thumb I pressed in on the knurled end of my Colt, at the same time rotating the barrel bushing a quarter turn clockwise to free the plug and recoil assembly. I removed the assembly and then rotated the plug in a counterclockwise direction, freeing it from the recoil spring.

My hands began operating on their own, disengaging themselves from my mind, my fingers dancing without any conscious thought. I rotated the barrel bushing counterclockwise, disengaging it from the slide, and continued disassembling the Colt without even looking at it.

Carefully, I polished the surfaces with the scarf and then set about reassembling the sidearm. When I finished, I started the process all over again, and then again, and again.

I don't know how many times I did it, but my hands didn't get tired, and every time the action became faster, almost to the point where I couldn't follow it with my eyes in the half dark.

I finally began feeding the rounds back in the magazine, then slapped it home and jacked the slide mechanism back, holding it at inspection arms. I stood there in the two-handed grip as I thumbed the lever, and the thing slid home with a menacing click, the hammer hanging back like a fang.

I carefully folded the bandanna and tucked it back in my jacket. I stood there with the battle-ready pistol hanging from my hand, allowing the energy to seep into my limbs and mind, thinking about the things I was going to have to do.

I went inside to find Vic asleep on the sofa and sat on one of the overstuffed chairs with the .45 on my knee.

Tomorrow would be the beginning of a quest, but for now the sky was still dark. I wanted morning, but I wasn't going to get it anytime soon, so I did what soldiers had always done — I drew the darkness closer and rested.

Then there was a noise, the sound of weight being distributed on the balcony outside.

My hand came to rest on the pistol.

I waited, but there was no more noise.

Carefully, I uncoiled from the chair, the air sucking back into the cushions like the furniture was attempting to hold its breath. I pivoted toward the deck with the .45 in front of me like an antenna. It was still dark, but with the streetlights, I could see two people ducking down the steps.

Vic was sitting up with her Glock aimed toward the door, and I'd just started for the bedroom when I noticed that Henry Standing Bear, Headsman of the Dog Soldier Society, Bear Clan, had filled the opening.

I put a forefinger to my lips and then watched as he turned back and made the same gesture to Lucian. The Bear pointed toward the window in Lola's room and then at the doorway where he stood and slid the same finger across his throat, indicating to Lucian that he should stay and protect her;

then he carefully closed the door behind him.

The three of us stood there in the middle of the room. "How many?"

I whispered back. "At least two."

"How?"

"Vic and I will go out, but you stay here. If they get past me, I want at least two more stops before they get to Lola."

He nodded, slid the stag-handled Bowie knife from his back, and flipped the handle in his hand until satisfied with the grip. The light glimmered on the blade like it had on my Colt, just as beautiful and just as deadly.

Vic and I quietly walked toward the door. Turning the knob and gently pushing it open with my free arm, I waited. It was possible they were gone — maybe they had heard me assembling and reassembling the weapon, maybe they'd looked in the windows and seen me sitting there armed.

Like I said, it was possible, but it wasn't likely.

Staying near the jamb, I unlatched the storm door and pushed it open wide. There was still nothing, so I took a small step out, panning the Colt across the deck. Someone sat whistling "This Train."

Keeping the gun on the figure, I came the rest of the way out.

"No need to worry; my friends are gone."

The rasp of his voice struck me like a whip, but I didn't respond.

Backlit by the streetlights, he gestured weakly toward the steps. "There's no way I could've made it up here on my own, so my friends were kind enough to carry me."

I said nothing as Vic came up beside me, also aiming her weapon.

"They were very quiet, but I assured them you'd hear." Gesturing toward Vic, he continued. "Or your friends would." He paused. "You look good, Walt, better than the last time I had the opportunity to kill you."

He shouted to be heard over the thunderous internal combustion of the locomotive. "Surprised to see me?"

I started to reach a hand up to massage my neck, but he stopped me, jamming the muzzle of the stainless Smith & Wesson into my forehead.

The wig was gone, but he still had the facial delicacy that had made him a beautiful woman and the husky voice that had helped give him away.

Kim LeClerc sat back in the engineer's seat and studied me as I studied him. He still wore makeup, but now it was smeared in a sad parody of femininity. The pantsuit and heels were gone; he was wearing the insulated coveralls and logger boots that had been in Gibbs's toolbox.

I shouted back, "I don't suppose you're going to let me shut this engine down."

"No."

"Then we're all going to die."

He gestured outside where the freezing night rushed by. "You can jump."

I started to turn and sit up, but he leveled the .38 at me again. I slumped against the brakeman's bench seat and shouted to be heard above the noise of the engine. "Thanks for the offer, but no thanks."

"I let the engineer and crewman off. If you'd been here I would've let you off, too. I don't like killing the innocent."

"Really? There's a whole trainload of them behind us." He didn't seem to know what to say to that. "I'm going to stand up, and I'm going to pull that lever back, and we're going to let all these people live because this has gone far enough." I took my hand and shoved his boot off my chest. "Now, you can shoot me if you want, but that's what I'm going to do."

He leveled the revolver at me again. "No, you're not."

I ignored the pain in the back of my head.

"Look, one of two things is going to happen here pretty soon — either this thing is going to blow apart or it's going to hit the curve at Walcott Junction and skip the tracks, so one way or another I'm pulling that lever."

"No." He shrugged. "Sacrifices are going to have to be made. The one that could did nothing about my sister and now they're all going to pay."

"The sheriffs?"

"Yes."

"Like Marv Leeland?"

He paused, turning in a little from the cold or maybe his feelings. "I didn't want to kill him, but he was about to find me out."

I waited, giving him the opportunity to tell his story. I'd found that few people give up the chance to explain themselves, no matter what the reason or environs.

"She was my sister."

"Melanie Wheeler."

"Yes."

Moving a hand behind my back, I started to shift my weight, but he aimed the S&W at my head and placed the work boot back on my chest. "You knew?"

"Eventually."

"Bullshit, there's no way." He studied me, trying to get a read on whether I was telling the truth or not. "How?"

"The conversation I had with Ed Schafer at the Asylum for the Insane." I sat up a little, noticing my .45 lodged near his feet along with the paperback, far out of reach. "Ed said that both he and his brother left your sister alive that night."

His eyes widened a bit.

"The night you killed her."

He said nothing.

"For whatever reason, you were there and saw your sister with the two of them and then killed her." I sat up a bit, and my hand bumped into something under the seat. "Why, Kim?" Carefully, I ran my hand along the length of the big box-end wrench that the brakeman had left underneath his seat. "Was it because she was a woman and you weren't?"

"Shut up."

I lifted the big wrench just enough to slide my fingers underneath, tightening my grip. "Was that how it started? You killed your sister and then killed another young woman on that same date for the next five years in some sort of crazy memoriam?"

"Shut up."

"But when John Schafer arrested his own brother last year, you had to stop or risk giving yourself away."

His breath heaved, and he didn't deny it.

"So, you attempted to get on the train with Schafer — yep, he told me — and when he wasn't game, you went with McKay?" I raised my voice, even louder. "Or did you just get so desperate you decided to kill every sheriff on the train?"

He sat there looking at me.

The wind was deafening, and the train shifted again, shuddering as it tried to stay on the tracks. "You killed Marv Leeland because he was figuring things out and then you killed George McKay with Lucian's weapon, and when that wasn't enough to muddy the trail you chopped his arm off to convince us that he was Leeland."

I waited for some sort of response, but none came. "You killed six young women, and now you've killed two more people; I'm not going to let you kill an entire trainload simply because you can't come to terms with the fact that you killed your sister." I felt the weight of the chromed steel in my hand. "You're sick, Kim."

"No."

"You need help."

The elongated snub-nose revolver shifted a little, so I swung the wrench at him as hard as I could. It struck his cheek, and the gun went off, firing a round up and behind me. I grabbed his leg and pulled, then grasped his wrist and slammed it against the metal floor. The .38 slid away as I placed a knee on his chest and held him there clutching his face and sobbing, the blood leaking from his fingers.

Scooping up my Colt, I stood and kept it aimed at him. Reaching up, I slowly pulled the lever back, and the screaming of the engine began dying down, our speed immediately diminishing.

I looked at the frozen landscape and thought about the body of the one-armed sheriff still lying out there somewhere. Then my eyes dropped to the man at my feet and the paperback lodged under his side, and I thought about what Leeland had said: that there were only so many permutations to the whodunit — he did it, she did it, nobody did it, and they all did it.

As I lodged the .45 in my jeans, sat on the brakeman's bench, and listened to Kim Wheeler, aka LeClerc, weep, I thought, *I guess she didn't figure on this one.*

"Where is my daughter?"

He wheezed. "I'll get to that, but how have you been, Walt?"

I ignored the question, still holding the muzzle of the Colt aimed at his so-called heart.

"C'mon now, it's been so long since we've talked. I mean, you can't count all those parole hearings where we were sitting opposite each other in a courtroom." He sighed and paused a moment, trying to catch what was left of his breath. "Before I forget, I've got something for you." He extended his hand, a small, stiff piece of paper between his fingers.

I reached out and took what appeared to be a postcard, tucking it in my shirt pocket without looking at it. "Where is my daughter?"

"You might want to read that." He sat there, fumbling with something in his lap, then looking back to me. "Now, is this any way to greet an old friend? I've gone to a lot of trouble to get here to see you." He turned his head and sighed. "Made a lot of deals. . . ."

"Who with?"

"The devil, I suppose. . . . But I'll get to that." He turned his head and laughed. "A meeting decades in the making." As his face swiveled back to mine, the streetlights caught the dented portion of his cheek where the wrench had hit him and ruined his face. "You know, I don't think I knew what I was doing when you and I had our confrontation all those years ago — letting you take my life."

"Where is my daughter?"

He coughed, and then his voice sharpened. "I guess we're not in a giving mood, huh?" His gaze turned to Vic, standing beside me. "Hello, young lady, and how are you?"

"Fine. Actually, trying to decide if I fucking shoot you now or later."

"You work with this brute, or is it more than that?" He choked a small laugh and adjusted himself on the railing, where I could now see that he held a small semiautomatic pistol.

"Where's my daughter?"

His head dropped, as if I'd disappointed him by reintroducing the subject. "Let's not talk about that just yet." He sighed deeply and looked back up at me. "Do you ever lie awake at night and think about the lives you've ruined? I mean, I thought my life was bad before I went to prison, but do you know what it's like in there for someone like me?" He stared up at the dark sky and almost lost his balance. "I've waited my whole life to do something *more* to you that would damage your life as badly as you've damaged mine."

Vic leaned in. "More?"

He sat there silent for a moment. "You

don't know?"

She re-aimed her 9mm. "Know what?"

"She doesn't know; I guess you're not that close after all." He turned back to me. "So when the Asociación Punto Muerto came to me, it just seemed like a gift."

Vic insisted. "What *more*?"

He shook his head. "The Dead Center Association, a little dramatic, don't you think? There was a member of the organization in Rawlins who put me in touch with Bidarte. They had plenty of leverage and money, and I was able to provide them with something that they couldn't seem to get access to — you. You've made a lot of enemies over the years, Sheriff. You'd be amazed at the lengths people are willing to go just to get a piece of you." I took a step toward him, but he raised the pistol, not directing it at me, but reminding me that he had it. "No, I've waited too long. This all has to play out the way I want."

"It didn't last time." I heard a slight noise behind me but wasn't worried, knowing the only person who could've possibly been that quiet was the Cheyenne Nation.

LeClerc leaned to the side, looking past me. "Hello." He coughed again and grimaced. "Sorry, they tell me I haven't got long, and I guess they're right." He nodded his head and leaned forward, and I was almost sure he was going to slip from the rail. "Where were we?"

"My daughter."

"They really wanted your granddaughter, and I know he wanted to do it on your watch so it would be more personal, but I guess that was becoming problematic with this gauntlet of protection — especially the noble savage behind you there." He shrugged. "He never goes with something simple, so he chose me to accomplish a common vendetta. They arranged for me to take a medicine to fake the heart condition, but then the doctors discovered the cancer."

"Where is she?"

"Oh, but you see that's the beauty of it: I don't know. They took her, but they didn't tell me where, so I can't help you even if I wanted to." He coughed some more and then caught his breath. "You killed my family. My parents, they died of shame after what you did to me."

"You're insane, Kim; your crimes killed them, after you killed your sister, and eight other innocents in an attempt to run from the responsibility, or maybe because it felt good."

He ignored me and gazed into the dark, his voice almost wistful. "Now I'm going to be that itch you can't scratch for the rest of your life, that thing that hangs over your every hope and desire."

"Where is my daughter?"

"I've really got only one more thing to do." Resignation overtook his voice. "I thought it would be more frightening than it is, but all this talk is just making me tired. I just want it to end." He looked directly at me. "You're never going to see her again, and you're never going to know what happened to her — whether she's in some concrete cell being raped and beaten every day like I was or if she's already dead and lying in a grave just a mile from where you live." Slowly, he began raising the pistol. "You're never going to know."

He'd almost gotten it up to where he could take aim when I fired.

He couldn't have weighed more than a hundred pounds, and the slug from the .45 hit him like the train that had carried the two of us all those years ago. Propelled by the impact, his chest blew backward and his limbs followed like fringe as he dropped from sight and landed on the surface of the alley, two floors below.

The echo of the gunshot rang off the buildings and you could see lights coming on all around us as I walked to the edge of the deck, my Colt trained on the lifeless body. I don't know how long I stayed like that — I only became aware when Vic reached out, dislodged my fingers, and took my gun.

Epilogue

The snow was bad on Elk Mountain, but the wind was worse, as it always is in Wyoming, and the caprice of that wind scoured the train's passage clean, allowing The Western Star to climb her way through like a parting gift.

There was no shortage of sheriffs ready and willing to buy me drinks — some I accepted and some that I didn't — and there was an almost holiday spirit that overtook the train as it chugged its way downhill out of the Vedauwoo territory and into Cheyenne.

Sheriff Connelly sat with me in the dining car as Gibbs, who stood by the table, refilled our glasses and then retreated to the galley. "How did you know?"

I took a sip of the Rainier beer that was growing on me since I'd gotten back. "Know what?"

"How the holy hell did you figure out Kim

LeClerc was a man and that he was really Kim Wheeler?"

I grunted a laugh, knowing full well that would be his first question. "My investigative experience in Vietnam. In some Asian cultures it's an art form, the ability to mimic women. The armed forces were concerned primarily with prostitutes, but they also wanted us to know about the pretenders. They taught us to always look for the Adam's apple, which is more prominent in the male, and the hands, which are usually larger and more masculine — everything else is pretty easy to hide but not those two." I took another sip of my beer. "I suspected, but at that point it didn't mean anything. I mean, what'd I care what McKay's tastes were?"

"You think he knew?"

"Not right at the start, but eventually — he must have confronted LeClerc, which led to him killing McKay and cutting off his arm to get us to think it was Leeland. That way, we would think only McKay was missing, when in fact he had killed them both. I suppose to put the blame on any of us since Marv had suspicions about the sheriffs' cabal."

"Then why kill Leeland?"

"I think LeClerc was telling the truth —

Marv was pretty shrewd and was beginning to put two and two together, that Kim was a man, and LeClerc jumped the gun and killed him. Did they find Leeland east of Fort Fred Steele?"

He nodded and looked out the window. "That, they did." He stroked his chin. "How'd LeClerc get my gun?"

I lowered my voice. "Probably Gibbs let him in our cabin by mistake. After the first mix-up with the rooms, I noticed Gibbs never really looked at the numbers when you asked him to unlock and I'm betting LeClerc noticed, too." I set my beer down. "I figure he shot Leeland with your gun because rather than take me head-on, he'd implicate you and get rid of me — of course, that was after he'd hit me in Medicine Bow." I shrugged as the older man shook his head. "We might stop him; he was planning on wrecking the train and killing all the sheriffs on board, at least that's the idea his mixed-up brain finally came to." I lodged my elbows on the table and made a double fist, resting my chin. "I'm no psychologist, but I'd say it's a case of what they call transference; in the heat of the moment Kim killed his sister, and it felt so good he found himself killing another woman on that date every year." I glanced out the window. "He had to stop to keep from giving himself away after Schafer arrested Ed, but he couldn't deal with the guilt and wanted to kill again, so he blamed the sheriffs' association and started going after us."

Lucian shook his head.

"The clippings that Schafer had in his suitcase mentioned that Melanie Wheeler had a brother, Kim, but there was no mention of a sister." I watched as we pulled into the all-but-empty station. "Then there were Gibbs's missing coveralls and boots; why would anybody else want them, they wouldn't fit?" It was late, and the cold had finally arrived in the state capital, driving the denizens inside until spring.

"So, this bullshit sheriffs' cabal that Marv Leeland was going on about, it doesn't really exist."

"Maybe, maybe not — we agree that Marv was pretty shrewd."

We sat there in the uncomfortable silence as Lucian sipped his hard liquor in response to my hard words. "Well, we might have to do a little more investigative work, then, huh?"

"I'm sorry, Lucian." I took the final sip of my beer and then gently placed it on the table. "The job wasn't the reason I was staying."

I could feel the wave of words building up in the old bull as he pulled out his pipe again and began stuffing the bowl with tobacco. "I'm gonna tell you something, and you can listen or not." His eyes went to the window. "When I was younger and full of piss and vinegar, I got a call about some bootleggers up on Jim Creek Hill, the Extapare brothers, and let me tell you, they were not unserious sons-a-bitches. Well, I headed out there all by my lonesome and got the drop on 'em red-handed, but I got cocky and wasn't watching where one of 'em was puttin' his hands, and Beltran, the older one, pulled out a shotgun and damn near blew my leg off."

As proof, he reached down and tapped the bottom of the bowl of his pipe on the hard, prosthetic leg, settling the tobacco. "Well, I laid there on the cold ground thinkin' about all the money I was gonna save on socks when Beltran walks over after loadin' as much of the contraband in the back of their truck that would fit and leans down to have a look at his handiwork. That old Basquo's eyes were black as coal, and I figure his heart wasn't so far behind, and he says to me — Lucian, I doubt you're going to make it, but if you do, I'd advise another line of work."

He lit the pipe, puffing as the flame from the wooden match flared.

"But you did make it."

"For a fact, I did. After lyin' there for a while thinking about what he'd said, I decided that I didn't particularly need a change in occupation and got to moving. I drug myself back to that old Nash I was drivin' and tied a rifle sling around my leg and drove back in to Durant, where they cut the damn thing off."

"What happened to Beltran?"

He puffed his pipe and blew smoke toward the window as the train finally came to a stop right about where we'd started this adventure, what felt like light-years ago. "I arrested the son of a bitch three weeks later and stuck his ass down a hole in Rawlins for a five spot."

"And the moral of the story is?"

He studied me. "Well, as I was lyin' there lookin' up at the sky at them stars all that ways away and bleedin' into the frost, I got to thinkin' about what Beltran had said and decided I was pretty damn lucky."

I leaned back in my chair. "Lucky."

"Lucky." He squinted. "Most people go through their lives doin' whatever it is that comes along, but every once in a while we stumble onto what it is we're supposed to do." He sat back and puffed his pipe.

I stood. "I guess I haven't found it yet, Lucian."

"Oh, you found it all right; you just don't know it."

"Well, maybe I will in some other place."

He stood, too, and extended his hand. "Their gain, my loss."

We shook. "You'll say my good-byes for me?"

"All but one."

That took me by surprise, and I waited till the little tremor of adrenaline faded before trusting myself to speak. "Yep, well . . . I don't think she wants to hear from me anytime soon." I reached down and picked up my duffel. "You want to walk me off the train?"

"In a hurry, huh?" He sat and smoothed the white tablecloth with his powerful hands, his fingers lingering on the edge. "No, I think I'm gonna sit here and drink my bourbon and chat with Mr. Gibbs about a bygone era, this bein' the last time they'll be runnin' this train."

Threading the strap of the duffel onto my shoulder, I nodded. "The times are changing."

He stared at the tablecloth and the place setting with the silverware, and then at the green velvet curtains, golden swags, and the single rose in the tiny glass vase held by a brass bracket attached to the wood paneling. "Indeed they are, and possibly not for the better." His eyes stayed looking out the window, and I was pretty sure he was looking at something, something specific, but from my vantage point I couldn't see what it could be. His hand moved toward the vase and plucked the white rose from the glass and handed it to me. "Here, take this."

It seemed like a strange gesture, but I took the thing.

He patted his shirt pocket. "You change your mind, I'll keep this star for you."

"Give it to somebody worthy."

We smiled at each other for a moment, and then I turned and walked away.

Gibbs was waiting for me at the galley with a paper bag. "I packed up some supper for you, Mr. Longmire."

I tucked the sack under my arm. "Thanks, Mr. Gibbs, I may need it." I stood there fidgeting, ready to go, but still not sure where I was headed. "I'm sorry to have turned out to be so much trouble for you."

"Oh, you weren't any trouble, sir. You were the solution."

I offered him a hand. "Thanks, Gibbs."

"You take care."

I pushed my way through the double doors to the bar car so that I could make my escape onto the platform, but certainly didn't expect to see the twenty-one surviving Wyoming sheriffs gathered there.

I stopped, wondering what kind of kangaroo court this was going to turn out to be, when Schafer himself stood and began clapping. After a moment, Tillman and Brown stood with him, and it wasn't long before the entire car joined them.

Feeling my face turning red, I nodded and stared at my boots and then tried to quickly make my way along the side to the other exit, but they caught me with handshakes and slaps on the back. By the time I got out of there, my shoulders were sore from the pounding and I was glad to step out onto the concrete platform; only one of them had followed me.

"Thank you."

I nodded and took John Schafer's hand. "You need to get your brother out of there. Even if he killed that guard, I believe there must've been some sort of mitigating circumstance, and with this kind of miscarriage of justice I can't help but think a wrongful imprisonment hearing might be in order."

He nodded. "Hey, hey, hey, I think I owe him a lot more than that."

There was a cluster of Cheyenne police officers at the next doorway, along with a cadre of Laramie County deputy sheriffs, probably there to get an eye on the individual who had killed their boss.

I wasn't tempted to stay and take part. Since I no longer had a badge, I figured I might as well get on with my life — whatever that was.

Crossing the platform, I pulled open the heavy glass door by the brass handle and stepped inside. The newsstand where I'd bought the Agatha Christie was closed, the metal grates rolled down, but I couldn't help but pull the paperback from the pocket of my jacket and leave it on the counter for the next passing traveler.

Remembering the rose Lucian had given me, I pulled it from my pocket, a little the worse for it, and placed it on the book, then started off.

"Giving up reading?"

Her voice echoed off the marble floor and through my internal organs, and I stopped and turned slowly. She stood in the reflection of the golden glow of the streetlights outside, where the snow was falling in a gentle flurry, only marginally diminished by the revolving red lights of the CPD cruisers.

"Just mysteries." I walked toward her and could see she was wearing the same outfit she'd had on in Evanston, still accessorized with the blanket I'd given her, courtesy of Grace. "Speaking of, where's your partner in crime?"

"Waiting. Sitting out in Lola."

I nodded and looked down at the wooden bench where I'd first met the president of the Wyoming Sheriffs' Association. "Waiting on who?"

"Us."

"Us?"

Her head came up, and if she so much as pressed a forefinger against my chest I was going to fall over backward. "How are you, Walt?"

I tipped my hat forward and rubbed the back of my head. "A few bumps and bruises, and I broke my watch, but I'm fine."

She snuck a glance at me between butterscotch locks, and then looked out the big plate-glass windows at the cop convention. "I'm afraid, Walt. I'm afraid we're doing something stupid, and then I'm afraid we might not do something stupid."

"When given the opportunity, I always go for stupid."

She smiled, even though she didn't want to, and she thumped a blanket-covered fist off my chest.

"Martha, I don't think anything I'd ever do to be with you could be construed as stupid." Adjusting the strap on my shoulder, I swung the duffel away and took off my hat, bending forward to give her a kiss.

There was a commotion on the platform as the two inside doors opened and a troop of assorted lawmen escorted Kim LeClerc/Wheeler through the lobby of the depot toward the vehicles in the parking lot.

He had looked better, what with the bandages wrapped around half of his head, and he was unsteady as he trudged, handcuffed, between a deputy and Holland, toward the door beside us.

I took a step forward, and I guess Holland must've thought that I wanted to say something to him. So he pulled up short and turned the prisoner toward us. LeClerc cocked his head sideways and tilted it back so that I could see the one eye still marred by smeared mascara.

I should have seen it there in that eye.

I should've known.

There really isn't anybody more dangerous than somebody who has absolutely nothing to lose, and Kim LeClerc was that person — so with all the force he could muster, he brought his knee up into my wife's abdomen.

Placenta abruption, that's what they call it. Generally damage of this type can only be done after the first trimester, when the uterus begins to peek above the pelvis, and that was where Martha happened to be at that time in her pregnancy. We lost the baby.

"Hey, buddy, would you mind moving along?"

I took another step forward in the line at the ticketing desk at Denver International Airport, adjusted the duffel strap on my shoulder, and clutched the handle of the hard case.

I thought about the questions that I'd been peppered with in the last week, the amount of people who'd been able to read that it must have been something more than the murders that had made me maintain a personal vendetta against Kim LeClerc for so many years, even if they didn't know the specifics.

I took another step forward.

Henry and Vic had driven my truck home to deposit my grandchild in the safest place

I knew, deep in the heart of the Northern Cheyenne Reservation, and then they would join me.

I was traveling light and would likely be for some time, at least until I got the job done. It was a dirty job, but that's okay because I was in a dirty mood. I pulled the linen postcard from my shirt pocket and studied the hand-tinted, grainy photograph of the two sentinel rock spires and the singular word printed on the back.

I glanced up and found myself looking at one of the airline's smartly dressed young women. Stepping forward, I placed the hard case on the counter and the duffel by my boots. Stuffing the postcard back in my shirt, I handed her my badge wallet, flipping it open to the ID card. "Walt Longmire."

"Can you remove that from the wallet for me, please?"

I did as she requested and handed it to her.

"Hey, cowboy. . . . What, you've never flown before?"

I turned and looked at the Captain of Industry behind me, with his three-piece suit, red power tie, carry-on bag, and briefcase, just long enough to find his polished loafers interesting and then turned back and thumbed the lock on the hard case, popping open the container and turning it toward the young woman. "My name is Walter Longmire. I'm sheriff of Absaroka County, Wyoming, and I am declaring an unloaded Colt 1911 semiautomatic pistol and two full clips of .45 ammunition in a separate container." I pulled the weapon and slid the assembly back, flipped the lever locking it home, and lowered the hammer in one dexterous move, assuring her that it was, indeed, empty.

I placed the Colt back in the case and closed it. "You'll find the orange manifest card on the lid there." I scooped the case up and carefully lifted the duffel onto the scale and unzipped it, placing my sidearm inside. "Anything else?"

She glanced around, then stepped through the opening where the scale was, careful to avoid my bag like it was rank death with a luggage tag. "Here's your ID, Sheriff Longmire. Do you need a boarding pass?"

"If you would, please."

She printed it out and then glanced at a workmate. "Jeannie, can you cover for me?" She looked back at me with a perfunctory smile. "Sheriff Longmire, I'm going to need to accompany you to a TSA agent, where they can examine the weapon and case."

I followed her, patting my shirt pocket to make sure the postcard, the only clue I had, was still there. I knew she was alive because he wanted me, and the only way he'd get me was if that was the case. And I found it hard to believe that Alexia was involved, figuring they wanted Cady to have one familiar face, at least that was what I hoped.

As we went toward the center of the walkway, the ticket agent blithely asked, "Business or pleasure, Sheriff?"

I stretched my neck, looking up at the peaked roof that was meant to mimic the Rocky Mountains soaring into the blue sky but that always reminded me of teepees. Riding the escalator down, I know it was the thunder of the jets taking off and landing that rattled the surrounding glass — but I could've sworn I heard drums.

"Business."

ABOUT THE AUTHOR

Craig Johnson is the *New York Times* bestselling author of the Longmire mysteries, the basis for the hit Netflix original series *Longmire*. He is the recipient of the Western Writers of America Spur Award for fiction, the Mountains and Plains Booksellers Award for fiction, the Nouvel Observateur Prix du Roman Noir, and the Prix SNCF du Polar. His novella *Spirit of Steamboat* was the first One Book Wyoming selection. He lives in Ucross, Wyoming, population twenty-five.